CRAZY BLACK AND BLUE

CRAZY BLACK AND BLUE

SUE HILLARD

THREE HEART BOOKS

Custer, South Dakota

This is a work of historical fiction. Fictitious characters interact with historical legends in sensible, yet fabricated encounters based on thorough historical research and the author's imagination.

Crazy Black and Blue

Copyright 2023 by Sue Hillard

Library of Congress Cataloging-in-Publication Data is available.

Three Heart Books, Sue Hillard, PO Box 511, Custer, SD 57730

Edited by Clara Howell. Cover by Dale Stradinger.

Art by Beth Harden Cooper, Dana Sordahl, and Sierra Sky.

ISBN: 978-1-943646-03-6

First paperback edition, 2023

DEDICATION

To my black lab, Lucy, who with her final breath of unconditional love, somehow nudged me to bury all that needed to be buried.

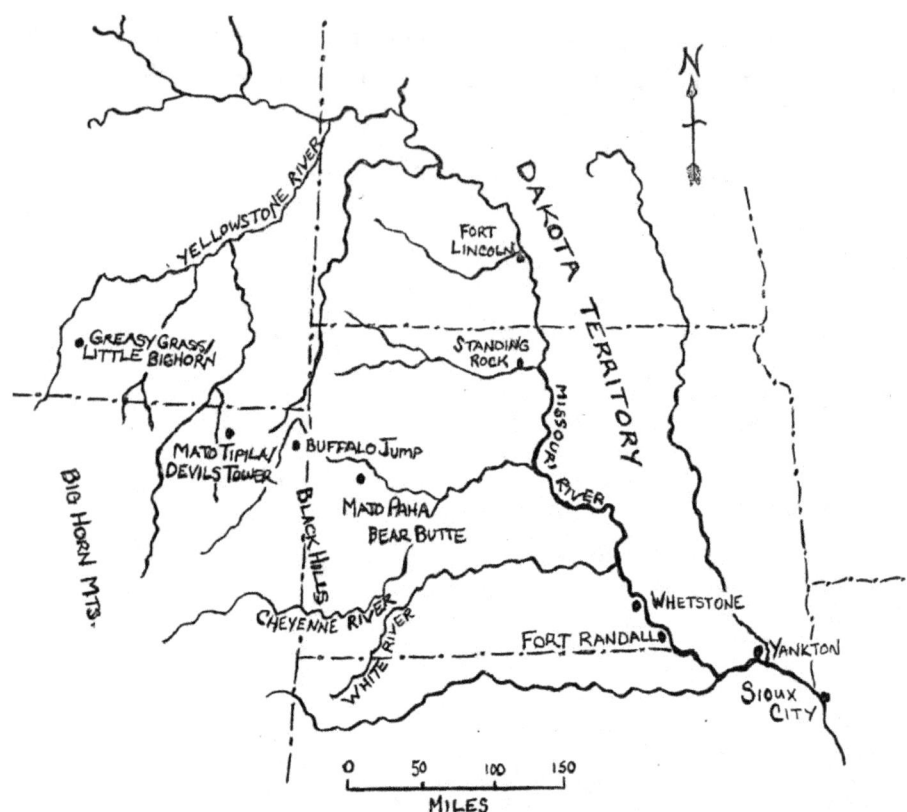

On June 25, 1876, General George Custer led the United States Seventh Cavalry into a battle with thousands of Sioux and Cheyenne warriors. Within an hour, Custer and 210 men were wiped out across the smoke-filled ridge and Little Bighorn River Valley, which is located in present day southeast Montana. The two-day battle killed and mortally wounded at least 262 soldiers and scouts. Approximately 41 Lakota and Cheyenne were killed, including six women and four children. The brawl is the most controversial engagement of the Great Sioux War, where the United States Army fought to gain western territory, carrying out President Ulysses S. Grant's orders and breaking previous treaties. The Army eventually forced the Lakota Sioux and Cheyenne people onto Sioux Reservations in Dakota Territory.

CHAPTER 1

SARA

JULY 1876

DAKOTA TERRITORY

"I DECLARE TO YOU THAT WOMAN MUST NOT DEPEND UPON THE PROTECTION OF MAN BUT MUST BE TAUGHT TO PROTECT HERSELF."
~Susan B. Anthony

When a red-hot piece of metal presses into live flesh, the stench is unforgettable. "I'm sorry," I whispered, studying the slick scar surrounded by gray hair at his shoulder. If I worked quickly, then the smoke would not draw attention. His loyalty consumed me, yet I hardly hesitated before forcefully pressing the red glowing steel to his shoulder, melting stubs of hair and bubbling his flesh. He groaned and flinched with each wound I inflicted, wide-eyed in disbelief and confused by my betrayal. Our nostrils spontaneously flared at the repulsive odor. The troubling cost of concealment.

Blue and I had traveled along the lowlands, invisible to any soldiers in the area, winding along streambeds and through ravines. We were merely a single shadow as we journeyed east across the prairie, leaving behind the eerie smoke-filled air that still hung over the rancid battlefield. I doubted I would ever see something so disturbing again, though one thing I had learned in the last months was how unpredictable life could be.

Blue was a cavalry horse, assigned to my dad on a piece of paper stuffed somewhere back in a file at Fort Randall. I could not stomach losing the only thing I loved which had not yet been torn from me. The military brand on his shoulder had to be concealed before crossing paths with anyone. Yesterday, the healed US brand identified him as a cavalry horse and me as a thief. Today, a piece of metal that likely dropped from a 7th Cavalry supply wagon offered a solution. Pulling the metal from deep within the hot fire of glowing scrub oak branches, I crafted the scarred US mark into an oozing blistered 08. A pink stream of fluid rolled down Blue's shoulder.

I put out the fire and hurled the cooled piece of branding metal into a narrow ravine. Crawling onto the horse's back again seemed like an insult after what I had just done, but Blue solemnly paced along, bearing my load as I avoided touching his raw left shoulder.

I questioned my decision to leave the Lakota funeral tipi. Deserted by a culture that had never embraced me, I wondered if crossing paths with Ohanzee, and spending those months together were only chance events. And as Sitting Bull said, I was not welcome to continue with his people. Yet, I no longer had a simple affiliation with the Army because my heart was now divided. I saw things differently and chose to ride away from a predictable life of constant compromise—the life Mother chose. I would find my way, with Blue.

I glanced back when I heard rustling but only swaying prairie grasses waved in the wind. Blue occasionally looked to his left, where Ohanzee previously walked, leading us mile after mile, in search of his people. It offered a sense of comfort to ponder if Blue possessed a spiritual awareness that I could not feel.

I shielded my eyes from the sun and watched a golden eagle glide peacefully above. Pain shot down my arm when I looked up to the sky. Injured from a physical assault by two prospectors, my menacing neck pain and numb hands were a constant reminder of the dire situation I experienced and how Ohanzee saved me.

I wondered what kind of God would allow the things that had happened to me? How could God stand by and watch me be assaulted? How could God allow my loved ones to die? Had I been alone on the prairie? During the blizzard, perhaps God was there? Or was it only a matter of luck that I survived? What forces nudged me to continue on? Was it God's will or simply personal fortitude I never knew I owned?

As a matter of custom, Ohanzee's tribe rejected a white girl. Understandable, only the white girl was me. Was it merely the rejection or was it grit which placed me on the back of Blue, riding calmly away from the battlefield? It was not by choice that I left Ohanzee gravely injured and in the hands of a chanting Lakota medicine man who packed Ohanzee's rotting wound with crushed sage and purple coneflower. The gray streaks of infection running up his leg were ghastly. Rejected and unable to stay at his side, uncertainty would always surround the timing of Ohanzee's last breath.

Blue had already gained a bit of weight over the days he rested. The prairie grass was long and green near the Greasy Grass River and rewarded his voracious appetite. A new fat layer covered his deepest valleys of protruding ribs. Without the burden of my contemplation, Blue left our past behind, not haunted by the unanswered questions of our ordeal.

With a lingering raw throat from the smoke and dust of the previous day's battle, I reached behind and pulled water from my pack. Ohanzee and his people left me well-equipped to survive. Apparently, they anticipated my disobedience to their "wait for white soldiers to arrive" command. I initially sipped from Dad's Army canteen throughout the day. But when the last bit of warm water remained, I took a final loud gulp with my mother unable to judge. She couldn't. She was dead. So was my dad.

The first night alone was unsettling. Most animal calls were easily discounted as non-threatening even though a persistent faint whimper left me staring to the outer reaches of firelight, searching for the source. Surely, it was not a danger, though I had sensed something following us all day. An injured Lakota would not whimper. A tracking soldier would have been impatient, announcing himself much earlier. Pushing apprehension aside, I spoke softly to the wind and the stars, luring out the one who stirred in the darkness.

Resting untied, only fifteen feet from my blanket, Blue softly whinnied toward the whispering prairie grass. What would the coming days deliver? Would I feel rain against my face? Would the back of my neck burn and blister from the afternoons of intense western sun?

As I lay beneath the vast sky dancing with stars, a skinny brown puppy appeared at the edge of the fading campfire light and then retreated. I reached beyond Ohanzee's bow and deerskin quiver holding seven arrows. His people left a large pack filled with my canteen, buffalo cord, a water bladder, fire-making tools, a cast iron pan, pemmican packs, a blanket, my pocketknife, a cavalry holster, a belt with a Colt 7-shot revolver, a bag of ammunition, and gold. Two large bags of gold.

I retrieved a pack of pemmican[1] and flung a chunk toward the puppy, who re-emerged cautiously, desperate for the food resting between us. Three more carefully tossed pieces narrowed the gap. Now closer to the firelight, I recognized my follower. She was the puppy who crawled under Ohanzee's tipi and cowered beneath my blanket during the battle. Later, a boy named Black Elk[2] carried the puppy away and I feared she became a Lakota meal. Unlike General George Custer and his soldiers, the puppy somehow evaded the wrath of death.

I tried for another hour to convince the puppy of my good intentions before I faded into light sleep. Somewhere deep in the night, when only embers glowed, the puppy gained courage in the cool air. Half-awake, I did not startle when she burrowed under my blanket, decorated with quilled edges.[3] The puppy spooned my back for the rest of the night and her occasional snores eased the tension on my gritty face. Drifting in and out of sleep, the restlessness to stay safe was overpowered by a growing obsession to protect my gold. I could not allow circumstances to unsettle me. I could not feel guilty for taking the gold from prospectors intending to steal my purity. They deserved nothing and I needed a solid plan to retain the only benefit of the assault. The next morning, I packed up my camp while the puppy chased grasshoppers that occasionally clung to her sides.

"What's your name?" I whispered hoarsely. She tipped her head and stared in my direction. "I could call you Stew. Lakota Stew." Her attention diverted while I pondered if anyone else would find humor in the name. "Okay then. How about Shadow? It's English for Ohanzee." The puppy stopped in her tracks and met my gaze, her mahogany eyes full of introspection and soul. "Well, you chose to follow a white girl instead of a Lakota, so Shadow it is."

Over the course of nine days, I followed game trails toward the morning sun until Mato Paha[4] rose from the prairie floor on the eastern horizon. To the south, were the Black Hills. I crossed worn trails which guided trespassing prospectors toward their dream of fortune. Complete solitude cleared my head and I recognized it was not enough for me to be brave, but I must also be wise. Perhaps if I traveled to one of the mining camps, I could trade in my gold for U.S. Notes. I could blend in until I knew what to do next.

I turned Blue south, where red ledges of rock formations peeked between the thick pine trees. Claustrophobia enveloped me as the surroundings went from expansive prairie to a narrow winding trail through a young forest. My neck throbbed from turning my head, scanning the high hills for danger as Blue worked our way between the ridges. Dropping my focus to the ground, I searched for tracks of predators, man or animal.

With Shadow balanced across Blue's withers, I ducked under low branches, thankful Blue was not any taller. As the sun disappeared, so did the branches. I grimaced as one tore at my cheek. Suddenly, Blue's ears perked forward in unison, distracting me from the scratch. Then he whinnied, a lonesome call into the unknown.

"Hello?" a man's husky voice called out. "Hello?"

He did not sound afraid or threatening, only matter of fact. Yet, I was hesitant to respond. I thought of jumping off Blue and standing my ground behind the cover of a tree, but the white man appeared before I could hide.

"Well, well. What do you know?" he asked, not waiting for a reply. "Lordy. Lordy. Sometimes the oddest things appear right before my eyes."

I frowned back at the man without speaking, attempting to hide my bow and quiver behind my back.

"Hello, young lady. I'm Henry Smith. Preacher Smith."[5]

I nodded silently as he stepped closer and twisted his ankle on a loose rock. He grimaced, exclaiming, "For the love of God. He sure makes this journey a bucket full of challenges, doesn't He?"

I continued to defensively stare, but a grin slipped into the corners of my lips.

"Where are you heading all alone, miss? No disrespect, simply not safe in these hills. When the sun goes down, it's more black than white around here. Or shall I say, more red than white."

Void of emotion, I answered, "I'm not afraid," in a tone which surprised myself.

"Well, maybe not you. Nor am I because the Lord watches over and protects His sheep. But evil is evil and you can never be too careful, mostly for a young lady pretty as yourself. How about something to eat or drink? I'll start a fire."

I swung off Blue and balanced the puppy in my right arm while dropping Blue's reins with my left. The man's eyes scanned me from head to toe and repeated the process up and down Blue. I stepped in front of my horse's freshly branded shoulder, hoping the man had not noticed. Then, self-consciously, my eyes dropped down at my body and I realized the strange sight we offered. I tightened my grip on Shadow, holding her in front of me like a shield. As the man measured me, I reciprocated. He was tall, perhaps six feet with the proportions of a working man.

Preacher Smith suggested I look for branches to help build a fire. He limped from tree to tree, bending over stiffly while gathering dried pinecones. After lowering Shadow to the ground, I collected kindling, arranged the sticks, and started the fire with a spark from Ohanzee's fire-making tools.

"Well, well. This ain't your first campfire, I see," said the preacher.

The sun had set, yet the fire cast enough light to allow us to study each other.

"So, where are you heading? To Deadwood?"

"Yes," I answered, realizing I had not thought through my reintroduction into the white man's world.

"It's a tough camp. Mostly for a girl. How old are you, if you don't mind me asking?"

"Eighteen," I lied, adding a few years.

"Family waiting for you there?"

"Yes," I lied.

"With no disrespect, in these parts, when someone introduces himself, the other person offers their name as well."

"With no disrespect, what business is my name to you?"

"Ahh. I see. Fair enough. How about just your first name? You must have one of those."

"Sara."

The campfire burned hot and the coffee brewed quickly at the expense of casting off significant smoke for an enemy to see. We were not in a ravine and I had not taken time to pick the driest kindling, but I was not sure who to trust at the moment and did not feel compelled to practice obscurity as I had when I was alone on the prairie.

The preacher handed me a tin cup half full of coffee. "I'll quit asking questions, but you can't make me stop talking. It's a preacher's greatest sin. Or at least it should be," he mumbled as his calculating eyes trailed off to the woods around us. I offered nothing.

He took another gulp from his cup. "So let me tell you what I think. I think you are running away from something. I think something happened to you because you are wearing Indian pants and a filthy blouse no self-respecting woman would wear if she had the choice. I think you stole that horse of yours. I think you're tougher than the average woman because you haven't whined about the gash on your cheek. I think you don't have a dollar to your name, whatever your name is for that matter. I think you are a scared little girl inside a young lady's body." He paused and added one more thought, "And do you know what else? I think you should be scared. I think you need to go back to where you came from because Deadwood is no place for a young lady."

"I'm not going back and I can manage on my own," I answered, slinging the last bit of my coffee across the flames and handing him the cup. "I must be going." I climbed on Blue.

"Listen, I don't need to know your surname or anything about your past, but it's dark out here and you should come with me to Crook City for the night. The Wagners were murdered near here just the other day. Bodies stripped. Young man carrying mail was jumped and killed. Cattle are stolen quick as they're brought in. This is dangerous, young lady. Come with me tonight and I'll escort you to Deadwood in the morning after my service."

"Your service?"

"I live in Deadwood but travel around to preach. Prospectors are like flies in these hills. They're everywhere. Making it easy for them to hear the good word. So, God willing, I'll preach in Crook City in the morning. Then I'll head back to Deadwood. I do this trip every week. Ease my mind and come with me. Two is better

11

than one in these hills. Plus," he paused long enough to haphazardly kick dirt over the small campfire and heave his pack over his left shoulder. "Plus, you need to get a different set of clothes if you don't want to cause a stir in Deadwood when you ride into camp. Not a good way to start a new life."

I peered down at my buckskin pants and moccasins. Reluctantly, I turned Blue to follow the man. Compounding my reservation, Preacher Smith veered onto a different trail, which followed a narrow ridgeline instead of backtracking to the prairie. Preacher Smith paced quickly and he attentively scanned our surroundings. Blue followed comfortably behind the limping man, never pulling to overtake him.

"Keep up Sara, not the safest out here but can't even say it's safer in camp. Just a week ago, a duel in Crook City left lead in a man."

"No doubt fighting over a woman?"

"Actually, an unpaid loan. Best not to loan money unless you never expect it back."

At the outskirts of Crook City, an unorganized encampment of wooden shacks and white canvas tents lined the trail. The smoke-filled air hung at the tree line as men squatted around separate fires, eating from tin cans and drinking from glass bottles. Most nodded or raised a finger in recognition of Preacher Smith. Only one man curiously stared at me as we passed by. The darkness protected my secret.

"Do you have bedding?" Preacher Smith asked.

I nodded. He pulled the pack from Blue's back before I could refuse his help.

"Awful heavy quilt, young lady. What else ya got in this bag? Rocks?"

My eyes bore holes through the man but Preacher Smith rolled his eyes and untied an oiled canvas tarp from his pack. He spread it out, flattening the tall grasses underneath. Then, with sturdy branches collected from the ground nearby, he raised the center of the tarp. The sides of the canvas draped to the ground on three sides and hung from a tree branch on the other.

"Welcome to Smith's Crook City Hotel. Won't cost you a thing. Don't bother looking for better lodging. Won't find it."

I stood beside his makeshift tent, not knowing what was appropriate and then realized I was already socially compromised. After all, I spent months alone with a Lakota, sleeping beside him under the stars. To most white folk, that permanently labeled me as dirty. Without hesitation, Preacher Smith stepped a respectable distance from the tent, unrolled a blanket and placed his pack as a pillow.

Blue grazed beside the tent, never venturing far. Relatively safe, I curled up under the canvas but a sense of nothingness came over me when I could not gaze at the stars. Finally, my eyes grew heavy with Shadow's already deep breath methodically pressing ribcage against ribcage.

I awoke to the movement of my tarp and a barely audible growl from Shadow. In the darkness, I blinked hard to focus and saw a masculine hand reaching under the flapping barrier. I grabbed the gun beside me.

"One more move and I blow your arm off," I hissed.

"Whoa, whoa, girl. It's me. The preacher. Settle down. I brought you clothes. Women's clothes."

"Oh, you startled me," I gasped.

"Well, you startled me. Not exactly planning on meeting my Maker tonight. Now go to sleep and we'll talk in the morning."

I put my gun down and took a deep breath. And another. My eyes were fully adjusted to the moonlight and a pile of carefully folded fabric rested beside me. I reached out to touch the calico print but could not feel what appeared delicate and soft. I picked up the fabric and rubbed it across my face. Closing my eyes again, the ballad of slurred campfire conversations lulled me to sleep.

Morning sunlight flashed into my eyes as the flap of the tarp swung in the breeze. I unfolded a long skirt and pulled it over my Lakota pants, creating awkward calico bulges. Retrieving a small handful of gold flakes from my pack, I dropped them into the side-seamed pocket of my new skirt.

A group of twenty prospectors gathered around the enthusiastic preacher. Rather than draw attention to myself by walking into the middle of his service, I led Blue the opposite direction to a creek with Shadow wandering behind.

With men about, I did not dare bathe. Instead, I watered Blue and searched for herbs along the creek bank, noticing an unnatural

14

heap of placered stones left beside the creek after someone sifted for gold nuggets. I found a few stems of mint and snatched a handful of sharp pine needles, crushing them together. Back inside the tent, I tried to cover my pungent body odor by rubbing the rough mixture against my armpits.

Once the service was over, Preacher Smith returned as I was picking packed mud from Blue's soles.

"Mighty fine gray you got there. Stunning as a matter of fact," Preacher Smith said. "Seems to have a strong spirit but you handle him well. Not too tall. Perfect for you and one hundred other horse thieves." He grinned. "Skirt's a little lumpy. Say, I'm heading back to Deadwood. You sure you want to come? Like I said, it's not what I would call civilized for a young lady such as yourself."

"I'm sure. I would like to try my hand at prospecting."

"Prospecting?" he chuckled. "Dirty work, my friend, and most of the good claims are spoken for. I can't even keep at it long, have to throw in a little carpentry and wood chopping to rest my back. You done this before? California?"

I did not reply as he searched my face for an answer. Then I blurted, "You may find humor now, Preacher Smith. Yet you'll find I can take care of myself. I'm fully capable."

"Okay then, Miss Capable. Deadwood it is. Help me break camp if you will."

CHAPTER 2

SARA

JULY 1876

DEADWOOD

ON EVERY HILLSIDE, ON EVERY MOUNTAIN TOP,
IN PLACERS AND IN QUARTZ. IT IS THERE FOR
THE POOR MAN AND FOR THE CAPITALIST." ~
New York Times

"How exactly do you plan to keep your claim? It's one thing to buy one. It's another thing to work it and protect it," Preacher Smith said as he paced ahead, still limping.

"Preacher, I can wrap your ankle for support if it bothers you."

"You a doctor too? A prospector and a doctor, huh? Guess you have it all covered," he said, chuckling. I grinned as he continued, "No bother on my ankle. I'm fine. Not much further. I'll take you to the claims office."

We entered Deadwood Gulch from the north with a steady uphill climb. The narrow trail weaved in and out of hillsides choked with fallen timber. The path opened to a grassy meadow with a creek running its length. The camp was squeezed into a crevice between two sharp ridges. More white canvas tents dotted all relatively flat ground. Horses and mules were scattered about. Then, beyond the meadow, it narrowed into a tight gulch. Uncertainty, noise, and overstimulated senses elicited self-consciousness.

I glanced downward at my new skirt, bunched up awkwardly around Blue's backbone. My emaciated calves and ankles were protruding like dead branches from a tree, exposed below the Lakota leather pants. Odd as it appeared, I felt safer with the extra layer, as if more protected from the lingering stares of men along the dusty road. A variety of pine-framed shacks lined the edges of the steep hillsides. Growing more paranoid, I slid the bulk of my skirt in front of my leg to conceal the brand on Blue's left shoulder. Shadow sat inquisitively in front of me.

"This is called the badlands," Preacher Smith said. Men stared from behind loose tent flaps and from the doorways of new buildings.

"Is that a hotel?" I asked.

"Not for someone as innocent as you. You need a respectable place to rest your head till ya get back on your feet."

"I'm already on my feet."

Preacher Smith ignored my comment and we continued riding south on Main Street. "Ya know, Miss Capable, the man at the claims office will need to know your name. Your real name."

"What does a name have to do with anything at all?"

"It's a legal matter. For papers. You don't want someone stealing your claim from you later just because you gave wrong information."

"I wouldn't think of such a thing."

"Didn't say you would," Preacher Smith retorted. "Best put your stolen horse in the alley." He guided us to a tying post between two buildings. I flipped the reins over the post and Blue knew what to do. He would stand until I returned, trained by my dad, his enlisted soldier Jake and others in the cavalry.

The preacher glanced down as we walked back to Main Street with the puppy held across my chest. Preacher Smith curiously reached for Shadow and delicately slid my Saint Michael medal from her mouth. She obediently let the attached medal drop to the bottom of the chain. Shadow was teething.

"Saint Michael medal? You believe?"

"Not sure what I believe."

"Then why do you wear it?"

"It was a gift. Sort of."

"Amen. A beautiful gift."

We kept walking.

"Looks like you have a limp of your own, Miss Capable?"

"It's nothing," I replied. He could not see the void in my right moccasin where three toes were missing. I recollected the excruciating pain as they were severed with a knife. Distracted, I blurted, "Your assistance was most helpful, Preacher, but I can take it from here."

He paused and stared kindly into my eyes, searching for something he did not seem to find. Before disappearing down the street, he hollered back over his shoulder, "If ya ever care to hear the truth, the real truth, I preach over there, in front of the Bent and Deetkens store. Remember, Sara, it's easy to get lost in Deadwood."

Immediately, I regretted my independence. With no boardwalk in sight, the street was hard to navigate, filled with trash and manure. Men congregated in random small groups, rolling tobacco and kicking the dusty ground while telling stories of gold nuggets pulled from Whitewood Creek. Their eyes rolled down and up and down again at the obvious newcomer. I felt dirtier than the ground I stood on.

"How about a shot of whiskey for my new girl?" A man whispered, leaning toward me as I walked past. "First one is on me, then you gonna work for it."

I had no way to gain my bearings. I ducked through the nearest door, thankful it was a legitimate business. The Big Horn Store smelled of recently tanned leather and pickles. Numerous shelves with gaping bare spaces suggested heavy demand. Canned beans and rice were the staples, flavors I had not tasted in months. A dill pickle barrel stood in the corner and straight-edged razors were behind the counter. Tobacco and a jar filled with horehound candy rested on the countertop beside a stack of Black Hills Pioneer newspapers. The headline caught my attention, "EXTRA! GENERAL CUSTER MASSACRE – DETAILS EMERGE"

I continued to wander through the store toward the back wall where prospector attire was stacked in piles. A far table held a few bolts of cloth and sewing supplies. Two ready-to-wear dresses hung from a rope in front of a mirror attached to the wall.

A clean-shaven, well-dressed man appeared from the back room. He was slightly pudgy but stood proud and sucked in his stomach while filling his chest with air as he spoke.

"Good day, young lady. May I help you?"

"Just looking for a dress or skirt. I lost my trunk a few miles back."

"We all have our stories, not sure you can beat mine."

"Not likely," I mumbled.

He continued without my prompting. "So, on my way here, one night it was dark as could be. I found the softest ground to lay my head for the night. Next morning, I woke with my head on the grave of a man who was murdered by the damn Injuns. Had no idea I slept over a dead man. He was probably still warm. God rest his soul. Doubt you'll top that."

"No, sir, I won't even try."

"Oh, lordy, lordy. Another woman in distress," the man mumbled, barely moving his lips as he spoke. "And with a puppy no less. Least you could have brought a cat."

"What exactly do you mean by that, Mr.?"

"Name's Gushurst. No offense but cats are in demand. One dollar apiece, easy. I'd pay triple to stop the mice from eating my inventory. Hell, I'd buy ten for that matter. Pardon my language."

"Well, Mr. Gushurst. I have no cats and I'm not a woman in distress. You are mistaken to take me as one."

"No offense. Just seen your type wandering into camp, looking for a man, or at least his money, and your type seems to leave a month later, completely broken and used up."

"My type?" I thought. "In distress?" I was certain of few things and one was that nowhere in Dakota Territory was another woman my type. If only the proprietor knew the contents in my pack.

"I would like to try on the purple printed dress. I would also like the …"

"Don't tell me you are planning to stay? Even after the massacre? Bound to get worse with the Injuns before it gets better."

Thunder interrupted our conversation and we glanced out the storefront window at darkening skies.

"Pull the curtain for privacy," he mumbled as he pulled it for me.

I was left in a makeshift dressing area. Alone with the full-length mirror and a new dress. I placed Shadow on the floor and stripped down, shocked at the image before me. The nomadic Lakota lifestyle had rendered me unrecognizable. I was lean and tan from the endless days walking across the prairie. The Lakota diet suited me fine, yet I knew most white men would consider me too hard and angular for their taste. The dress was beautiful, but extra fabric hung where other women had curves. I pulled my dirty clothes back on.

Sliding the curtain back, I gathered the purple dress, a few cans of beans, and a white tarp, placing them on the counter with a copy of the newspaper.

"So, how did the dress fit?"

"It'll be fine, thank you."

I completed my transaction with gold flakes from my pocket, which raised the corner of his left bushy eyebrow.

"Where did you get your hands on that?"

I had no acceptable answer. "Excuse me, but is that a proper thing to ask a lady?"

Mr. Gushurst let out an exasperated sigh and continued barely above a whisper, "As I see it, someone already got to you and paid for it in gold. What a shame. But just pointing out, young lady, if you are working so hard for it, then you shouldn't let the dust slip through your pocket seams. Here. It's on me."

The man reached under the counter and pulled out a tiny bag with a leather tie. The leather was silky smooth and would have held liquid if tasked.

"What's this, leather?" I asked, intrigued by the texture.

The proprietor stuttered, "No need for a young lady to inquire as to such things. Please, accept it without questions. It's only on the house if you stop with the questions."[6]

I nodded and Mr. Gushurst placed my gold on his scale, clearly flustered.

The skies opened, but I did not wait inside. Instead, I stepped from the Big Horn Store and raised my smudged face to the showers. Shadow whimpered when thunder rolled overhead and echoed through the gulch. The loitering men fled down the muddy street and I followed, less conspicuous than before.

An empty bathhouse was on the right. A few blocks down, a vivacious saloon was packed with energetic banter which nearly drowned out the piano player. Above the saloon entrance, a wooden "Nuttal & Mann's" sign hung from creaky chains in the breeze. Tobacco smoke slithered out of the swinging doors as I glimpsed card games in progress and a few fancy dressed women attending to men. Uncomfortable with my lingering curiosity, I ducked down the side street and untied Blue, who seemed to enjoy the moisture. We rode out of the camp, into the hills.

The rain gloriously soothed my parched skin, but Shadow tucked her head under my blouse. We rode for just shy of an hour on a narrow trail until I felt comfortable veering up a secluded draw following a narrow stream. The draw opened into a meadow, flanked by ridges on each side. Camp was made efficiently with my tarp stretched overhead as Preacher Smith had done the night before. I opened two cans of beans with Dad's pocketknife: one for me and one for Shadow. Blue grazed nearby.

With only a few hours of muted light remaining, I pulled out the newspaper and read the headline again, expecting it to be different than before. It wasn't. I crawled under my blanket with the paper at hand.

"EXTRA! GENERAL CUSTER MASSACRE – DETAILS EMERGE. DISASTER IN THE INDIAN COUNTRY. GENERAL CUSTER AND 261 MEN THE VICTIMS. On the 25th of June General Custer, with the 7th Calvary regiment battled 2,500 attacking Sioux warriors on the Little Big Horn River in Dakota Territory. Gen. Custer and five companies were separated from the rest of the force before the fight and all were killed. No man lived to tell the tale. Only one horse survived, the mount of Col. Keogh, and he is believed to have been transported to Fort Lincoln on a steamer with the injured from Major Reno's companies. Major Reno was surrounded by the savages. However, the timely arrival of Gen. Gibbon's force caused the Indians to flee. A total loss of 14 commissioned officers, 2 surgeons, 237 enlisted men, 5 civilians and 3 Indian scouts. Gen. Custer was an experienced officer, with much dash and bravery and this is the greatest disaster the Army has met in Dakota Territory. By some, Gen. Custer was considered rash and his death is to be ascribed to this quality. Still, the massacre arouses a universal feeling throughout the United States that Indians should be severely chastised. The Secretary of War will likely call an immediate conference to address the Indian war and future campaign against the savages."

I threw the paper to the ground and a steady trickle of rainwater pooled underneath the typeset of lies. A massacre? How could they call it a massacre when the cavalry rushed in and attacked the Indians? The cavalry's assault was not provoked by Ohanzee's people. My face flushed. I knew the truth. After all, I was there.

I snatched the paper again. A few soggy sections clumped and stuck to my fingers. Colonel Keogh was dead. I reread the story, this time focusing on the lone surviving horse named Comanche.[7] Colonel Miles Keogh and Comanche. I remembered my encounter with the handsome tall man, heavy with an Irish accent. When I lived at Fort Randall, he rode in with General Custer, standing apart as he cared for Comanche. The horse was no showpiece, but if any horse deserved to survive, it was Comanche. With short legs and an aging, slightly swayed back, the fourteen-year-old's partial mustang pedigree was obvious with his thick neck and a dark stripe down his back. They had been a team for eight years and Colonel Keogh purchased Comanche from the Army because he couldn't imagine ever parting with him. His words echoed through me, "Best money I ever spent, ninety dollars for a heart of gold. He never gives up. It's quite amazing." He told me that Comanche earned his name during a Kansas battle. Comanche meant bravery. With arrows in his rear, he didn't quit. He gave all he had for the entire battle and Colonel Keogh was certain the horse spared his life. Not this time.

The next morning, I bathed in the nearby stream, washing weeks of dirt from my emaciated body. I pulled off my deerskin pants and slid on my new purple dress. Without a comb, I fingered through my thick brown hair, swirling it into a bun and securing it with a twig. I repacked my belongings and headed back to Deadwood.

About a mile from town, a man on horseback approached. A black medical bag dangled from his saddle horn. He raised his hand to acknowledge me, only to rush on.

At the claim's office, I tied Blue to a tree behind the building next to a water trough and placed the puppy on the ground.

"Okay, Shadow. You need to stay." She followed behind. I picked her up and walked her back to Blue. "Stay, Shadow. I mean it." She stayed.

I stepped inside the busy office where five grungy men were arguing over a specific gold claim area.

"The only claims left are long shots. But gentlemen, plenty are out there for sale. Just ask around," said a plump man in a tight suit. His desk was piled with papers and a propped metal sign which read "Claim Recorder."

"Ain't fair," one man grumbled. "What about a lottery? Ain't got enough money to buy one from someone trying to get rich. They all want too much."

"The lottery is long gone. All the good claims been recorded months ago," the claim recorder hollered, only inciting two rank smelling men, who grunted and challenged each other, bumping chests until one finally yielded.

I stepped around the agitated men and faced the man in charge.

"Excuse me, sir, how do I go about staking a claim?"

The entire room fell silent.

"Well, what do you know? How do you go about staking a claim? Are you crazy?"

"Perhaps, but if so, looks like I'm in good company."

The man scanned the room of sweaty, disheveled men and grinned. "If you wanna fight with the rest of 'em, then you can bid up a claim someone wants to sell. If you ain't got it in you, you can look at the map for an undisputed claim, it's over there on the wall. None are much good though. Maybe two cents of gold per pan. Might be wise to stay close to town if you know what I mean."

I squeezed past the men and carefully studied the map, concealing my thrill to recognize an open claim near my creek campsite from the previous night. If God was truly in charge of my journey, then perhaps He was nudging me to commit to that creek. I liked to think I was not alone making random choices.

"I would like this one, sir."

The men's lice-ridden heads turned to see where I was pointing.

"Quite a ways out of town. Sure?" He stepped closer and whispered, "Not seen much luck up there. Not a bit of quartz running through that meadow. You need a solid quartz vein. Nothing clumping up in that creek much either. Plus, the Injuns are stirrin'."

"I'm sure. What do I do now?"

His voice raised, "One dollar to me. I record your claim. Gets ya 300 feet of stream and rim to rim on the ridges. But ya can't just sit on it. Post your notice on boundary trees. You gotta work it with a pick and shovel at least twice a month."

"Not an issue."

I handed him my smooth pouch of gold flakes. Both eyebrows rose above his crooked bangs. He turned his back, weighed and separated the appropriate flakes to satisfy the charge and quickly completed the paperwork.[8]

"Nobody picked this one yet 'cause it ain't suitable for a wagon. Your pretty little back will be hauling everything out on foot or horseback. Just a hint of an Injun trail up there. Name, young lady?"

"Sara Capable."

"Odd name," he muttered under his breath, shrugging and finishing the paperwork with no additional scrutiny.

With the claim in hand and four claim notice placards, I left. As I retrieved Blue, a handsome young man barely older than me was tying his horse next to Shadow who was sleeping against the water trough. When the puppy stirred, the man's horse spooked, rearing up and throwing his over-stuffed pack to the ground. White powder spewed from the pack. The man groaned.

"Aww. Mah floor. Darn cuddie."

His heavy Scottish accent caught me off-guard. "I'm terribly sorry. It's my fault. My dog caused the disruption." Shadow started licking the flour.

The man collected his emotions quickly as I held Shadow at arm's length and scooped what I could back into his canvas bag. His arms brushed against mine as he took the pack and placed it back on the rump of his calmed horse.

"Nae worries ma'am. Jist an adventure anyway. It was a hunder poond adventure. Noo it's an eighty poond adventure," he sighed. "Nae bad feelings. Phillip's mah nam. Guid day." He tipped the short brim of his flat cap and walked into the claim's office.[9]

On our way out of town, heading directly to my claim, we crossed paths again with the man with the medical bag. He was less rushed upon his return. He raised his hand again with half a grin and an added nod of recognition. I kept Blue's right side to the man, shielding the raw brand. Surprised when he introduced himself as "Doc," his disheveled appearance raised my suspicion that we were both imposters.

"Was up tending to a man who was hit on the backside of his head by an Injun, no doubt. Doesn't remember a thing. Woke up with blood everywhere and his horse missing."

"If he doesn't remember a thing, then how are you certain it was an Indian?" I asked.

"Who else would it be?"

"Did you stitch him up?"

"Sure enough," he answered with curiosity emanating from his sparkling blue eyes. The man's face showed nights without sleep.

"Did you wash your hands before you stitched him?"

"Uh," he stumbled. "I did not catch your name," he said.

"Miss Capable."

"Do you come with a first name?"

"Sara."

"Okay then, Sara Capable. Looks like you're heading up the wrong trail. The same Injuns might want your horse and certainly would like a night or two with a young thing like you. And they wouldn't likely wash their hands first," he grinned.

"I'll be fine," I answered, desperate to change the subject.

"Why not start out early in the morning? Come stay with me tonight."

"Certainly not," I replied, although his demeanor seemed kind.

"No, no. I did not mean in my cabin. Of course not. Not appropriate as I'm alone. Not lucky enough to have a wife waiting for me. What I do have is an extra stall in the barn to put you up. It's no problem," he said, maneuvering his horse close enough to reach over and pet Shadow. "Cute pup. All I ask is you clean up behind the horse in the morning." He smiled.

As we rode side by side, he casually inquired, "Why did you ask about washing my hands before I stitched up the man's head?"

"Because the risk of infection drops if you wash your hands."

"How do you know that?"

"Learned it from other doctors. I want to be a ..." I thought carefully as the word "nurse" failed to escape my lips.

"You want to be what? An undertaker?" Doc asked, laughing at his own joke.

"No. I want to be a doctor." My heart raced by saying the word.

"Huh. None 'round these parts. Lady doctors, I mean. Then again, not many feminine types around at all for that matter. Unfortunate fact for me, but that's a story for another day."

We rode on quietly for a few minutes.

"So as for your doctoring, guess I don't know why not. We have seven doctors in the hills, including me. Personally, I could use a little help. What's your experience?"

"Broken bones mostly."

Doc smiled. "Easy enough to get experience if you been in these parts very long at all. So, you done your share of amputations, huh? Above the joints?"

"No. No amputations."

"Oh, simple breaks?"

"No, compound fractures."

"Well, young lady, I haven't had much luck with saving lives when the bone pokes out. Might as well lop it off well above the break. Gives the fellow a better shot of not passing from infection."

"I was taught to set the break and keep everything clean, sometimes packing it with herbs, until it heals."

Doc looked at me funny and said, "Well, we can talk later. Let's set you up for some shut eye. You look whipped."

With two arms full of quilts and a lantern, I was shown to his four-stall barn and we unsaddled his horse, who rested in a clean, roomy stall. As I was settling Blue into his stall, Doc excused himself. A short time later, I heard fiddle music coming from his cabin.

Self-designating another empty stall as my own quarters, I emptied my pack and placed the gold bags to the side. Paying for things with unearned gold flakes had not been wise. Even so, what was done was done. Once I worked my claim for a period, I could justify purchases in gold. With no other means of support, I needed to live frugally and as inconspicuously as possible. I picked a handful of gold flakes and small nuggets out of one bag and refilled my pouch. Then I carefully sealed the two large bags of remaining gold, each still weighing thirty pounds.[10]

A shovel, pickaxe, and hay fork leaned against one inside corner of the fourth stall of the barn. I chose the cover of my horse stall to shovel a two-foot-deep hole at the edge of the wall. Digging was slow, trying to minimize the sound of metal slamming into the rocky soil. Eventually, one bag of gold filled the bottom of the hole and was covered with dirt. I jumped up and down on the loose soil, compacting it until little give was left. I kicked away the extra soil and scattered straw bedding around randomly to conceal my secret. The second bag of gold went back into my pack, doubling my chance of losing some yet minimizing the risk of losing it all.

Exhausted, I did not change from my dress and immediately fell asleep on the sweet-smelling quilts. I was startled awake by a man knocking frantically on Doc's cabin door. Peeking through a crack between warped boards of the barn, I saw panic before me. Anticipating a house call, I quickly saddled Doc's horse. As Doc rushed into the barn, he saw what I had done and glanced at Blue.

"Sara, come quickly. I need your help. There's been an Indian attack." Doc hardly uttered the request before I left my pack on the stall floor, bridled Blue and hopped on his back, ready to ride. Doc noticed I was riding bareback, with my dress bunched up over Blue's withers. He said nothing. He kicked his horse into a lope and Blue followed. Our short but frantic pace took us up the main trail to a well-worn road. Each horse raced faster and faster off the other. As we rounded a bend in the trail, chaos echoed ahead. A red stagecoach was on its side. Bodies were crumpled in limp, contorted positions. Those able to walk were milling about, trying to help the ones crying out in pain. Doc dismounted and crouched at the nearest casualty. A child's desperate cry drew me to the side of the trail.

"Papa. Papa. Oh, Papa," the blood-stained boy repeated over and over. His father lay dead and the wiry boy stood above him, afraid to touch the lifeless bloody form.

"What's your name?" I asked.

"Chance."

"Chance, I need your help. Can you please come hold my horse for me?"

"But my papa?"

"He doesn't need your help anymore."

Chance glanced down at the side of his father's crushed skull and sobbed without words.

"I need to help the others. Chance, can you hold my horse?"

The boy nodded and his eyes wandered.

"This is Blue. He has special power. He can hear you even if you don't talk. He can hear your heart."

The boy nodded again, fixated on another injured man.

"Now take care of him until I get back, okay? Blue needs you to talk with him, okay?"

The boy's head bobbed in agreement.

Placing the reins in Chance's hand, I turned toward the bodies before me. Frozen in place, the stress mentally transported me back in time to the battlefield scattered with General Custer's soldiers. The memory of blue uniformed contorted bodies flooded over me, with flies swarming from open wound to open wound, laying eggs in the flesh of each silent fallen soldier. I could almost smell the gut-wrenching rot in the air.

"Stop," I ordered my mind, realizing the flashback was not the present. "This is not a battlefield. It is an accident," I convinced myself, pushing the past back to the past.

A man lay bleeding profusely from his abdomen. He groaned a distant guttural sound of impending death. Another screamed in pain - his foot heading in the wrong direction. A few were beyond help and had already slipped to their Maker. The doctor was already back on his feet and stepped beside me.

"Just pick one, Sara. You can't save them all."

I moved toward the screaming man. Wide-eyed and irrational, he demanded the doctor as I approached.

"Not you. I want Doc. A real doc."

I squatted beside him and cut off his pant leg at the top of his thigh, exposing an injury nearly identical to the compound fracture I had experience mending. To the rhythm of his heartbeat, blood spurted from the gaping wound where his thigh bone had snapped apart and escaped the skin. I thought of Ohanzee.

"It's not about me, it's not about me. Don't stare. Just help," I thought to myself, swallowing the gag reflex crawling up my throat after the man's warm blood sprayed across my face.

"Take deep breaths. You need to settle down and I can help you," I calmly said, trying to follow my own advice.

"Help me," he begged, realizing I was his only option.

"You're okay. I've done this before," I said. My reassurance did not include the poor result for my previous patient who suffered as infection permeated his body.

"You better have. Can't lose my leg. Would rather die."

I grabbed his calf and twisted his lower leg so the direction of his feet matched. Glancing above, the exposed femur rotated, even though the splintered bone did not disappear under the skin.

The man screamed, then cussed. "You're a stinkin' girl. I want Doc."

I ignored him and braced myself against the man's other bent knee and pulled on his fractured leg quickly and decisively with every bit of mustered strength.

His weak thigh muscle stretched and I was fairly certain I reconnected the ends of the jagged bones. Blood gushed from the open hole and stained the ground a dark red. The man screamed again, then moaned in agony and passed out. I felt for a pulse, wondering if he may be dying. When I found a strong and steady beat, I manipulated the swelled, blood-soaked thigh and was confident his femur was reset.

I hollered at Chance to fetch a straight stick from the pines surrounding us. When he did not respond, I found one myself and snapped the splint to match the injured leg. I pulled the man's knife from his hip, and cut away five strips of fabric from the skirt of my dress, leaving only tattered edges above my knees. Repeating the process with the white lining underneath, I wrapped the wound in the white cotton and then tightly bound his leg to the stick with the purple fabric, reminding me of shiny ribbons adorning presents under a tree. The man remained unconscious.

Merchants from town gathered at the edge of the chaos as word spread of the accident. They loaded their empty buckboard supply wagons and carried the wounded to Doc's cabin for more care. The dead were slumped over the backs of spare horses and taken away.

I glanced at the thinly built boy, now sitting on Blue and asked, "So Chance, where's your mom?"

"Don't right know," he answered, confused.

"When did you see her last?"

"Don't right know."

"How old are you, Chance?"

"Ah, ten. No, nine. No, eight."

He was too thin and short for a ten-year-old. "Did you see how many Indians attacked you?"

"I think about ten. Or maybe only one or two."

I turned to Doc for guidance.

"Looks like we have another guest tonight," Doc replied. "We can clear this all up in the morning. Let's get going."

Doc gave me a leg up on the back of Blue, in front of Chance. My ragged dress no longer gathered at Blue's withers. When Chance reached around my waist for balance, his ribs pressed against similar protruding bones on my back. We plodded behind the rickety wagons of wounded, moaning men and the malnourished boy wept.

CHAPTER 3

SARA

JULY, 1876

DEADWOOD

"WHITES LOOKING FOR GOLD KILL INDIANS JUST AS THEY WOULD KILL BEARS AND PAY NO REGARD FOR TREATIES."
- General William T. Sherman

Hours turned into days. Days turned into weeks. I patiently cleaned wounds and tended to the injured men. All but one man healed and moved out of Doc's cabin as soon as they were mobile. One man lingered. Rusty Reynolds was slow to recover from the compound fracture, which I had set the night of the accident. Abrasively, he continuously grumbled in pain when others would be stoically grateful for having both legs. Most were surprised Reynolds survived. As he lived to see another day, and another, rumors grew in town that Doc's young new assistant had miracle healing in her hands.

Doc ignored the town talk and saloon gossip that I was half Doc's age and may not be sleeping in his barn. He shrugged it off and urged me to assist on each of his house calls in exchange for food and the use of his barn. It seemed an easy trade until I could display income from legitimate means. We bantered with light-hearted conversation as we rode from patient to patient. He told me the key to becoming a good gold rush doctor was to be confident enough to act quickly with nothing else to go on. "That's why they call it medical *practice!*" he chuckled.

At least once a week, I rode to my claim and panned for gold. The disturbed soil near the creek where I had buried the other bag of gold became less obvious as the days went by. Sometimes Chance followed on foot with Shadow at his side. He rarely spoke and appeared confused at times. Doc and I assumed Chance had struck his head in the accident. Or was he simply mourning? When he did speak, it was mostly in questions. He asked over and over again where his father was.

"God is the keeper of your pa's soul," Doc told the boy. "He's with God."

"But I want him here with me."

"He is here with you, Chance. He's in the air and the trees and the sunrises and in Blue's warm breath against your cheek," I said.

Chance choked up. "If he's here, why do I miss him?"

He shook with emotion while I patted his back. All the while, sorrow sucked air out of my lungs as I grieved with the boy for what he lost. For what I lost.

On days Chance accompanied me to my claim, I went through the motions of prospecting so he believed it was productive. Eager to impress, Chance did most of the heavy work, insisting he was a man. In truth, he had the build of a young sapling, bending to the breeze. Still, Chance shoveled down into the stream. I appreciated his efforts because the work was difficult for me. My arms went numb and my neck burned from bending over in the water. As many warned, it was back breaking work, even for a man without an injury as mine.

Chance was simply full of energy. He scooped out a shallow hole. A shovel-full of gravel and dirt went into our two gold pans, eighteen inches across and four inches deep. Mr. Gushurst from the Big Horn Store instructed me to let the bottom of my pan rust so it would hold the gold dust in place.

With chilled hands, Chance and I squatted at the edge of the stream and submerged our pans full of gravel. We slid them side to side and the light silt washed downstream. Then we lifted our pans, swirling the gravel in circle after circle. The angled sides of the pan allowed sand to flow off. On sunny days, when most of the sand was gone, remaining garnets shimmered translucent burgundy and rose hues. We saved the brilliant garnet gems and discarded gray pebbles. More and more of the contents slid over the edge of the pan until almost nothing remained. Then, the moment of truth came, with one quick flip of our hands, as the contents spread out where we could poke around for a flake or two of gold. We pleaded under our breath with the God of gold strikes, praying for a rare flake or an even rarer nugget.

"Awe, not again, Miss Sara. Not even a speck," Chance complained.

"Me neither, Chance. But Shadow wants to play. Why don't you throw a stick for her? Take a break. I'll shovel out our next batch."

As Chance played fetch with Shadow, I scooped more gravel from the stream. After glancing back to be sure he was not watching, I pulled my pouch from my pocket, quickly seeding the newly filled pans. Chance returned later and worked his pan, oblivious to my scheme.

"Look, Miss Sara! It's a good one! Look at the flakes! That one's almost a nugget, wouldn't you say?"

"I think so, Chance! Things are looking up."

A few evenings later, when I walked to Main Street for supplies, a few nodded their heads as I passed. One man, who seemed shady, mumbled to his friend, "That's her. Sara. The girl who put Reynolds back together. He said she never seen the elephant and she's hittin' it big on a lousy claim.[11] The boy helps her pan and they have better luck than most of us."

It was then, behind them, I saw the mule tied to the rail in front of the Nuttal & Mann's Saloon. One brown eye and one blue eye. A white stripe down his chest. I gasped for breath. The mule with unique markings was likely owned by the prospector who knocked me unconscious and assaulted me three months earlier. The only blessing of the horrid night was how I had the constitution to steal the prospector's bags of gold as I was rescued by Ohanzee. I recalled the man called JoJo, cowered at their

42

campfire, hollering for his partner who dragged me into the trees to steal my purity. I wondered if Ohanzee was ever honored with an eagle feather for counting coup on JoJo.

I impulsively marched straight into Nuttal & Mann's Saloon, confident I could recognize the man who had planned to take every part of me. During the assault, he was drunk and we were shadows beneath the night sky. I was unsure he would remember me months later, though his voice was seared into my mind. I scanned the congested room. My eyes adjusted to the dim light but I gagged at the combination of putrid body odor, stale ale, and spittoons overflowing with snuff. My memory of JoJo could have described at least thirty of the men in the saloon: Tall, skinny, canvas pants with suspenders, a grimy white shirt and filthy nails.

A wall of liquor was neatly lined up like soldiers behind the long walnut bar. The burly bartender with a thick gray mustache was the iron cannon in front of the troops. "Howdy, young lady, what do you know?" He glanced down at my new royal blue dress.

"I was looking for someone," I professed under my breath.

The bartender was a stout, olive-skinned Italian man in his forties, and wore gray trousers with a soiled white shirt and a worn-out vest. The breast pocket was stretched tight, holding two cigars. He made eye contact with a lady in a low-cut shimmering red and black dress seated at the end of the bar, then tipped his head toward me, giving her a signal. Slightly staggering, she moved toward me. The extremely tight-waisted black bodice of her dress made me wonder how she could breathe. Grabbing my arm, she pulled me to the far end of the bar, away from the groups of men either playing cards or talking whisky tales of new bounties on Indian heads. Distracted, she listened with me as I rolled my eyes at their claims.

"Nonsense," I murmured, under my breath.

"No, Honey, it's true. The county commissioners placed a $25 bounty for Indian heads."

"What?" I gasped, envisioning Ohanzee's head severed from his body by a miner's pickaxe.

"That's what they voted cuz too many Indians are sneakin' into the hills. They're killing prospectors, all riled up after murdering Custer and all those poor soldiers. I'm Annie. What's your name?"

"Sara," I said.

"Lookin' for a job here in the saloon? Been told to scout out a new supply for the men, if you know what I mean. You're pretty. Young. Just a tad thin. Not like me, outta commission if you know what I mean. Good money if you're interested. Nine of ten people breathin' here are men. Gives you good odds at makin' lots of money."

She was older than me but not wrinkled or gray; just a bit plump in her mid-section and her face was drawn. She seemed to have trouble with her green eyes, squinting a bit as one eye diverted from the other.

"I'm quite busy working for Doc. And I have a claim."

"Oh, nursing for Doc are ya? Well, know this work is here if you get in a bind. Not sure what's best, fixing fights, standing in frigid

44

water siftin' mud or doing the dance with drunk men. Each girl here decides for herself who she wants to be."

As she spoke, I noticed the bartender weighed gold dust differently for his intoxicated customers. While placing the dust on the bar scale, he consistently ran his fingers through his greasy hair, certainly carrying an ounce home with him at the end of his shift.

The rest of the conversation was a complete fog. If it was profitable to cut the head off of an Indian, then what would those who walked the streets of Deadwood think of me? I traveled with an Indian. I watched the battle between red and white. I did nothing to stop the Indians as they sent each soldier to his Maker. Would I be hated as an Indian sympathizer? Would I be found guilty of stealing a cavalry horse and end up swinging from a tree beside many a horse thief? I started to hyperventilate.

"Excuse me, ma'am."

I rushed past the inebriation surrounding me and Annie hollered after me, "You'll be back, Sara. I bet my life on it."

As I ungracefully slammed out of the saloon doors, the last person I wanted to see was standing face-to-face with me. Preacher Smith.

"What do you know? So, that's where you ended up, huh? Just as everyone speculated."

"What's that supposed to mean? Who is everyone?" I asked, trying to keep my voice from quivering.

"Not for me to say."

"I was just looking for someone in there."

"Perhaps yourself?"

"Don't tell me you never slipped into a saloon."

"Not lately. Won't let myself step into the darkness, though the pull is true. It don't feel right to indulge, being a servant of the good Lord."

Preacher Smith was too old for me to feel attraction, yet his physique was admirable. He was solid and had a way about him.

"Still hiding?" he asked in a soft-spoken manner.

"Hiding what?"

"I don't know. You tell me, Sara. Might help to talk it out sometime with someone you trust. If it ain't God, then I've been known to listen and I don't start rumors, no sir. I see it like this: Life happens, Sara. You choose how to go forward. Same thing for me. I left my wife, children, and church to step into this calling. So now, what do I choose? I miss them, but I left for good reasons, even if it looks wrong today."

"You left your family back east to survive on their own?"

"I know it looks bad, but I couldn't drag them out here until I knew it was safe."

He saw my doubting eyes. "Least you can do is send some of God's money back to them," I said sarcastically as I walked away.

I solemnly picked up more supplies at the Big Horn Store and walked back to Doc's barn, unsettled in my heart and mind.

The next day, Chance asked if he could camp with me for a few days on my claim.

"If I pan a lot of gold and if I find a big nugget, can I keep it?"

"What do you want a nugget for?"

"To pay for my trip home."

"Do you know where home is, Chance?"

"Um. No. I can't remember exactly. Doc said I have to start saving money so when I remember, I can go home."

That afternoon, I slipped extra gold into Chance's pan.

As we settled into camp, I told Chance to stay under the tent with Shadow as I collected extra branches to fuel the fire throughout the night. I climbed up the sharp hillside, loose with slick shale. Out of breath, I reached the tree line above the ridge and collected wood for our fire. I heard Shadow rustling behind me. She had taken to chasing squirrels rather than keeping Chance occupied.

Then, in the opposite direction, I heard a low mumbling of unintelligible words, flowing together like springs into a narrow stream. I walked toward the source. There, under cover of thick spruce, was an Indian, softly calling out a painful song over a body partially covered with rocks. Only buckskin pants and worn slick moccasins protruded from the steel gray stones. More quickly than I could react, the warrior turned and sprang on me, taking me to the ground with a knife pressed against my neck.

"Oun she la yea," I whispered, begging for his compassion on me.

Startled at my broken Lakota, he pulled the knife from my neck. "Oh ya lay hey?" he asked, questioning who I looked for.

"Ohanzee. Lakota."

"Ohanzee, Minniconjou?"

I shook my head yes.

He puckered his lips in affirmation. "Taku eniciyapi hey?"

"Sara."

"Say-Rah?"

I nodded.

The man rolled off me and diverted his eyes. I had interrupted his private mourning.

"Akicita?" I asked.

The protection warrior nodded. He methodically spoke in Lakota and I understood less than he thought. Stepping away to pick up another rock, he carefully placed it over the exposed legs of his companion. Something terrible had happened so he would not be able to fight in the afterlife. I could not understand the details. Nausea overcame me when I sensed it may be Ohanzee. I backed away on my hands and knees. The mourning warrior did not watch me leave and his chanting grew faint as distance separated our worlds.[12]

48

"We need to put up the sides of our tarp, Miss Sara," Chance said as I returned to our camp.

"It's a clear night, let's just look at the stars."

"Can I go back to Doc's?" he asked, looking into the darkness with apprehension. Vivid stars shone at each treetop opening, offering space to catch my breath and contain my wild thoughts. The mourning cries sang harmony with distant howling wolves echoing between the ridges.

Chance shivered with his back against mine.

"You aren't scared, are you?" I asked.

"Naw. Just cold."

"Tell me what you remember of your home?" I asked, trying to distract him.

"Don't rightly know. Why ain't ya afraid of Injuns?"

"Goodnight Chance."

"Ain't cha afraid they'll take you away and do bad things to ya?"

"Goodnight Chance," I repeated more forcefully and the rasp of crickets turned still.

The next morning, I dropped Chance at Doc's cabin and went to town. Once again, the newspaper headline caught my attention while resupplying at the Big Horn Store. Mr. Gushurst saw my not-so-subtle glances and gave me the newspaper for free. Tucked between two buildings, I sat on the dirt beside Blue, immersed in the story, now on a side column of the front cover.

"MORE DETAILS ON CUSTER MASSACRE. SQUAWS MUTILATE AND TORTURE SOLDIERS. DEAD VICTIMS ROBBED. BRAVE MAN HAILED FOR SAVING LIVES. As the Army reorganizes against the Sioux after the massacre killing Custer and his men, heroes are immerging from the bloodshed. After the fight, Grant Marsh, the captain of the steamer, Far West, risked his life and steamed up 674 miles of the savage infested territory of the shallow Bighorn River. He rescued injured men from the battle and the lone surviving horse, Comanche. When the men were finally loaded at 2 a.m. on June 28, Marsh navigated nine hundred miles in fifty-four hours to bring survivors to Fort Abraham Lincoln for medical treatment. His bravery inspires all as we wait for additional action from the Army."

Grant Marsh. I hardly believed my eyes. I knew Grant Marsh, with his thick mustache and dangling cigar. Nine months earlier, I was a passenger on one of his other steamboats. His piercing eyes exuded perseverance. Of course he would have risked his life to rescue the wounded soldiers.

"It's absolutely wonderful out here," he had said. "It's a thrill. *Josephine* and I work together like a marriage from heaven. Actually, I have another wife too, *Far West*. She's upriver right now. Waiting for me."[13]

I remembered how Mr. Marsh spoke of confidence. He explained how he would tell himself over and over again, when faced with danger, to not be a coward but to be brave. If the newspaper comments about him were true, then he lived by his words.

I walked into the Nuttal & Mann's Saloon and found Annie in her usual place at the end of the bar. Before we could talk, a mob of men plowed through the door, some cheering and others trying to see around the crowd at the sun-worn man in front, who swung a decapitated head with blood-caked shiny black hair and dull half-opened eyes onto the bar. "Where's my prize? The bounty is mine," he said with a heavy Mexican accent and a slimy smirk on his face.

I nearly vomited on the sawdust-covered floor after glancing at the head. Orange paint in the shape of a sun clung to the dark-skinned cheek. I recognized the tribal features of the sharply chiseled cheeks and straight nose. But he had been older than Ohanzee. I gasped for fresh air and rushed outside.

The crowd seemed to follow me and reorganized in the street as they argued about who would pay the man for the Indian head. The foul-smelling Mexican hopped on his horse and rode up and down the Badlands, swinging the head by his long hair, whooping so loud that it echoed off the gulch walls. I bent beside a water trough and threw up, realizing the irony of a man native of Mexico feeling superior to a man native of the Black Hills. When I rose to wipe my face, an agitated man from the crowd noted my distress.

"Looks like the greaser just proved we have a white Injun in Deadwood."

"Not a white Injun. Just human, you sick bastard," I blurted.

"Th' lassie is reit. Boonty fur a heed is sick," were the heavily accented words, which came from beside the gathered crowd. I glanced over to a six-foot man wearing a white scarf around his neck. It was Mr. Phillip from beside the claim's office. He was unshaven and deliberately moved through the crowd, confidently dividing the men in half as he slowly approached me.

Men hollered out, "Injuns are animals. Shootin' us and scalpin' us in the dark. They murdered Custer and his men in cold blood."

I bit the inside of my cheek and could taste the blood.

"Government ain't even trying to keep us out no more. Six months now. These hills are good as ours," another man hollered. The comments continued.

"Heard Phillip wants to make a baby with a squaw."

"Looks like the girl wishes she was a squaw."

"Ya don't like the bounty? Then you don't belong here."

"Not leavin' in fear, boot nut a place for da laddie," said Mr. Phillip, grabbing my arm and safely hustling me from the growing mob. "Yoose best all rot away, just sayin'."

CHAPTER 4

SARA

AUGUST 2, 1876

DEADWOOD

"PROBABLY HICKOK WAS THE ONLY MAN WE
HAVE YET HAD IN OUR MIDST WHO HAD THE
COURAGE AND OTHER QUALIFICATIONS TO
BRING SOME SEMBLANCE OF ORDER TO THE
LAWLESS ELEMENT OF OUR CAMP."
~Black Hills Pioneer

Doc never turned down a case, whether the injured or sick had
money or not. He was right. The town offered unlimited training
from injuries and illness. Stitching knife wounds was not even
worth mentioning. Tying off spurting veins was more challenging.
Those with head injuries could only rest because time alone
would determine if they recovered. Most never did. Abdominal
wounds were best left to Doc. They never seemed to end well, no
matter what he did to treat them. I watched Doc stitch up holes
the size of my fist. I sponged the oozing fluids from wounds he
left open. Either way, I watched most of the men die.

In my opinion, Chance spent excessive time with Mr. Reynolds in Doc's cabin as the man's leg slowly healed. They smirked whenever I passed by, becoming more indignant each day. Finally, enough was enough. Late one afternoon, I walked to the doctor's porch where Chance was alone, playing with Shadow.

"How are you doing, Chance?"

"Can't talk with you," he said.

"What do you mean you can't talk with me?"

"Mr. Reynolds told me not to talk to you. You love Injuns. You wish you were one. You probably help them kill us. You probably sneak guns to them or something."

"What in the world are you talking about?"

"I seen it. I followed you up the hill at your claim that night. I saw you talk in Injun to that Injun."

"Chance, someone cut off his friend's head for a bounty."

Reynolds had been listening from the cabin's open window. Using crutches, he wavered from the doctor's door, dragging the toes of his broken leg for stability. Reynolds glared into my eyes, wobbling from either whisky or something Doc gave him.

"Ah, there she is. The skinny white girl who wants to be an Injun."

"I don't know what you are referring to, Mr. Reynolds."

"Ah, but you do. When Chance told me, it all made sense. How you ride bareback, then the boy said you secretly talk in their language. I dug in your pack in the barn and found all your Injun stuff. You a spy for them, huh, Sara?" His intoxicated, bloodshot eyes failed to track as he pulled a blue cloth from his pocket and wiped the snuff juice from his lips.

"How dare you go in my bag."

"Whatcha hiding, Sara? Guilty of something? Don't want to be found out?" He swallowed hard. We stared at each other and his eyes swayed with the hot breeze. I doubt he saw the bead of sweat trickle down my cheekbone.

"So it's simple. You give me half of the gold you take from your claim and I don't mention a word of this to anyone. Otherwise, you'll hang from a tree, Sara. If that's even your name."

"You are pathetic. You deserve no more of my time. I have to go check on Annie. She isn't feeling well."

"You mean Anytime Annie? Nice company you keep, Sara. Suppose you'll start moonlightin' to fill in for her at the saloon? Won't have any other choice if I tell what yur up to. First, we thought you might be a miracle girl. We were wrong, 'cause you just an Injun lover, spyin' for 'em."

"You are full of yourself."

"Hell, this is quite a twist to our botched job," he said, before catching his tongue. He staggered to the house, leaning on it for stability.

"Our botched job?"

"Never mind that, I'll confess when your ears no longer hear as your white Injun corpse swings from a tree."

Chance panicked and stepped to the side of Sara, grabbing her hand. "Don't hang Miss Sara, she didn't hurt nobody. You're the one who jumped the wagon and killed my papa."

"Shut up, boy," the drunk man yelled.

"You killed my papa!" Chance screamed, repeating, "You killed my papa."

"I didn't kill nobody. Comes with the work, bound to happen eventually when you hold up enough stages."

"What?" I asked. Chance started to cry.

"Gotta do something to pay for my whiskey. Can't be a bandit now with a busted leg. But lucky me. Now I know your Injun secret. Keep quiet about the stage. Slip me gold from your claim and my lips will stay sealed. It's a good option for you, Sara, 'cause I'd rather just hang your pretty hide on my wall," he cackled.

"You deserve to rot in hell."

"And you'll burn beside me if I tell the town of your red tendencies."

I turned to leave, trying to process his words; angry at myself for weaving a web so easily destroyed by one evil man.

"Hey, Sara, ya can curse me all you want, but fact is, I'll brag forever that you took your dress off for me."

"A gesture I'll forever regret," I answered. Disgusted and sweating, I walked away and went about my routine in town as if nothing had happened. Two newcomers were setting up a hardware business and I nodded as I passed. Slipping along the alley beside the saloon, I climbed the exterior staircase two steps at a time. After knocking, I opened the door without invitation.

"Annie? Annie?"

When no reply came, I walked into the room where I examined her the week before when she whined of stomach cramps. She lay unresponsive, curled up around her distended stomach. An empty bottle of the drug Laudanum rested on the floor beside the bed.[14]

I flinched when a gunshot echoed through the rafters. Commotion rumbled below my feet. "Find a doctor! We need a doctor," echoed through the floor. I touched my right hip to assure myself that my belt held my seven-shot revolver. Charging toward Nuttal & Mann's, I paused at the entrance. No men were standing at the bar. They all gathered, six men deep, around one table. Some were silent. Others were busy speaking but nobody listened. A prospector I did not recognize grabbed me at the door, pulled me through the men and halted at a lump on the floor. "Sara's here. Good as a doctor."

"Don't matter if she's a doctor or not," a man said, losing his footing as he slipped in the crimson pool of blood and overturned booze. "The miracle girl ain't workin' her magic today. No bringing him back."

I reached over the mess and checked for signs of life but the man had been shot point-blank through the back left side of his head and the exit wound was through his right cheek. "Who was he?" I asked as my insides churned.

"Girly. Girly. Where have you been? He's Wild Bill Hickok. Yes sir."

The biggest legend of the west was crumpled on the floor with his leg caught in the stool he fell from. His Smith & Wesson Army revolver was still tucked in his belt in old cavalry fashion with the butt facing forward. He was dead as dead could be with a blood-soaked pair of black aces and black eights stuck in his hand.[15]

"I think I'm shot," a man standing above me suddenly announced. With his uninjured right hand, he reached for the drink of the dead man and took it in at once. "Saw smoke then heard the shot. Ah, gin and bitters."

Another town doctor, Doc Pierce, was summoned quickly since he lived nearby. I had finished wrapping the injured man's shattered left wrist with the community towel from the bar.[16]

"Doc, can you handle this man? He's been shot. I have another patient to tend to." Blood was soaking through the towel. I rolled my eyes up to the second floor where Annie waited. He nodded and I disappeared up the stairs.

Annie's door was ajar and the stench of vomit forced me to breathe from my mouth. She was still alive but unconscious. I used the wash basin beside the bed to clean up the front of her dress. The lacy lingerie draped over a red velvet chair in the corner was washed yet not appropriate. I left her in the soiled dress and kept her covered by her blanket. I stared at the calico pattern wallpaper for an hour, tracing the pattern over and over until Annie slowly regained her senses. She moaned, cried, and finally opened her droopy eyes.

"Annie, Annie. What on earth?" I asked. "What can be so bad that you take your life?"

After another half hour of listening to Annie's shallow breath, she let out a long sigh and wept. When words finally came, they were ugly.

"You don't know, Sara, what it's like to have a hidden life. My entire family back east thinks I'm an actress, dancing and singing for Mr. Swearengen.[17] He promised to help me get a foothold in acting and dancing. Said there was lots of money in it. Lured me out here and now I'm stranded with no respectful means of support. So, I'm an actress all right. Between the sheets."

"You can always do something else. I can help you. You can help me on my claim."

Annie smirked. "The girl with all the answers. It ain't so easy to fix me, Sara. I gotta babe coming."

"I can see that," I answered, looking at the bulge below her ribcage. "It's not a disaster, Annie. I can help you. And the baby."

"Baby's doomed. Don't even know who the daddy is. Never will. No market for me now. Nobody to lean on. I'm finished."

"That's not true, you need to be strong for your baby. The baby needs a mama."

"I ain't no mama, Sara. Don't know how to care for a child. Will ruin me. Who wants a pregnant woman? Best to die now and take it with me to the grave."

"No, Annie. Please don't. You aren't alone. You have your baby. You have me. Just take it moment by moment. The moments will turn into days. Then weeks. Then months. Then you'll have a beautiful baby in your arms."

The door swung open. It was the madam who ran the upstairs brothel.

"Annie, you aren't making me any money by laying around crying. Get on with it, the men will be restless after the murder. They're drinking up a storm downstairs and you know what comes next," she callously said and walked out.

"We can work through this Annie." I said halfheartedly, wishing I knew the answers.

"Easy for you to say, Miss Miracle Doctor. Ya ever wonder how the men look at us differently? You're respectable. I ain't. I slip into town on the Utter wagon train and start spreadin' dark diseases.[18] You waltz into town a few weeks after me and start healing people. Funny thing is, we both take care of them prospectors, just in our own ways."

I left Annie and walked outside as the daily stagecoach arrived. Groups of men, already high with energy from the murder, stood around, kicking at the ground, restlessly waiting for the contents to be revealed. Most expected mail or freight. Two finely dressed men stepped out of the coach. Then, a woman with a heavily powdered face and two small children cautiously stood on the top step, wavering as her boys leapt to the ground and ran into the arms of a freshly bathed prospector.

One young woman remained inside the stagecoach, nervously peering out the window. When the driver demanded her out, the glistening plum dress fought to remain in the confines of the coach. After her fancy lace-up boots hit the ground, she tugged and readjusted her waistline, wiping a sweaty curl from her eye while dirty blonde ringlets framed her beautiful face. A group of men watched her fidget with her attire in the street, still scanning the crowd, searching for someone. Where had she traveled from and why did her grand entrance turn bad? Unable to leave her alone, I approached in a friendly manner.

"Can I help you find someone?"

"It will please me if you will," she said under her breath. "So perplexed as to why he isn't awaiting my coach?"

"Who?"

"My fiancé, Jack. He promised to meet my stage. Said waiting for my arrival felt like lifetimes passing before his aching heart. So why isn't he here?"

"I don't know why. And I don't know of a man named Jack. What does he look like?"

"We spoke not of his appearance as I chose him for deeper reasons. I am certain he is handsome and he is clearly a gentleman, with values far beyond the gloating eyes I see staring this direction."

I spun around and saw the crowd of curious men growing.

"His whereabouts are of great concern for me at the moment, but to be perfectly frank, I have little to go on."

"What? Do you know where he lives?"

"Not precisely. He just said in the ad that he wanted an adventurous companion and a good mother to our future children. I know he has a prosperous claim, a beautiful log cabin, and six lovely dogs." As she spoke, her eyes sparkled with optimism. In the sunlight, I saw blue and green and gray. She was close to me in years and was strikingly beautiful, though she did not seem to recognize it.

"He has six dogs?"

"Well, actually, once he learned of my passion for dogs, he purchased six just for me. And three cats. That's how much he loves me and pleases me with my every wish."

"You have never met him?"

"Not exactly. Nonetheless, our love is true and it shines through the letters."

"You're a mail order bride!"

"Hush, not an ordinary mail order bride. His love is real." She whispered and clasped her hands together as if to gain more confidence. Her voice wavered as she asked, "This is going to work out just fine, right?"

"Um. Right," I answered, unconvinced. I had not seen one cat since leaving Fort Randall six months earlier. The beauty's story was weakening by the moment.

"It's getting late and Deadwood is not the best place for you to be alone tonight. You're welcome to stay with me in Doc's barn."

"A barn? You must be kidding? What do you think I am? A cow?"

"More like a broodmare from the sound of it."

She placed both hands on her hips and blurted with a raised voice, "How dare you Miss, Miss, Miss."

"Sara. Just tell it like I see it."

She curled up her lips to her nose, searching for a response. None came. A man standing in a group of three spoke up, "Woooo weeee! We have a feisty one, boys."

"She's a doll," the next chimed in. The last one watched through dark squinty eyes as he methodically rolled a cigarette between his fingers. He merely snickered with a snuff-stained crooked smile.

"Ah, Miss Sara. Your barn seems to be the accommodation I will stoop to tonight," she whispered. "Where's the sheriff when you need him, anyway?"

"No sheriff in town," I answered.

Walking to Doc's barn in unending conversation reminded me of how deprived I was of female companionship. Her name was Rebekah and she was not short of fancy words. She came from Georgia, the youngest child of a wealthy family of eleven. Her parents never gave up on their dream for a girl, even though it took nine tries. As Rebekah explained, an all too predictable affluent young man diligently courted her. He was soon to inherit a vast and prosperous plantation. Rebekah's family, and their entire circle of wealthy equals, were pressuring her to marry him. They insisted love would come later and she could not pass up his land inheritance which was ten-fold the size of Rebekah's family plantation. Even though he claimed to be madly in love with her, Rebekah could not muster the same feelings in return. She felt nothing romantic for the young man and could not stand the thought of compromising on love to gain wealth. She waited and waited, hoping a dormant seed of love in her heart would grow and blossom. Instead, anxiety and doubt flourished with each passing day.

In a moment of great desperation, weeks before she was expected to accept his request for engagement, Rebekah pulled her father's Savannah Morning News from the brass container of kindling beside their meticulously bricked fireplace. She thumbed through to the classifieds, curious of the opportunities for the less privileged. An advertisement in the bottom left corner of the classified section read: "Bride Wanted. Prosperous prospector with a beautiful log cabin near Deadwood, Dakota Territory, looking for a wife who will tolerate the frontier and be a good mother to our children. Please write and send a photo."

Rebekah immediately notified her affluent suitor that she could not be the wife he envisioned and she would not accompany him at the altar. She secretly corresponded with the prospector from the ad and fell deeply in love, or so she thought. Upon learning of her intentions, Rebekah's parents vowed to disown her.

"So you come from wealth?" I asked.

"No, I *came* from wealth. No going back. I packed my bags and left with only fifty dollars in my pocket."

When we finally reached Doc's cabin, I introduced him to Rebekah, sensing disappointment when he saw beyond her silky skin and purple dress, recognizing her tender age just as mine.

"Girls," he said. "You have both had quite a day. I'm happy to trade places with you for the night. You can stay in the cabin; I'll stay in the barn."

When I refused, even with Rebekah glaring at me, Doc graciously handed over extra blankets and we retreated to the barn. My curiosity overcame the unspoken Deadwood Gulch rule of not asking personal questions about someone's past.

"So, did you send your photo to Jack?"

"Of course, and he said I was the most beautiful girl he ever laid eyes on."

"Oh, how sweet."

"He said the moment he glimpsed at my photo; he knew that we were meant to be together. I took his breath away. He said I had sparkle in my eyes."

"Sweet as honey, he sounds," I said, wondering if I would ever find someone as adoring. "So, perhaps he was confused about the date of your arrival? I'm sure he has a good reason for not meeting you at the stage."

She shrugged. "Jack promised he would wait at the stage stop every day in August until I was safely in his arms. He said he fondly yearned for days when we would picnic on a blanket and bask in the sun. Isn't he charming and romantic?"

"Um. I suppose. I'll take you back tomorrow," I promised.

"And how did you end up here?" Rebekah asked.

"Long story, better for another time."

"Serious? It must be extraordinary."

"You could say that. Goodnight."

"Goodnight," she echoed.

A few minutes later, I cleared my conscience. "Rebekah, I'm sorry I insinuated that you were a broodmare. I didn't mean to offend you."

"That's okay, no offense taken," she replied. Long after I assumed Rebekah had fallen asleep, she followed up, "What's a broodmare anyway?"

CHAPTER 5

SARA

AUGUST 3, 1876

DEADWOOD

"SHOULD IT EVER BE OUR MISFORTUNE TO KILL A MAN ... WE WOULD SIMPLY ASK THAT OUR TRIAL MAY TAKE PLACE IN SOME OF THE MINING CAMPS IN THESE HILLS."
~Black Hills Pioneer

"What do you think you are doing wearing a purple dress?" Rebekah groggily asked, squinting through swollen morning eyes. Natural golden ringlets still framed her face. "It's me who is to steal the show on this day, not you."

"It's new. Replaces the one I tore apart. I want to wear it to the funeral today."

"Tore one apart? Surely a story for later. But I have nothing near as fancy as my purple dress and my love must cast his eyes upon me for the first time, looking as lovely and alluring as he deserves."

"Then we shall both wear purple."

"Fine," she pouted, under her breath.

I delivered Rebekah to the stage stop where she thanked me while staring into the dense cathedral pine trees lining the gulch.

"Are you okay?" I asked.

"I fear he will change his mind," she confessed.

"You're beautiful, Rebekah. He won't change his mind, as long as he shows up."

I told her to wait while I checked on Annie. The madam stopped me at the first room of the brothel and explained that Annie was busy. I asked how she was feeling, but the madam shushed me and escorted me to the door, which she promptly shut behind me. I returned to the busy street where a crowd gathered for the stage's arrival.

Rebekah's dress glittered like a purple kaleidoscope as a man held her in his arms and spun in circles with unrestrained delight. Mostly relief but a tinge of jealousy spread across me, thankful she was not left in the street for another day of dashed dreams, but also envy toward the carefree adoration showering upon her.

"You, Rebekah, are beautiful!" he hollered in a familiar voice that I could not place. I stepped closer. His back was to me and Rebekah grinned from over his shoulder. She was happy. Rebekah waved for me to join them, seeming oblivious that loitering men were smirking and commenting how they should order up their own cure for loneliness.

"Sara, I am pleased to introduce you to Jack, my fiancé," she said over his shoulder. And then, he turned his head toward me.

"Jake?"

"Sara?"

"Not Jake, Jack," Rebekah corrected.

"Jake?" I said again.

Jake dropped Rebekah before she could gain her footing. She flopped down at our feet and instantly flared her right nostril in complete confusion.

"Sara?" Jake asked again, as if questioning a ghost.

"I thought you were dead," we said in unison. We hugged awkwardly.

"What's going on here?" Rebekah demanded, rolling onto her knees and onto her feet. "Have you prior acquaintance?"

"Uh, it's a long story," Jake said.

Indignation filled me. "What on earth, Jake? Were you so desperate you had to buy a mail order bride?"

"Not desperate. What about you? I thought you were dead."

"Well, you sure didn't mourn very long, did you?"

"What do you insinuate? I was never for sale. I am not what you think I am," Rebekah demanded, red-faced with a set jaw.

"That's all you are. An easy, warm body to keep Jake horizontal."

Rebekah slapped me. I returned it, twofold in strength.

"Now, now ladies," Jake said, stepping between us. "Let's not overreact here."

"Overreact?" Rebekah hollered. Merchants and prospectors on the street stopped and stared. "I'll show you overreact! She's ruining everything!" I barely had time to flinch back to evade Rebekah's right punch. Her clenched fist narrowly cleared my nose and hooked up to directly meet Jake's left eye. He dropped to the ground.

"Oh my goodness. Oh my goodness," Rebekah repeated over and over again. She crouched over Jake and tenderly stroked his reddening face with her silky-smooth porcelain hand. "I am terribly sorry, my love. Shame and rage overcame me."

Jake regained his composure and stumbled to his feet. While Rebekah was distracted, picking bits of straw and dirt from her dress, Jake angled his body from her and whispered near my ear, "Don't say a word of this to anyone. We'll talk later. Not a word. Understand?"

I nodded. He turned back to Rebekah, who appeared confused but less angry.

"I'm sorry Rebekah," I said quietly. She did not respond.

"Come now, my beautiful princess, it'll all be fine," Jake said, placing Rebekah's hand in the crook of his bent arm. "We need to get something for this shiner and headache of mine." His dimples appeared with his steadfast smirk.

They walked toward the Big Horn Store, leaving me standing alone in the middle of the street. Preacher Smith stepped from the crowd and approached cautiously.

"Well, Well. What do you know? You okay?"

"Yes."

"Couldn't help but see what happened," the preacher offered.

"You and the other thousands in town," I said, slightly embarrassed.

"Don't worry about them. Just a little tussle, not a shootout. I take it you know Jack?"

"I thought I did," I answered with surprising disdain.

"Come now, Sara. He's not a bad young man, even listens to my sermons now and then."

"Well, he didn't have the courtesy to meet his mail order bride yesterday. He didn't even care enough to show up at the stage when she arrived."

"Sara. Sara. He was busy yesterday, helping move Wild Bill's body to Charlie Utter's camp for the funeral. Wasn't like he was part of the group who let Broken Nose Jack off the hook. Or should I say off the noose? "

"What's that supposed to mean?"

"Didn't you hear? Where have you been? The miners held a trial for Broken Nose Jack.[19] Down at McDaniel's theatre."

"And?"

"Well, he said he was avenging his brother's death. Claimed Wild Bill killed his brother years ago. In cold blood. So, the miners declared him innocent and told 'em best to leave town, which he did in a hurry. On a rather nice horse, I might add."

"So now random men with their own agendas are the law?" I asked unemotionally.

"Who else can do it?"

"I don't know, but it doesn't seem right. Nothing seems right. Are you going to Wild Bill's funeral?"

"Of course, was heading that way when I saw two purple dresses fighting over a man."

"I wasn't fighting over a man."

"Sure seemed that way but if you say so. Why don't you walk with me to Charlie's camp? Funeral starts at three o'clock. We can talk along the way."

The ground was packed hard from hot, dry days. Still, we weaved around occasional patches of wet sludge from people throwing dirty water and waste onto the street.

"Sara, seems like you had something special with Jack back there. Felt the energy between you. But if he's in love with another girl, then you don't need the drama."

"I never said I had something special with him."

"I know, Sara. Just saying what I saw. If God wants you to have a man, He'll drop a good one into your life. You don't have to go searching. Your only job is to trust God and discern if your suiter is speaking truth or not."

"I'm not searching," I stated emphatically, consumed with a confession I longed to release. "Can I tell you something?" I asked.

"I'm listening."

"I'm in a bind."

"Aren't we all," he said, chuckling.

"Preacher Smith. I'm not who you think I am."

"Yes, you are."

"No, I'm not."

"Let me tell you who you are. You're a child of God and nothing you tell me right now will change that fact. No, sir."

Confused and rootless, I reiterated, "But I'm not as I appear."

"Never thought you were."

"I'm not 18. I'm 16."

"Hmm. That's it?"

"And my name isn't Sara Capable."

"Hmm. What is it?"

"Sara Taylor."

"Okay. What else?"

"I did not steal Blue."

"What? That's your first confession that surprises me."

For the first time since assuming my life of lies, the truthful details of my last year spewed out, accompanied by tears and a runny nose.

"My dad was in the Army. We were at Fort Randall, but then set up an outpost at Whetstone. My dad and most his men were ambushed and killed."

Preacher Smith offered his grubby handkerchief, which I declined. He wrapped his arm around me and pulled my shoulder closer in an uncomfortable half-hug.

"Yes, yes, I believe I read about Whetstone in the paper. All perished. Some weren't identifiable after nature took its course."

"What do you mean nature took its course?"

"Sara, I really shouldn't go into it. It was weeks before the Army could pass through the drifts of snow left by the blizzard."

"Tell me."

74

"Ahh, Sara. They said some of those who perished could not be identified 'cause animals, wolves or something, had fed on them. It was a blizzard, Sara. Animals were starving."

"You think I don't know that? I was there. It was living hell. Pardon the curse."

"Forgiven."

"That's how I know Jake. Or Jack. Or whoever. He was at the outpost. My dad sent him back to Fort Randall for help, but he never returned. Neither did my dad. Sergeant Zito decided to make a run for Fort Randall because the blizzard wasn't letting up and we were starving to death. My mother froze first. We left her with Blue because she couldn't go on. Our compass failed in the cold. Sergeant Zito blocked the wind after we collapsed from exhaustion. When I woke up, Sergeant Zito was frozen. Frozen dead. He had taken off his coat and placed it over me to keep me alive." My voice shook. "He sacrificed himself for me."

"A good man. God rest his soul," Preacher Smith added while waiting until I composed myself. "Do you want to tell me more?"

I nodded.

"So, Ohanzee led me across the prairie."

"Who's Ohanzee?"

"Oh. Sorry. He was a Lakota prisoner at Whetstone. We caught him trying to steal a cavalry horse. When Sergeant Zito decided to try to walk back to Fort Randall, Ohanzee somehow escaped and followed us."

"Sounds like a whole nuther story, yes sir."

"So bad things happened while we were searching for his people." I started to cry again.

"Did he rape you?"

"No, he didn't touch me. Two prospectors tried, though. It was horrid. Ohanzee put an arrow through one of them as he tried to take it all from me. I believe the other man is back here in Deadwood."

"Is that why you're here? For revenge?"

"No. I can't tell you why."

"Oh, Sara. Sara."

"I ended up saving Ohanzee. He broke his leg real bad and I somehow took him to Greasy Grass to meet up with his people."

"So you saved an Indian?"

"At least for a while. Till he was back with his own people."

"That might not look so good to some of the locals here."

"I know. I know. Still, that's not all."

He sighed. "Okay. What else?"

"I was at Greasy Grass when General Custer attacked Ohanzee's village. I saw the battle with my own eyes. I saw how it actually happened. It wasn't as the newspaper said."

This time he did not say, "Okay. What else?" Both eyebrows raised and his eyes bulged, before exhaling all air from his lungs.

"You didn't warn the cavalry?"

"How could I? I was in a tipi."

"You didn't try to help the wounded soldiers?"

"How could I? I was a prisoner. Sort of."

"I don't know, Sara. I don't know. I wasn't there. How did you escape?"

"I didn't escape. They left me behind. Sitting Bull said I couldn't come with them."

"You wanted to go with the Indians?"

Self-consciousness and guilt enveloped me. "Never mind."

"Sara, how can I help you?"

"I'm living a lie. I thought I could start new here, but now there's Jake."

"Who else knows?"

"Chance saw me speaking Lakota with an Indian in the woods. He told Mr. Reynolds. Now Jake knows I'm alive. I'm ruined."

"More than ruined, Sara. They could hang you for stealing the horse."

"Or the gold," I thought.

"I'm not sure I should know more, Sara. At least not right now."

"But what should I do?"

"If you have a real reason to stay here, which I don't understand, but if you do, all I can say is you need to keep this a secret. Work through it with God, but don't tell anyone else. I'll take this to my grave. Talk with Jack. Or Jake. He seems like a good young man and may want to work through it with you. But honestly, Sara, Deadwood is full of inner-focused souls who want someone to step on. Maybe this is not the place to start new. Maybe you should move on."

People around town said Wild Bill was a lawman at heart and believed in right and wrong. His funeral offered no insight into the man's faith and left more question than answers. With the lack of religious symbolism, Wild Bill's friends tearfully placed him in the hole as bystanders like me stoically averted our eyes. I suddenly regretted I did not eat before the service. The temperature was stifling with no breeze to dry the sweat from my forehead. Over four hundred under-bathed bodies surrounding me, and the sad affair left me woozy and weakened. Not personally familiar with Wild Bill made the afternoon merely a matter of respect. After all, he was alive one moment and gone the next, a product of the enemies he acquired along his way.

While some deeply mourned the murder, others walked from the grave talking about a raffle of Wild Bill's two guns. Before his corpse had time to cool, people were taking a 25-cent chance on the raffle of his 44 Caliber Colts cap and ball and his 32 Caliber Rim Fire.

The town was basically back to normal by the time I returned. Some men who had not gone to the funeral were strolling about. Store owners were reopening their shops. Newcomers arriving on the stage had no idea of the turmoil Deadwood Gulch offered.

I walked into the Big Horn Store. Mr. Gushurst greeted me now.

"Good day, Miss Sara. What do you know?"

"It's one of those days which you wish never happened."

"Aww. Sorry to hear that. No idea you were close to Wild Bill."

"I wasn't. Just bad after bad all day long. I need something to eat."

"Haven't had a chance to grab something myself. Could I interest you in my leftovers from last night? A few cold potato cakes and cured bacon? We can eat a bite or two and talk."

CHAPTER 6

SARA

AUGUST 18, 1876

DEADWOOD

"MY OWN RELIGION HAS BEEN TO DO ALL THE
GOOD I COULD TO MY FELLOW MEN, AND AS
LITTLE HARM AS POSSIBLE."
~William W. Mayo[20]

The gold seekers kept arriving like ants on a hill before a storm.
Framed houses and two-story businesses replaced tents. Day after
day after day, the streets filled with scurrying bodies focused on
personal agendas. Grinding screeches of ungreased wagon wheels
filled the air as drivers swerved around broken whiskey bottles in
the street in front of the saloon. Cat calls and lurking eyes gawked
toward any female that dared step onto Main Street.

As prospectors flooded into the hills, Doc needed me more than
ever since the dream of quick money and fortune attracted the
careless. The lawless town attracted the lawless. Lawlessness

created injuries, from bar brawls to gunshot wounds. Unsanitary living conditions spread colds, the flu, and smallpox. Deadwood needed more doctors.

I divided my nights between Doc's barn and my claim. Logically, I should have felt safer in the barn, with the faint music from Doc's fiddle lulling me to sleep. Instead, I felt trapped. Where I should have felt vulnerable at my claim, I felt peace.

Occasionally I was met by a golden eagle, who whistled and skimmed over the top of the ridge on my claim. He typically stalled above me; his three-foot wingspan supported by the invisible stream above. He usually dropped, swooping onto a branch close enough to draw the breath from my lungs. His sharp talons held tight as moss-laden bark fell to the ground. It was as if he was watching my creation of lies, layering one on top of the next. His beady eyes seemed to wonder why I panned for gold in an unproductive stream when I had two bags filled already. I glanced up at him.

"It's complicated," I blurted, as if he would understand.

I slept under stars with no cover and kept my Colt revolver close, even when I bathed in the creek. I took time every day to brush Blue's mane and stroke his face. I rubbed the grit and fly eggs from the hairless spot at the center of his belly. His gentle eyes soothed my soul and put breath in my lungs.

After a few days alone at my claim, Blue and the golden eagle eased me back to a place of serenity. When I returned to Deadwood, my peace was short-lived.

As I rode Blue down Main Street, the pain was as sharp as an arrow, piercing my heart. Jake and Rebekah passed on the opposite side of the street. Her delicate arm looped through his. Rebekah did not seem to notice as Jake's eyes locked on mine. A staggering woman stumbled and fell to her knees in front of Blue, who halted and threw me into his mane. I slid from his back. The woman, wearing buckskin pants and a man's shirt, smelled of whiskey. Her eyes were unfocused and her words pathetically garbled. Urging her from the center of the street, I propped her against a building.

"Ain't no use," she slurred.

"You're okay. You're okay. Nothin' can be that bad."

"You ain't lost nuttin' as important as Wild Bill. He's why I breathe."

From a seated position, she turned her head to the side, leaned over and vomited.

Annie appeared over us, looking pale and unbalanced. Her left bloodshot eye did not track with the right.

"Poor thing," Annie said, watching the woman wipe her mouth with the front of her sleeve.

"Annie?" the woman asked, looking up.

"Yes, Calamity," Annie answered.

"Help me. I'm gonna be sick," the woman moaned. Her face was flat and swollen from her binge, exuding the thick features of a man.

Annie pulled me aside and whispered that Calamity was on a drunken binge over Wild Bill's murder. I suddenly realized I had met this woman before. Calamity Jane.[21] Annie tipped her head, gesturing me to go about my business. I turned to Blue, standing motionless in the street, reins dangling at his feet. I walked him to a hitching post between two buildings.

"Sara, may you cast aside our contention. I need to talk with you," Rebekah whispered, startling me from behind. She was nervously looking around as I draped Blue's reins over the rail.

"Rebekah, I have nothing to say to you. I do wish you the best, but I must be going."

She grabbed my arm with desperation and accidentally brushed against my revolver, only to quickly pull away. "He lied to me. Jack lied to me."

"Well, welcome to Deadwood."

"He doesn't possess what he said he did," Rebekah continued, starting to tear up.

"What doesn't he own?" I asked.

"Six dogs. Three cats. Or a successful mining claim. Or a cabin."

"I'm sorry, Rebekah," I said. "He told you what you wanted to hear. What men see as an adventure, most women see as hardship. He sweetened the pot 'til it looked better than it was."

"It's incomprehensible, though. I should be fuming at the betrayal. Instead, he looks in my eyes and I still feel like a princess."

"Well. He's got that going for him then."

"Do you grasp my situation?" she asked.

I gulped, unwilling to answer. "Have you thought about trying to make it on your own, slowing it down a bit with him?"

"What do you mean? Cancel the wedding? Leave Jack? Why would I?"

"To know you can."

"I don't need to know that. I need to just, just, just, swallow my dreams and, and accept my fate, and dig in and forget who I thought he was, and, and, and, and..."

I saw the compromise in her eyes. But I also saw love.

"Any dogs at all?" I asked.

"Three skinny excuses for dogs, came running down when he took me to his tent. Jack said they scavenge for scraps like Indians camped at a fort gate."

Sara explained where Jake camped and asked if I thought he would ever build a cabin. When I did not speculate, she sighed, "Well, I need to go, Sara. He'll wonder where I am."

Before she reached the corner of the building, she spun abruptly, "So can we talk again? Can I come find you?"

"Of course."

She took one more step and stopped again. "Sara, will you come to my wedding? Preacher Smith said he will marry us, soon as we can, to keep it holy."

"I'm quite busy, but we'll see, Rebekah. Might not be the best idea."

Doc intercepted me as we stepped from the shadow of the building. A man was in terrible condition after being shot the night before. Doc asked me to follow him to the man's tent. We examined the man, and Doc whispered, "We need to remove the slug if he has a chance in hell. Pardon my language." He turned directly to the despondent man and said, "Who did this to you?"

The prospector only made a few guttural sounds. His pleading eyes begged for help, for relief from the pain, yet he did not have the strength to speak. Doc placed an ether-soaked rag over the man's ruddy face.

"We need to wash our hands," I insisted.

"Of course we do," Doc agreed and we scrubbed with a dirty bar of soap beside the man's wash basin. Doc pulled back the blanket and cautiously pulled out the blood-soaked cloth which had been jammed in the man's distended belly like a cork. Doc stuck his finger in the open wound, tracing the bullet's path.

"My hands are too big, Sara. Can you do this?"

With a tightly clenched stomach, I stuck my index finger into the injured man's warm stomach cavity. His bowels were floating in fluid.

"Reach in deeper, Sara. You have to find the slug."

The opening was tight and I could not push my entire hand into his body. Doc pressed his scalpel into the edge of the wound to widen the hole, but he went too deep in the process, puncturing the bowel.

"Oh, my Lord," the doctor sighed. The slick intestine oozed green and brown mucous into the abdominal slurry like swirling moss in a stagnant pond.

"We'll need to clean this out or he'll die of infection," I said, breathing from my mouth. Against the back of my fingers, a muscle spasmed. I swallowed hard with gathered mental focus and searched for the slug. My fingers were still numb from when I had been assaulted, so I was lucky to press the slug against an organ. Doc smiled as I pulled it out. He handed me a threaded needle and I sewed whatever seemed to need sewing. Once the intestines were stitched, Doc poured a pitcher of water into the gaping hole while I moved the heavy, slick intestines back and forth as if washing clothes in a bucket; only the bucket was the man's belly. The fluids oozed over his sides, down to our feet and across the uneven ground.

"This will have to do," Doc said, running out of water. "Can you sew up his belly or do you want me to?"

"I can," I answered and made even stitches as if I was sewing a quilt. Doc pulled the ether rag from the man's face.

"I don't give him more than a day. He's more dead than alive. But ya never know for sure. Worth a try. Ain't a thing more we can do for him. In the good Lord's hands from here."

"Who did this to him?"

"Don't rightly know," said the doctor. "Who knows what he said for sure."

"Did anyone see the shooter?"

"Not that I know of."

"So another killer goes free," I replied with disdain. "What about his family? Is there someone he wants us to contact?"

"None that I know of. Could search through his belongings, I suppose. Hope to find nothing, though, 'cause it only causes more suffering," Doc answered.

I wandered onto the dusty street. Preacher Smith was in front of Bent and Deetken's drug store, speaking with a gathering of men. Chance stood at the back of the crowd, listening intently. I paused and faintly heard something about healing, which drew me closer. Leaning up against a hitching post out of exhaustion, I listened. Chance approached.

"Miss Sara," he whispered.

"Not really looking for company right now, Chance."

"But Miss Sara, I need to tell you something. I been lying to you and Doc about not knowing where I came from. Mr. Reynolds told me I'm worthless to him and I can't stay with him. So, I figure I best come clean."

"Okay," I responded.

"My mama died when I was a baby and I know where I'm from. Rochester."

"Minnesota?"

"Yep. My dad and I lived in the back of a store where Dad worked before Mr. Reynolds talked us into coming out to Dakota Territory to rob stages. I used to explore the woods with my neighbor, Charlie. I ate dinner with his grandma and grandpa when I had nothing else to eat 'cause my papa would be gone for days."

"What are their names?"

"Grandpa and Grandma Whiting. Charlie is my friend. Charlie Whiting. Can you find him for me?"

"I'll do my best. I'll look into it."

Chance bounded away and I refocused on Preacher Smith.

"He came to heal the sick. He came to heal the wounded. He came to heal you, each and every one of you. You don't need to come to Him already clean for He will bathe you in his spirit. I say to you. Yield of your sinful ways and walk in His Word."

He held his Bible to the sky as he spoke. When the crowd dispersed, Preacher Smith walked to me with a smile on his face. "So, my sweet Miss Capable. You ready to listen?"

I faintly shook my head, downhearted. "Just finished sewing up a man."

"Oh, I see," he replied.

"My hand was in his warm belly. He's gonna die."

"So, so sorry, my girl. Can't say anyone should have to do the work you do. Not even a man."

"It didn't even bother me. That's the whole problem. It was surreal; my hand searching around for the slug while his heart beat right against me."

"Ah, Sara, Sara. Are you sure you're being called to this? Might be you haven't grieved the loss of your parents and friends yet. Sooner or later, if you don't heal and seek the Lord's guidance, you'll fall into a pit of bitterness."

"I'm not bitter. I try to listen. I'm just distracted," I answered.

"Distracted by what?"

"By all the things I do every day: taking care of the animals, helping Doc with his patients, panning for gold at my claim, shopping, cooking, cleaning, starting a fire. Life seems to get in the way of working through the hard stuff."

"Ah, but it is Satan who distracts you. God won't force you to listen. You must seek Him. Are you filled with clear divine direction?"

"Nope. It's all clear as mud."

Preacher Smith paused and then continued, "Sara, I have to mention, whether you want to hear it or not. I see a young woman who has a past that's not letting go. You are so quick to tend to the wounds of others, still you ignore your own."

Preacher Smith patted me on the back, catching my loose strands of hair between his fingers. He carefully pulled them free and said he needed to go home to prepare a sermon for the next morning.

"Sara. Sara. You're welcome to join me in Crook City tomorrow. Never know what the Lord might have in store. Might be simpler than you think. You might just need to listen 'cause the Spirit will wash the mud from your eyes."

"Easy to say but not to actually figure out."

"Well, come with me and we can talk about it on the way."

"Thanks for the offer, but I need to get back to my claim. Oh, before you go. Are you going to marry Jake and Rebekah?"

"Unless you can tell me a reason not to. At this point, best they dive in, don't you think?"

I was speechless.

"Sara. Look at me, girl. The good Lord will never cast you aside. He's all you need. I promise you," Preacher Smith smiled with the sincerity I had not recognized since the last smile from Sergeant Zito. I hoped he would not notice my quivering lip. "It'll all be okay, Sara. See you soon, Lord willing, of course."

CHAPTER 7

SARA

AUGUST 20, 1876

DEADWOOD

"WE BELIEVE THAT GOD IS NEARER TO US IN
SOLITUDE...THE HOLY SILENCE IS GOD'S VOICE."
~Ohiyesa (Charles A. Eastman), Santee Sioux[22]

Saturated from the morning rain, I sat in silence with my eyes
closed, searching for the voice of God to guide my empty heart.
Wind rarely reached my claim because the gulch was protected,
yet a strong gust of summer air crossed my face as the sun crested
the ridge. Blue raised his head from grazing on the tender shoots
of wet grass and his ears rotated in a swirling dance. Shadow
growled. Branches snapped under heavy feet.

"Sara? Sara? Don't shoot. It's me. Jake. Can we talk?" he asked
cautiously, peeking with his dimpled grin from the cover of a pine
tree. Jake was sporting a two-day beard, blue canvas pants, and a
white button-down shirt. Shadow approached, smelled his legs
and snorted, likely from Jake's musky cologne. She wagged her

tail as Jake stroked her back and mumbled something I could not understand.

"I'm not stopping you," I answered flatly, feigning disinterest.

"Come on, Sara. This is crazy. I've been looking for you in town for a few days, but you're avoiding me."

"Been busy here."

"I need to explain. You need to understand. I need to understand. What happened to us, Sara?"

"Don't know, Jake. Or is it Jack? You tell me."

"Come on, Sara. It's just a name."

"Just a name? Only the name doesn't belong to you. I thought I knew you."

"You *do* know me. I had to get out, and to get out I had to take a new name," Jake retorted.

"You deserted?"

"It's not like I'm a rustler or holding up stages."

I interjected, "You told me commitment was commitment and you would never desert. What did you have left to serve? Two years?"

"Just over a year now."

"You said you'd save your wages, marry the right girl, and be set for life."

"Well, things change, Sara."

"And how about you telling me I'm the most beautiful girl you ever laid eyes on; that we were meant to be together? Surprise, surprise, you told the same thing to Rebekah."

"That's not fair, Sara."

"Oh, isn't it?"

"I meant everything I ever said to you. Hell, how can you second-guess me? I risked my life for you."

"Did you really? Is that why we were left starving to death at Whetstone Agency? You never came back for us, did you Jake? I thought you would keep your promise. Remember? You kissed the back of my hand and said, "Wait here, Sara. I'll be back. I promise.""

"I tried, Sara. I tried. It's not what you think. My trek was bad, I nearly died. Could only move at night. The damn Indians swarmed around me, Sara. By the time I made it back to Fort Randall, the blizzard was full force and I collapsed, frozen at the gate. The commander saw my condition and refused to send troops out to rescue you. He said you would be fine at Whetstone as long as you stayed put."

"So what did you do, Jake? Nothing?"

"Ah, well…"

"Did you argue for our rescue?"

"I was just a Private. Who listens to a Private? Come on, Sara. What's wrong with you?" Jake frowned.

I did not speak.

"So, enough of all my shortcomings," Jake said, turning the conversation. "Let's just say it was all my fault and save us a lot of time. Curious, though. Why did you change *your* last name? And where have you been for the last four months? And how did you end up with Blue?"

"It's a long story."

"Ah, I see. A long story. Well, I have all day. And Sara, you know that Blue belongs to the Army, not you. You could be hung as a horse thief."

"How dare you, Jake. Maybe you'll be swinging in the wind right beside me as a deserter."

We patiently waited out the other. My eyes burned, still I refused to blink.

"Sara, you know I loved you with every beat of my heart, but when I found the left-over bits of your mom and Sergeant Zito, you can't blame me for assuming you were scattered beside them."

"You went back for me?"

"Of course. And I buried all I could find."

We stared at each other.

"So Sara, imagine this. I believed I was burying pieces of the first girl I ever loved. My heart physically ached. Why, if you cared about me at all, why didn't you write me and tell me you were alive?"

"I couldn't."

"Why not, Sara? Tell me now. I need to know."

"I can't."

"Fine then. If I have learned anything, Sara, it's that we all make mistakes. Sometimes with good intentions, sometimes without. If that makes me lesser in your eyes, then so be it 'cause you're lesser in mine for not having the courage to come clean. I'll go. This ain't resolving a thing. Sara, you gave up on me and don't ya ever forget it." Jake walked away.

"Jake," I hollered.

"What?"

"What is it about Rebekah? What makes her so special?"

"Have you heard her laugh? Have you seen her mysterious eyes, how they go from playful to gloom at the snap of two fingers? She's alive, and spontaneous, and willing to take a chance for the sake of love."

Jake's jaw had been set, but it relaxed as he spoke of Rebekah. I noticed how strikingly handsome he still was. He was clearly in love.

"I need to go, Sara. I had hoped we could talk it out. Maybe later," and he walked away.

I could not sit still and my nerves were on fire. I grabbed my shovel and dug up my bag of gold, removing four handfuls of flakes and rolling them into a white hanky. I reburied the rest of the gold in the same hole.

I slept poorly, trying to stay dry during sporadic rain while remaining alert to possible predators dancing between the trees. I watched night turn to day with each lightning strike. The burdens of the present could not cover the burdens of my past.

The ride to Deadwood was time consuming as Blue struggled through the mud, which clumped on his hoofs, only to break free when it weighed too much to stay attached. We arrived before noon and the town seemed eerily quiet. I was the only customer at James W. Wood Bank, placing the rolled cloth of gold on the counter and asking for notes in exchange. The banker stood behind the counter and it took a few seconds to mentally process my request. I stood eye to eye with him, although he had an extra one hundred pounds on his frame. His light brown, slicked back receding hairline exposed his wide forehead. A black bowtie held up a starched white shirt, beneath a finely tailored black suit.

"That is quite a bit of gold, Miss, Miss Capable, is it?"

"Yes, Sara Capable."

"You need to open an account here if you want to do business with your productive little claim."

I filled out one sheet of paper with the ink pen he offered. Under his breath, he said, "Who would have guessed?" He processed my transaction. "Our intention is to keep most of your balance at our bank. Of course, you can withdraw funds whenever you wish."

With a handful of bank notes, I strolled up Main Street to the Big Horn Store for supplies. The door was locked and a sign in the window said, "Closed for funeral."

My pace increased as I walked to the Nuttal and Mann Saloon and asked the bartender for Annie. He said she was at the funeral.

"Whose funeral?" I asked.

"The preacher," he answered casually, pouring a bottle of whisky into a drinking glass.

I approached the bar. "The preacher? What preacher?"

"Preacher Smith. What other?"

I gasped and pulled the glass of whisky from the bar, gulping it down. The rush went straight to my head and I quickly learned how it softened the edges of sharp pain.

"Whoa, Missy. Take it easy. This is a bad, bad road to start down." He leaned across the bar so no others could hear, "This one's on the house, Sara, but you need to leave. You don't need this. You are bigger than the rest of us."

Off-balanced, I staggered out the door in disbelief, sensing someone behind me. I turned and saw Old Frenchie, a black-skinned man who did chores for merchants and fought a losing battle against the slop and garbage thrown out the doors of restaurants, saloons and brothels.

"'Scuse me, Miss Sara? You okay?" he asked.

My vision blurred and the man's dark hands grabbed my arms to ease my collapse to the cesspool of polluted mud. "You be okay. You be okay," he said. He offered his hand for stability and I noticed his missing thumb and white scars sliced across his palm. He gently helped me to my feet and guided my shaking body to a pine bench in front of the new hardware store. Gasping for air, tears flowed from my eyes. Two men approached and I turned my head away.

"Take your hands off her," the younger man demanded.

"Just trying to help, yes sir," the dark man replied.

"No need, Old Frenchie, is it? We met yesterday. I can take her from here. Are you okay, miss?" the man asked. Old Frenchie [23] quickly patted my back and disappeared down the street. The younger man stood quietly and close enough to touch.

"Are you okay, miss?" he repeated.

"Yes, yes. Pardon me. I just learned of a friend's passing."

"Ah, Henry Smith. Or Charlie Nolan?"

I started to weep. "Who's Charlie Nolan?"

"The Pony Express rider killed the other day outside of Sturgis."

"I don't know him. I only know the preacher. What happened to him?"

"Ah, ma'am. He was shot by an Indian. They're stirrin' it up lately."

I stared at the dirt covering my brown leather shoes.

"Were you close, if I may be so bold?" the older man continued without waiting for a reply. He squatted beside me. Bushy eyebrows hung suspended above deep brown eyes. His invisible lips were concealed by the thickest black mustache I ever saw. "Seth Bullock's my name. I came here the first of August, own this new hardware store here. I want you to know, young lady, we'll find the savage who did this and we'll string him up from a tree. I promise you."[24]

"What happened? Did he suffer?" I asked.

The younger man nudged Bullock, "She's full of questions. Why not let her read your letter?" he suggested.

Bullock thought for a moment while carefully patting down his hair, which was parted oddly to cover a bald spot. "Not sure this is the wisest move, but you seem to care more than most," he said, and handed me the letter. "Drop it in the store when you're done so I can send it off. Oh, and don't forget, you owe me one."

"Dear Reverend J.S. Chadwick, August 21, 1876, It becomes my painful duty to inform you that Rev. H. Weston Smith was killed by the Indians yesterday (Sunday) a short distance from this place. He had an appointment to preach here in the afternoon, and was on his way from Crook City when a band of Indians overtook him and shot him. His body was not mutilated in any way, and was found in the road a short time after the hellish deed had been done. His death was instantaneous and he was shot through the heart. His funeral occurred today from his home in this town.

Everything was done by kind hands and a Christian burial given him. I was not personally acquainted with Mr. Smith, but knew him by reputation, as an earnest worker in his Master's Vineyard. He has preached here on several occasions, and was the only minister in the Hills. He died in the harness and his memory will be always with those who knew him. A letter from you which I found in his home causes me to convey this sad intelligence to you.

Signed, Seth Bullock"

As the words sunk in, my tears abruptly stopped and heat filled my cheeks.

"Who actually saw the Indians?" I asked bluntly.

"Nobody witnessed the actual murder. Heard the shot, though. Least he wasn't scalped, but them Injuns been stirring up a hornet's nest in these hills. If you don't see them, you ain't lookin', ma'am," said the younger man. I intended to glare at him but his eyes were the kind that made me forget to breathe.

"My name is Dillon McFoley. I work for Mr. Bullock," he cracked a cautious smile. A Colt single action 44 or 45-caliber hung from his right hip. Silver inlay decorated the ivory handle.

"I'm Sara. I work with Doc and I have a claim up the way."

"Well, nice to meet you, Sara. I wish it was under different circumstances. Were you close to the minister?"

"I guess you might say that. He was better than most. I struggle to even find words at the moment. Please excuse me."

Dillon stared at me with an intrigued glint in his eyes, offering his strong hand and helping me to my feet. I attempted to brush off the manure-infused muck on my dress, but it smeared. I thanked him and started down the street toward Blue.

"Miss Sara," he startled me. I stopped and turned around in time to see him rake his fingers through his thick brown hair. "Would you mind if I walked you home? You seem a bit flustered."

"I don't walk, I have a horse."

"Would you mind if I escorted you to your horse?"

He offered his arm, but I pretended not to notice. We walked side by side along the edge of the street. He spoke gently and at times I caught only bits and pieces of his pleasant voice. He said he arrived in Deadwood a few days earlier to work for Mr. Bullock in his hardware store. He rattled off a list of what they planned to sell: woolen blankets, rubber hip boots, Winchester rifles, Smith and Wesson revolvers, shovels, picks, gold pans, utensils for cooking, saddlery, hatchets, and tents. I had no immediate interest in his inventory, still processing Preacher Smith's murder. Dillon continued on, explaining that working in a store was not what he intended to do forever. He needed the stable income while he sent most of his money back east to his father, who was a struggling farmer.

When I stopped at Blue, Dillon's eyes grew.

"Wow, your horse is beautiful, yes sir. Where is your saddle?"

"I don't ride with one," I answered, untying Blue and gently stroking his warm muzzle before leaping on his back with minimal effort. "He likes it better as do I."

I squeezed my knees and Blue went from standing to a slow lope in two strides. Dizzy from the bouts of tears, fury and my first shot of whiskey, I needed to be alone, in solitude. It was as if someone had cracked me over the head with a pickaxe. Thoughts rushed between grief and the inexplicable distraction of meeting Dillon.

CHAPTER 8

SARA

SEPTEMBER, 1876

DEADWOOD

"IT IS ONLY THOSE WHO HAVE NEITHER FIRED A SHOT NOR HEARD THE SHRIEKS AND GROANS OF THE WOUNDED WHO CRY ALOUD FOR BLOOD, MORE VENGEANCE, MORE DESOLATION. WAR IS HELL." ~William Tecumseh Sherman

Preacher Smith's final thoughts pestered me: You are so quick to tend to the wounds of others, still you ignore your own. Never know what the Lord might have in store. Might be simpler than you think. You might just need to listen. The good Lord will never cast you aside. He's all you need. I promise you.

I could not make sense of his simplistic advice through the grief of losing such a man. His words churned and churned while awake and in my sleep. Saving lives? Treating the sick? Love? Revenge? Restoring relationships? Protecting others?

My brain juggled the confusion while I slept, and I suddenly snapped to consciousness after vibrantly searching for answers. I was driving myself crazy with the darkness of my raging thoughts.

One morning, half-awake, I heard a whisper in the breeze. A whisper calling me to my past without fear. Aware of dew and my breath permeating my blanket, I yielded to the pre-dawn consciousness and climbed barefoot to the ridgetop where my other world waited. Shadow followed a few steps behind. I crouched silently beside the scattered bones of the headless warrior, now blending into the landscape. Shadow offered no curiosity and simply sat next to me, her side against mine. I did not weep. I did not shed a tear. Silence. Pure silence.

As if a storm had brewed beyond the horizon, thunder welled from my soul and I let out an unrecognizable wail of grief. Shadow slid into a down position with a sigh and unfaltering loyalty. What had previously been voiceless anger became all-consuming. I screamed, reaching for a fallen tree limb to beat against a nearby tree trunk. Guttural sounds escaped my body as I gasped for breath. When the branch broke, I picked up rocks and threw them over the edge of the ridge. Then I kicked a nearby pine tree, wailing until my well ran dry.

Collapsing, I saw blood running down my shin and a wide gash at the top of my right foot, an inch above my missing toes. I rolled onto my back and for the first time in ages, felt my heart pounding in my chest. Clear as spring water, my directionless months made sense. I was surviving but I was not living with passion. I was simply going through each day with nothing to look forward to. I had deserted people and places, never resolving loss and disappointments in my heart.

I descended the hill. Without cleaning up, I pulled on riding pants and boots before I hopped on Blue and rode to Jake's tent, staked on a flat knoll at the edge of Deadwood. Rebekah described the location perfectly and he was easy to recognize with the Army canvas strategically placed in a way to buffer the unrelenting wind. Three scraggly mongrels, not weighing eighty pounds between them, were slumbering in front of the tent.

"Jake?" I called.

He did not answer but simply poked his head from the tarp. "Darn it, Sara," he whispered. "You gotta stop calling me that."

"Well, we need to talk."

Jake crawled from his tarp, shirtless. "Yes, we do. I go first, yes sir. You need to know; I miss them too."

"What are you talking about?"

"Your dad and Sergeant Zito."

I gulped.

"So it's not easy for me either. Not that you care."

"I do care, Jake. But so much is going on in my head. Can you put your shirt on? You're distracting me."

Jake's dimple appeared and he retrieved a shirt from his pack. "Do you remember, Sara, when your dad called me in and asked me to ride the message back to Fort Randall?"

"Of course."

Jake slowly pulled his shirt over his head, covering the lean slabs of muscle defining his torso.

"Do you know what I remember most of that day?"

"No idea."

"I remember your messy hair and beautiful brown eyes. I remember being the chosen one, to sneak through the Indians and lead back reinforcements to rescue you."

"My dad said you were his best scout. I remember. I remember how proud you stood."

"Remember how you wanted me to take Blue?"

"Yes."

"But I knew deep in my heart you needed Blue. Sara, if it weren't for Blue, you might not be here today."

"I wouldn't."

"So trust things will work out. They will."

"I need to go back and make things right," I whispered.

"With?"

"I don't know yet, but I need to go."

"So go. Nobody is stopping you," Jake uttered.

"Fine. I will."

"Fine. Good luck to you then, Sara Taylor."

"Sara Capable, Jake. I'm Sara Capable."

"Whatever."

"Where is Rebekah, by the way?" I could not stop the inquiry from leaving my lips, though I regretted it immediately.

"She's none of your business."

"Perhaps not, but I need to ask her a favor."

"Such as?"

"Such as, I need her to take care of Shadow."

"Don't know where she is staying. Says she wants to stay separate till I commit to our vows. But if she can't take care of Shadow, I will."

"No offense, but it looks like you're starving the three you have."

"I ran across these at a deserted Injun camp and pity got me this. Crazy. The damn savages would of thrown um' on the fire if they'd had any meat on 'em."

"What were you doing at an Indian camp?"

"Seems I could ask you the same question now, couldn't I? If the rumors are even half true."

"What rumors?"

"Not gonna mention them, Sara. Be careful 'cause a lot of eyes are watching you."

I was speechless.

"If you leave, what about your claim?"

"I haven't thought that through yet."

"I'll work it for you if you want. I'll do anything for you, Sara. Please, I'm trying to start fresh. I need to earn money working, enough to build a cabin for Rebekah, that is, if she'll have me."

I dropped my eyes and nodded my head in uncomfortable affirmation.

"I'll put off this wedding if you say the word."

I stayed silent.

"Just say the word, Sara."

"I can't."

"Because you don't love me?"

"Because you're in love with Rebekah. Yes?"

"I am."

"So that settles it. The past is the past. You and I will always be unfinished business. I wish you both the very best." My voice wavered but I forced out the words even though something felt more complicated churning inside me. "I need to finish some things up. Maybe go back to New York."

"How do you plan to get there? Please tell me you aren't riding Blue the whole way," Jake said gently. "Ride him to Cheyenne and take the Union Pacific from there. Under 200 miles for Blue that way. He's a darned good horse, don't wear him out before his time. I know a woman who can stable him for you in Cheyenne. She runs a fine livery barn. Her husband was killed at the Custer massacre. She's trying to make a living on her own. When do you leave?"

I swallowed, "In a few weeks. I need to see how it goes with Doc." I climbed on Blue and squeezed my heels against his side for the short journey to town.

When I was nearly out of range, Jake hollered, "Sara, I'll always love you."

I kept riding, with a pang of regret, pretending the wind had blown his comment the other direction.

I directed Blue to Doc's place and put him in the barn. Chance stood on the porch and hollered out, asking if I had found his friend, Charlie, yet. I borrowed paper, a pen, and an envelope from Doc and sat with Chance on the porch as I penned the letter, notifying Charlie's grandparents of the death of Chance's father and asking for any guidance regarding Chance. I addressed the envelope to: Mr. and Mrs. Whiting and his grandson Charlie, Rochester, Minnesota. I hoped it would reach the correct eyes in case numerous Whiting families resided in the area.

I walked to Deadwood's Main Street from the south, which was full of excitement and more energy than usual. Prospectors and business owners cheered at the sight of the soiled blue-clad foot soldiers and cavalry entering town. The exhausted men barely had enough energy to raise their hands or tip their campaign hats in response. Their horses were emaciated and limping which made me judge the riders who seemed able to walk.

"Who are they?" I asked a man as the soldiers marched up Main Street.

"It's General Crook. Word is, he beat them Injuns in a prairie fight."

The man did not look like a general. Although he maintained a squared and proud position on his horse, his thin-set gray eyes peered from tired, thin eyebrows. His bulbous nose overpowered the full face of unkempt, scraggly reddish hair, which parted in the middle, leaving two separate beards to cover the gold buttons on his uniform. He bowed stiffly at the hips from his unremarkable frame, tipping his rounded filthy hat at the locals lining both sides of Main Street. [25]

In the distance, Rebekah stood alone, watching the men file by. I worked my way through the crowd until I stood beside her. She said she was with Jake until he disappeared down the alley when he saw the troops approaching.

The soldiers were directed to the Grand Central Hotel where General Crook uncomfortably spoke from his balcony to the cheering crowd below. He explained how they destroyed an Indian village at Slim Buttes as part of the government's Indian campaign. Most of the crowd cheered, but a few skeptically looked on, including myself and the hotel's black-skinned cook, Aunt Lou.[26] She was best known for her happy disposition, her buttermilk biscuits, and her plum pudding. I thought of Miss Bee back home in New York, caring for my grandmother. She resembled Aunt Lou physically but her job as a servant seemed more passive than Aunt Lou would ever embrace.

As the day went by, the soldiers' lips softened from liquor and warm baths. Their interpretation of the Slim Buttes confrontation differed from that of their leader. All were exhausted. Some admitted to shooting their horses to ward off troop starvation. One man wept with a whisky in his hand, "Couldn't eat my own damn horse. I'd rather starve, yes sir. That horse saved me and deserved more than that. My buddies ate him anyway, hunger outshined guilt. They didn't say a word or look my direction as they swallowed him down."

Another soldier sat beside the man, consoling him, "Not even close to a victory march. More like a horsemeat march. Damn Injuns burned it all up to starve our horses. Smoke was terrible, a smoldering hell. Couldn't see nothin."[27]

Startled upon hearing a bottle break in the saloon below, the same man jumped from his bath, grabbing his issued Colt single-action revolver from the floor. He spun in circles, with wild eyes on his sights, dripping and naked, looking for an invisible enemy.

I followed the troops to Jack Langrishe's theater but kept to a dark corner of the large room, concerned a soldier might recognize me from Fort Randall. When the crowd asked for increased military presence in the northern hills, General Crook said it was our responsibility, as citizens of Deadwood, to form our own militia to protect ourselves. I heard mumbling in the crowd that we needed to travel in groups because the Indians preyed on lone travelers through the hills and on the plains. They said Indian braves were slinking through the hills, watching and waiting for opportunities to murder.

As I headed home, Mr. Gushurst called me into the Big Horn Store. At the front door, he whispered, "There's a lieutenant here who led the initial charge at Slim Buttes. He was trying to buy new boots and then I saw his feet. Can you help him?"

I paused. Were Ohanzee's people at Slim Buttes? Did the lieutenant shoot holes through them? And then it hit me, the stench of the soldier's rotting feet. I walked over and sat on a crate facing him. Soaked for weeks inside his muddy boots, numerous punctures spewed white infection.

"Tacks holding the top leather and sole kept tearing at my feet," the man said stoically.

"You're in bad shape. Quite bad," I offered.

"Suppose you expect payment for that diagnosis?"

"No. I simply question why you failed to care for your feet."

"Not my choice not to. I watched the horses go down, one after the next. Not my sweet one. I walked beside her as much as I rode her. Anyone with a heart would have done the same."

I nodded.

"Loosened one boot up as my foot swelled, but leading my sweet mare across a bog, the mud sucked my boot off my foot. Thigh deep in mud. Least the men got a chuckle watching me shoulder deep in the muck, digging down for it. Probably not what West Point expected of an officer. Different world out here. What's your name?"

"Sara."

"Beautiful name, Sara. I'm Fred Schwatka. Please call me Fred."[28]

Mr. Gushurst had placed a bowl of warm water and a clean piece of unbleached muslin next to the lieutenant. I gently picked the mud from his wounds and washed his feet until the water ran clear. For me, the store became silent as the intimacy of my work took root. The officer stared at the crown of my head until I had the courage to raise my eyes and embrace the handsome features of twenty-six years. His rugged ruby-red, wind-burned cheeks showed his months on the plains. His brown hair was messy with natural curls, one dropping into his kind, green eyes. Instinctually drawn to him for obvious reasons, our gazes locked for a moment. I resisted the awkward urge and refocused on his feet.

He broke the silence, "Where did you get your training?"

"Here and there."

"How do you know to keep it all clean?"

"Dr. Mayo. Back east. It's a long story."

"Ah. Must be a good one. I trained at Bellevue Medical College. It's in New York."

"I am familiar with it."

"Got a medical degree and a law degree last year. Knowledge glutton after West Point."

"What was it like?"

"What you would expect of a military academy."

"No, not West Point. What was medical school like?"

"Not all I had hoped for. Mostly nosing it in a book day and night. One cadaver for the whole school. Hardly touched it. Anatomy was useful, but I guess I shouldn't complain because this campaign is giving me plenty of hands on."

He stared at me again. "What do you charge for your services?"

"I beg your pardon. Not all Deadwood women are in that profession."

"No, no, Sara. You misunderstand. I mean how much do you charge for tending to my feet or fixing a broken leg for that matter. Simply something to chat about, not something that has me ducking from your right hook."

Embarrassed for misjudging him, I kept my eyes down and replied, "I don't tend to you for the money. I help you because it must be quite painful and I may relieve some of that."

"Well, how about a quiet dinner long after the crowds have moved to the saloons?"

My heart pounded in my chest. "I will have to see."

"See what? Flatter me. Say yes, Sara."

"Yes."

I finished cleaning and dabbing his feet dry, wrapping the worst infections with gauze. Mr. Gushurst provided a fresh pair of socks at no charge and Fred paid a discounted price for his new boots. With General Crook's column in town, the shelves at Big Horn Store were bare. Mr. Gushurst was in an exceptionally elevated mood because Captain John Wilson Bubb, the commissary officer, had been willing to pay nearly any price for staples such as flour, coffee, and bacon.

Fred waited on the top step of the Grand Central Hotel entrance. He watched me approach and I regretted not changing into a fresh dress. He escorted me to a small table at the back of the restaurant and Aunt Lou greeted us, apologizing for the limited menu. While she smugly grinned, I hardly focused on the choices listed on butcher paper. Fred's chiseled features and wide, square shoulders distracted me. He was not only handsome. He was a polished conversationalist offering enough, yet careful to not talk over me.

"I heard you were the first to charge at Slim Buttes," I said.

"Not as glorious as it sounds. Had 25 with me. Captain Mills ordered me to move their horses off since it's hard to be a warrior without a horse. The men flanking on each side were to come down the hills and take care of the rest. Were about 400 ponies and it wasn't quite light yet. The ponies heard someone and started stampeding toward the Indian camp. So we followed them in and shot up the tents as we pushed the horses past the Indians. It's like they had a shield of protection over them 'cause not one of our bullets hit an Indian when we shot up their tipis. Not one. Except later, when we got some as they fought back. American Horse. He came walking out of that gully and his guts were falling out of his stomach. He tried to hold them in. Darndest thing, he stood tall and brave and offered himself up if his warriors were set free. A man's gotta respect someone like that, even if he's an Indian. General Crook honored his request."

"Then what happened?"

"Dr. Clements and Dr. McGillycuddy tried to sew him up, but the hole was so big, it was useless. They told him he would die. Braver than I've ever seen, he refused morphine. Just bit on a stick. He died about the same time as Private Kennedy. Middle of the night. Is this hard for you to hear?"

"No. How many did you kill?"

"Ten, maybe twenty. Definitely the ones who massacred Custer 'cause we found 7th Cavalry gear in their village. Even so, still hard to stomach the dead women in the ravine. Seems they were used as shields. We thought they were all warriors till babies screamed out and women cried. Even after hearing it, some of us had to pull our other soldiers back, the ones that kept shooting. Not sure what got into their crazy heads. Battle makes men do shameful things. We were lucky to only lose three of our own."

"Why do you do it? If you're a doctor and a lawyer, surely you could help people instead of kill people," I suggested.

"I know, but complications abound. Pay back West Point time with my service and then see where to go from there. If you never tasted a battle, you can't know the exhilaration of wondering if you'll survive. Guess I'm a bit charged by it. Not your fault though, Sara, for not understanding."

"I understand perfectly," I thought.

"This whole situation is haunting at times. Broke my heart when a little Indian girl wept on her dead mama, right in front of us all. Not easy to get over." His eyes filled with tears, which he wiped away without shame. "I have a confession to make," he blurted.

"Okay," I murmured, wondering what he would divulge.

"I did not actually need you to tend to my feet. It's just that Mr. Gushurst divulged you were a lovely, unattached girl. He was right, Sara. There's something about you. Something very special. Not only beauty and strength. There's something more. I would like to get to know you."

I blushed.

Aunt Lou came out of the kitchen with a dessert we had not ordered.

"Plum pudding for the soldier and the doc," she said, winking at me.

"Aunt Lou, I'm not a doctor."

"Might as well claim it, Sara." Fred said, as he promptly took a bite and raved, "Delicious, ma'am. What's your secret recipe?"

"Oh, a handful of this and a handful of that," Aunt Lou said as she walked away and left us alone.

"Where did you come from, Sara? How did you end up here? And where did you get that Colt on your hip?"

"Can we just talk about you and not me tonight?" I asked, fighting back emotion.

"Now there, not meaning to pry. I'm sorry, Sara," he touched my index finger resting on the table before he carefully stroked it as he pulled back. "So, if those questions are too personal, let's stay superficial. What are your plans going forward?"

"I'm not sure. I love medicine. I love helping people. How about you?"

"I love helping people also, but after all this, I want to experience the world. When I commit, I commit. I consistently desire a life of adventure. I did it with my education. With the Army. With the Indian Wars, and now I want to experience the world. Battle the wilderness instead of man."

His eyes glimmered with intensity.

"I leave in the morning. May I write you?"

"Of course," came out of my mouth before I considered suppressing it.

After our meal, Fred walked me to Blue, patiently waiting at a hitching post. Fred's Army-issued mare was coincidentally standing beside Blue. I grinned at the thought they compared battle stories while they waited together.

"She's a beauty," I said. The horse stood fourteen hands high and was well-proportioned, with a baby doll head. Except for her ribs protruding from her deep gray summer coat, she seemed to bare the last few months without significant injury. Her coloring was remarkable, as if Fred had placed gray ash from a cool campfire into his open palms and blown the soot across the mare's face. The light gray faded to deep gray before it reached her shoulders.

Fred reached down and rubbed her underbelly where the loosened cinch rested. Her lips quivered and she turned to nuzzle his shoulder, as Blue did with me. "She was a handful in the beginning. I didn't fear being killed by Indians 'cause death may have been better than being bucked non-stop across the prairie. I kept her heading in the right direction and eventually, we became quite a team. Sara, someone stole your saddle," Fred said, smiling. He offered his hand for my foot and hoisted me on Blue's back. Fred's palm lingered on my calf and he smiled up at me.

"I had a wonderful evening, Sara. Thank you for taking me away from this chaos for a while." Every word he uttered was full of expression and satisfaction.

He glanced at Blue's brand and dropped his hand from my leg, lightly outlining the 08 with his index finger.

"He's tender, don't touch it," I demanded and Fred instantly pulled his hand away as if he personally experienced the burning flesh.

"Where did you get this horse, Sara?"

"From a ranch not far from here. The 08 Ranch. Blue was a handful, just like your mare. Bucked off their cowboys, so I took him off their hands. Gentled him down."

"I see," he answered, eyes rotating between mine and the brand. It seemed like minutes with no words and seriousness fell upon us.

"Please, Fred. I lost everyone I love. Except Blue. He's all I have," I whispered.

The lieutenant paused for another unbearable amount of time. A glimmer of intrigue and intimacy shone in his eyes.

"Battles do strange things to people. I can't say I understand, but I certainly know I'm not one to judge." He stepped to his mare's side and ran his finger along the edges of her "US" brand, whispering, "Your secret, whatever it is, is safe with me."

I audibly sighed in relief as Fred continued, "Sara, I know you have courage. Still, it would be wrong if I didn't mention how dangerous it is for you to ride home, alone in the dark."

Our eyes locked. Fred's straight white grin seared into my mind as I simply replied, "I'm not alone. I have Blue. Thank you for everything."

I rode home in silence, bewildered at my encounter. He was all I could imagine in a good man. Yet, as quickly as he came, Second Lieutenant Fred Schwatka was gone.

CHAPTER 9

SARA

OCTOBER, 1876

DEADWOOD

"LOVE IS JEALOUS, AND INGENIOUS IN SELF-TORTURE IN PROPORTION AS IT IS PURE AND INTENSE." ~Victor Hugo

When Lieutenant Fred Schwatka departed, he seemed to pull the heat from the hills. The chilly nights left frost shimmering on my tent canvas in the morning. On some days, the elusive sun allowed a bone-aching mist to hang in the gulch until noon. Other than the pines, the trees had dropped their pallet of yellows and oranges, standing bare and bracing for winter. The lust for gold and the spirit of determination sagged under the melancholy weather. Men packed up and left the hills, some with a pouch of gold and others with nothing but worn-out clothes hanging from their thin bodies.

Weeks passed quickly as I spent long hours with Doc. I focused on making frequent gold deposits into my bank account, growing the balance beyond numbers I deserved. No matter how busy, my mind consistently wandered to my favorite lieutenant. The distraction was not a burden, but an escape. Some important things fell by the wayside, however, such as Annie. Once I realized it had been quite some time since I last saw her, I paid a visit.

Construction along Main Street had progressed rapidly in the few months since I had arrived. Two-and three-story businesses lined the street with staircases clinging to the exterior walls, offering access to upper levels. When I was nearly up the stairs to Annie's room, I was met by a descending worker who stopped me, explaining Annie was not there. She thought Annie may be in Chinatown at an opium den.

I opened my mouth to ask why Annie had not been stopped, but snapped it closed before words escaped. I marched loudly down the stairs and continued along the street into the Badlands, the lower end of Deadwood Gulch. Over one hundred Chinese prospered in the small section of town, or at least they survived. Until then, Preacher Smith's warning had kept me from the dark area.

The night was crisp and as I walked, an odd essence hung low and clung to the street. I immediately thought of the burning sage and the pipe smoked by Sitting Bull, only this scent was heavier. With each breath, I became more light-headed. I passed Coon Sing's laundry, which was out in the open on the street. His hand painted sign said, "COON SING'S WASHEE-HOUSEE." A frail Chinese man stood at a rough-cut table and in broken English asked, "Washee, lady? Hun Hao, very good." I walked past.

Something was burning on the hillside and figures stood unimpassioned around the smoke curling wistfully into the sky.[29] I arrived at a rock building where only mud held the stones in place. A small Chinese man blocked the door.

"You looking for fun?" he asked, "Doctor lady looking for fun?" A dainty Chinese woman sat on a stool emotionless behind the man, her eyes meticulously painted in heavy black makeup and her porcelain skin looked like it had never met the sun.

"I'm looking for Annie. From above the saloon."

"Annie? She no want talk."

"Where is she?" I asked, pushing past him.

Resigned to my determination, he agreed and I stepped to the side. Without further hesitation, he led me down wood plank stairs, loosely set in notched-out dirt. Following him into a tunnel, I was confronted by tiny stone cells. A veil of privacy was suggested with the mere barrier of pulled soiled curtains. The unventilated subterranean passage sent shivers down my arms as I peered through a crack in the first room's curtain. A man reclined on a cot, mentally drifting somewhere else.

The second cell held Annie. I stood at her curtain, half pulled back, and could not begin to rationalize what was before me. Instinct told me to step in and care for her, while her odor made me pause. I suspected it was not only her, but the continuous stench of nauseated customers.

Annie's cell contained five things: a wooden cot, a scrap lumber table, an empty opium pipe, a bucket, and Annie. She could not see me or she did not care, profoundly retching over the edge of her cot into the bucket. I walked away, realizing only Annie could save Annie.

"You sell opium to a woman with child!" I said emphatically to the man as I stormed out. "You'll kill her baby!"

"I no know. I no know. No big deal. I make pain go. No break law. Yes, Doctor Lady?"

"Not safe," I answered.

"You no problem, Doctor, I give you free time. Me no selling opium. Me selling plates and bowls. Wood boxes, pretty knives. Yes?"[30]

"I don't want a free time," I shot back.

The sun was long gone and I walked briskly along Whitewood Creek, yearning to reach a familiar, safe street. The yellow moon faintly shone upon a man still prospecting in the late hours. Glancing up from his rocker apparatus at the side of the rushing water, he nodded as I greeted him. He never stopped oscillating the creek gravel back and forth like a baby in a cradle.

"What do ya know?" he asked, standing up stiffly. "Got somethin' for these hands, Doc? They're botherin' me somethin' terrible. Full of rheumatism."

I wondered how I recently became a doctor in the minds of the prospectors. I did not recognize the man but examined his gnarled and deformed hands. "This frigid water isn't doing them any good," I said, noticing an odd hue to his skin, like it had been burned. "Did you spill something on them?"

"Mercury bag broke when I was squeezing gold out of it. Not feeling the best ever since."

"What do you mean, not feeling the best?"

"Can hardly get out of my tent come mornings. Exhausted, ya know? Wicked headache from hell I suspect. Dizzy all the time."

"Can you rest a few days?"

"Naw. Winter creepin' in. Gotta find the nuggets before my boots freeze to the creek bottom."

Walking through the Badlands after dark was hard on my faltered reputation. The hillside had transformed from tents to one room homes. Since thousands went back east for the winter, empty lots were for sale at lower prices than a month ago. Still, 3000 locals were willing to call Deadwood their home and lots above the Badlands were selling for $25; view lots above upper Main Street averaged $500. I tried to envision myself living in town, but the thought did not last long.

"Sara, Sara?"

I stopped. In the darkness I could not see who was calling me from the back-alley door of Wagner's Hotel.

"Pssst, Sara. It's me."

I joined Rebekah in the shadows, where she stood, shivering in a conservative blue dress. She explained she had moved into the hotel until Jake found another minister to marry them since Preacher Smith was dead.

"How can you afford the room?" I asked.

"I work it off."

"Oh no, Rebekah, no. I can help you. It isn't worth losing your purity over."

Rebekah laughed. "Oh, Sara. I don't do that. I clean rooms and help in the kitchen."

Rebekah went on and told me Jake was only making $4 a day working at a prominent mine. "Deserves at least $6," she said. She explained everyone working at that low rate spiked the claim but Jake refused to steal. I asked her what that meant and she said the workers concealed gold flakes under their fingernails or slid small nuggets in their hatbands when the boss turned away. Then, abruptly changing the subject, she said, "I heard you need me to take care of Shadow."

"Oh, Rebekah, that would be great because I'm going away for a while."

"Where?"

"New York. I have things to do. If you and Jake want to live out at my claim while I'm gone, you are welcome to it. Might give you privacy being freshly married and all."

Rebekah's voice cracked. "That would be great, Sara. How long might you be gone?"

"I'm not sure."

"Why do you have to go?"

"It's hard to explain. I need to check on Miss Bee. She was my house maid. But she's more than that. She's my friend. She lives with my grandmother."

"When was your last correspondence?" Rebekah asked.

"I can't even guess."

"At all?"

"At all."

"Why not? If she is so significant that you would travel back to New York to see her?" Rebekah asked, inquisitively.

"It wasn't convenient."

"Nor is it convenient now, Sara. Pardon my confrontation, still, I must say you appear to be hiding something."

"Hiding something? Hiding something? Perhaps you should look at your future husband and ask the same question," I retorted.

"What do you mean by that?" Rebekah asked.

"Why do you think I call him Jake? Why do you think he disappeared as soon as the Army marched into Deadwood?"

"I don't know why."

"Maybe you should ask him before you marry him," I snapped back.

"Very well. I will."

Knowing her innocent nature, and that I may have upset her, I cautiously asked, "Rebekah, please. Are you willing to take care of Shadow and my claim or should I make other arrangements?"

"I told you I would. My word is my word. Still, what if you travel all that way and your friend isn't there?"

"I don't know," I answered, softening, hoping I had not sabotaged Jake and Rebekah's relationship.

The days had grown short before my eyes and the biting winds had taken on a life of their own, exasperating the urgency to get things done before winter set in. First, I stopped at the claims office to inquire about additional claims. The man said that given the winter facing us, a few good claims were up for sale, but the prices were in the tens of thousands. He said the Wheeler Brothers were pulling out over $1,000 of gold a day and Johnson and Company took out $70,000 in their first year.

I asked about claims on my stream and the man said the one just downstream from me was still available. He said, "Miss Capable, the Hills still got the fever, but ain't nobody seeing a quartz cropping by you. Who would honestly want that next claim? Not saying you ain't doing fine, but not sure where you're pulling it from. Plus, you're too far out of the gulch. Too many Injuns lurking in the trees. It's a wonder you ain't been found face down on the trail with an arrow in your back."

I purchased the adjoining claim under the names of Jake and Rebekah Wells.

Over the next week, I planned my travel back east. I included Ohanzee's parfleche as I packed my bag. Somehow, it felt as though he would travel with me, protecting my passage.[31] I decided to ride Blue to Cheyenne, where I would leave him at the livery stable Jake spoke of. Once I was convinced of his care, I would board a train for New York.

The last night at my claim was frigid and the pitch-black sky failed to raise my spirits. As the wind howled through the trees, I wished for more shelter than my canvas tent. Then, before daybreak, the air went still.

Jake, Rebekah and their three dogs arrived an hour later. Rebekah immediately picked up Shadow, kissing the top of her head. Shadow's lanky legs dangled from Rebekah's arms.

"I have a feeling about this claim," Jake said. "This place has a good feel. Might heal some hearts." Jake surprised me because he was rarely sentimental.

"I hope so, Jake. I hope so. Please listen, though. If I don't make it back, this is for you and Rebekah. And this is for your troubles here while I'm gone."

I handed them the piece of paper from the claims office that showed the claim downstream from mine belonged to them. I handed them a pouch full of gold flakes. "To help get you started. But you must know, this isn't quite as prosperous as you might hope. It might be better to simply live here and work in Deadwood."

"That's not what the banker is saying around town," Jake replied.

"Jake, now is not the time to doubt me."

"Fine," he grinned, both dimples reacting. "We'll be good neighbors."

"I can't think of a sweeter couple to live beside," I answered, stressing the word "couple."

Rebekah smiled and set Shadow down, introducing her to their three skinny dogs. One offered a high-pitched yelp as he vied for Rebekah's attention.

"Look at how sweet they are together!" Rebekah exclaimed, petting them as they maneuvered in and out of her legs. "Just like us, Jack. I mean Jake." She turned directly toward me and said, "We worked it all out, Sara. I know the whole story; how Jake changed his name because he deserted. He told me everything."

Jake stood behind Rebekah, wide-eyed, shaking his head back and forth, silently pleading for me to remain silent about our past. He relaxed a bit when I changed the topic to the care of Shadow.

"She needs her belly scratched. And don't let her wander too far because I saw wolf tracks the other day. And I'll write when I can. And feel free to use all of my tools."

"We'll be fine, Sara," Jake reassured me. "Go on. And Sara, I hope you find what you're looking for."

I hugged both of them and swung my leg over Blue. Riding off, I hollered back, "Don't forget to check for my mail. Oh, and don't shoot the golden eagle. He's my friend."

Blue and I intended to follow behind a stage from Deadwood to Cheyenne. The driver attempted to charge me $15 for the added security, but I refused as I had my own food, horse, and gun. The stage left town and I followed a few minutes later up Main Street. Annie peered glumly from her second-story window as I passed. I waved cautiously and she ducked behind the curtain.

At night I camped by myself, away from the other travelers and patiently waited until they departed each morning before breaking my own camp and following behind. The stage's pace was annoyingly slow and I decided to split from the group and ride ahead.

Alone, I focused on the scenery, traveling with my head up, always wondering if the golden eagle followed. He didn't. One morning as I veered off course to find water for Blue, a small speck at the top of a cracked jagged rock wall caught my attention because it was not natural. The closer I came, the more it grew and I eventually recognized a death scaffold. I thought of Ohanzee's grandfather on Mato Paha and wondered if Ohanzee met the same fate.

Pulled to the somber sacredness, I turned Blue up the narrow ridge where the light was blocked and a muted gloom prevailed. Parting the sweet-scented pines as we approached, I saw a man sitting cross-legged beside a body wrapped in buffalo skin. His wails mimicked the winds.

I slid from Blue and the man did not look up, innately sensing no threat. I extended my dad's canteen of water, which he refused. I pulled a piece of fire-roasted beef from my parfleche. Only then, his mournful eyes captured mine. I asked in broken Lakota if I could help him. He pulled a bitesize piece of beef from the chunk I offered. I asked if he knew Ohanzee, a Minneconjou. Barely visible, he shook his head no. Then, I asked "grandfather?" and gestured toward the scaffolding with my head. He answered in Lakota, "Wife." I nodded. "And baby," he finished. A solitary tear ran down his face.

Nine days later, Blue and I arrived at Cheyenne. I easily located the livery barn owner and she readily agreed to board Blue. She was a lovely woman running a tight business. I avoided asking about her deceased husband because it was too uncomfortable to think I may have seen his corpse on the hillside with General Custer. The woman seemed kind, and I felt certain Blue would be well-cared for until I returned.

"Would you like to clean up in my private room?" the perfectly kept woman asked carefully. "The gentile back east might not be used to a woman looking the way you do, no offense."

Embarrassed at my obvious lack of hygiene, I appreciated her accommodation and left an inch of dirt in her wash basin. I changed quickly into more ladylike attire, slipping into a simple green dress with creamy lace trim.

When I emerged, the woman hardly recognized me. Blue's nostrils flared, capturing my scent to validate my presence. It was a horrible goodbye, nonetheless. I shamelessly cried with my face against his jaw. Blue's haunting whinny followed me, echoing down the street.

The Union Pacific Railroad station was not busy and the eastbound track was empty. I purchased a coach seat and waited three hours on a short wood-slatted platform until my train arrived. Before we were allowed to board, the train was serviced. Coal was shoveled from the platform into the furnace and holding bin which would keep the steam engine pressurized during the trip. The engine hissed white steam from gaskets and loose pipe connections. Luggage and mailbags were thrown into the baggage cars. Finally, the blue-uniformed conductor called to the travelers, "Aaaaaaall aboooooooard!"

Stepping into the passenger car, I recognized it was identical to the one I rode in almost a year earlier. I remembered pressing my face against the windowpane, taking it all in as I headed in the opposite direction. The car was worn out but clean. Straight-backed wooden benches, like church pews, were covered with stained red-velvet seat pads. Some benches faced forward and the others in reverse. A coal-burning potbellied stove sat in the corner. I selected a window seat facing backwards and realized that this time my mother was not directing me where to sit. I lifted my bag onto the dented, gold-gilded shelving above. The benches facing forward remained mostly unoccupied.

People scattered from the platform after saying goodbye to loved ones. None drew my emotion as I watched from my window. A gas lamp flickered at the end of my car. I read a medicine journal Doc handed me when he learned of my journey. "That way, you'll have to come back to return it," he had laughed. Mile after mile of rough track jostled my core, yet I read and slept to pass the time. Days later, when I finally stepped from the train, the pages of the manual were creased and my head was filled with anatomy.

I hired a coach to my New York neighborhood and then stood in a shadow at the corner of Danbury Street, watching the commotion. It was as if I had never left. Clanking metal on horse-drawn wagons swerved to avoid people crossing the cobblestone street. Horses trotted in cadence with jingling brass from fine leather tack, pulling the affluent passengers to their destinations in elaborate carriages. The neighbor's calico cat still curled up on the brick window ledge of his home. Overwhelmed by the activity around me, I took a deep breath.

As I was about to cross the street and knock on the front door of my home, Miss Bee appeared, with Dad's gift from years ago, a worn ebony cane. In her other arm, she carried a package dangling from a white string handle. I did not cross to her or call her name, though my stomach jumped at the sight of her. Instead, I followed at a distance as she limped away from the house. She was still thick through her waist and hunched over with a black scarf around her head.

Miss Bee did not notice me as she navigated around obstacles, just as we had done on our rare escapes from my cynical home. I was invisible to her, perhaps because I was a significantly different person than she remembered.

She was purposeful as she walked, with a little less limp than I remembered, although her left foot remained contorted and stiff.

Miss Bee walked two blocks to the market. She did not linger, heading straight to the old man's bread stand. Her tight, black curls escaped from her scarf. The man spoke with her as friends, less formal than a year ago. They exchanged boxes and he gave her change, which she dropped into her skirt pocket, flashing him a magnetic white smile against her deep brown complexion.

Miss Bee continued down the row of the market and purchased a few pieces of fruit from a vendor I had never seen. The woman seemed pleasant, in sharp contrast to the one she likely replaced. As I followed at a distance, Miss Bee finished her business but did not take the most direct route home. When she came to my house, she scaled the steps, glancing each way before stepping inside.

I stood across the street and waited. The house was still well-maintained with winterized empty flower boxes and partially pulled white lace curtains. Geraniums peeked from the window, as Miss Bee rescued them from the frost-filled nights.

I had seen enough and marched up the steps, which had been swept of city dust and falling leaves. The front door was freshly painted bright red, a vast improvement from the solemn gray I left a year before. I raised my hand, hesitated for a moment, and knocked. She did not open the door. I knocked again, louder. And louder. Finally, I sensed her on the other side, but she could not see me, so I hollered through the door frame.

"Miss Bee. It's me. Sara."

CHAPTER 10

MISS BEE

NOVEMBER, 1876

NEW YORK CITY

"ALL MEN HAVING POWER OUGHT TO BE DISTRUSTED TO A CERTAIN DEGREE."
~James Madison, Constitutional Convention in 1787

When I heard "It's me, Sara!" I paused, perplexed. The thought of my only friend standing on the other side of the door rather than the image of her bones scattered across the prairie was worth the risk of responding. I cracked the door enough to see the transformed girl before me. I screamed, "I thought you were dead! I thought you were dead!" Sara smiled, standing strong and very much alive. I hugged her with all my might.

Earlier, when I went to the market, I felt someone might be following me. I kept my head low and minded my own business. The months of living an invisible existence were taxing, but I had few options. So when I heard the knock at the door, I ignored it as usual, silently praying the person would leave. But it was Sara.

The rest of the day and night was spent behind locked doors and pulled window curtains. I explained how Sara's grandmother had no will to live after Sara left with her parents and how she died in her sleep after contracting a brief lung illness. I had tried my best, but there was nothing else I could do to keep her alive.

Sara did not express emotion at the news. She shared what happened in Dakota Territory and I cried over the details not provided in the letter I received in early June from the War Department, addressed to Grandmother. Since she was on her deathbed, I opened the letter which said Sara's dad was killed in a brave battle against the Indians, and Sara and her mother perished in a snowstorm. They offered condolences without a survivor pension. I never told Sara's grandmother because the news would have killed her. I told Sara how sad I was her dad died because he was the first white man to treat me like a human.

"I didn't know what to do. Never was allowed to make decisions. So, Sara, I offer my greatest apologies. I thought you were dead, and I decided to continue on, day by day, pretending like I was still caring for your grandmother," I explained.

"Where is she buried?" Sara asked.

"In the backyard, under the garden, opposite the privy. I dug all night and placed her in her finest black dress, but I didn't have a coffin. Wrapped her in the sheet she died in. I hid inside for weeks, crying over you being dead and I was worried the neighbors would check on your grandmother. But they never did. Nobody even noticed she was gone. Sorry, Sara."

"Nothing to be sorry for. How have you been getting by?" Sara asked.

"Ashamed to say. I used your grandmother's stashed money at first. Her hiding places were easy to find for a few months, but I think I found 'em all - behind bricks in the fireplace, stuck to the back of her clock on the mantle, under loose boards in the floor. Felt guilt, but given you and your folks were dead, didn't see harm 'cept the heaviness in my heart. Then I found my own way. I sell a pie or two a day in exchange for food plus put cash in my pocket. Please don't judge my actions, Sara. I was just stayin' here 'til someone kicked me out on the street again. I'll pay you back, I promise."

"You already have," Sara said.

Late into the night, Sara told me about Fort Randall and Private Jake. She explained how they moved to an outpost and a blizzard set in. Her dad sent Jake for help. She told me how her dad was killed on patrol and how Sergeant Zito saved her from freezing to death. She spoke of an Indian named Ohanzee who cut off her frozen toes to save her life. He taught her how to survive on the prairie and took her to his people. She told me about the battle where General Custer perished.

The next morning, Sara talked of her gold mining claim in the Black Hills. She said she had a horse named Blue, a dog named Shadow, and a golden eagle with no name.

"Sounds enchanting," I said. "When I worked in fields as a young girl, we sang gospel to the beat of crow wings. Not exactly eagles but better than nothing."

"Well, Deadwood is not exactly enchanting," Sara said. "Dangerous, exciting, yes. Enchanting, no."

"Why did you come back? To sell the house?"

"No, I came back for you."

I was startled, "Why?"

"Because something inside told me to. I also need to retrieve Sergeant Zito's wife on Hart Island.[32] Her name is Rose. Their only child, Charlotte, died from the fever. They prayed and prayed, but she didn't recover. It made Sergeant Zito's wife crazy. He dropped her at the insane asylum on Hart Island, in the waters east of here. He couldn't take her on the Army assignment and he felt terrible about the conditions on the island. Sergeant Zito was only allowed to leave her with the clothes on her back and no valuables. He slipped a heart-shaped rock into her skirt pocket and hoped it would nudge her back to sanity. Sergeant Zito wrote letters and told her he would be back to pick her up. But instead, he gave his life for me. She's my responsibility now."

"How exactly do you plan to do this?" I asked.

"I don't know yet," Sara said.

I offered to help if the opportunity arose. She said she wanted me to escort her to the island, which made me a bit nervous. The next morning, Sara said we needed to go to the dress shop. The salesman told me to wait in a side room because my type wasn't allowed where the other women shopped. Sara was insulted and demanded I would be purchasing items and should be able to try on my own dresses, just as any fair-skinned lady. Since we were the only two in the store, he complied.

The salesman tried to increase his commission, commenting that Sara's figure was now in style. Thin builds and long torsos were the "most exquisite treat for the eyes of men." If only her mother was alive to hear it after all those years of complaining that Sara was not curvy enough.

Four dresses fit me equally well and Sara said I should select my two favorite. The prettiest dress dipped down in the back, exposing my shoulder blades. Since Sara's eyes lingered, boring holes through the uncovered scars across my back, I knew to leave the style behind. Sara was doubling my wardrobe so I took the opportunity with great contemplation. I would wear these outfits for years. I spun in circles before the mirror, flaring out the pastel pink dress like a fan. The cream lace around each layer accentuated my round figure and I had never felt so beautiful. The second outfit I selected was actually a skirt and blouse, suited for practical daily wear, and not worn to the last thread like my other stained outfits.

Much to the salesman's disappointment, Sara purchased one formal dress and one day dress, both with conservative necklines and practical skirts. "Such a shame, such a shame," he commented, wishing she selected something more revealing. He suggested she purchase a corset but Sara refused, saying they were a fire danger.

We walked to an accessory shop on our way home and tried on various hats and gloves until we settled on practical options. Before entering our neighborhood, a cobbler studio caught Sara's attention. Random pairs of leather boots and shoes lined on shelves. We stepped inside and learned they were worn shoes on display for resale because they had been repaired and never picked up by the previous owners. I couldn't imagine someone forgetting to retrieve their shoes until Sara clarified they probably had another ten pairs in their closet. The cobbler allowed Sara to slip her feet into the shoes but refused to let me try them on. Sara found fancy leather boots she thought would fit me and took her chances with the discounted price. Later that afternoon she returned them, requesting the cobbler to stretch my left boot, which improved the fit over my maimed foot.

We dressed carefully in the morning, remembering the years of fashion torture we endured with Sara's mother and grandmother. As we pulled on her tight-fitting bodice, Sara told me about burning her corset in the fire and we laughed. Her shimmering blue overskirt had enough fabric for two conservative prairie dresses and it draped beautifully behind her. I wore my new skirt, blouse and boots.

Sara seemed careless about her finances. She hired a buggy for the four-hour journey to the dock across from Hart Island. The further we traveled, the more disheveled the roads became. By the time we reached the ferry, we were stiff from the ride, but Sara tipped the driver generously and he promised to wait for our return.

The ferry was tied to the rickety dock and a rotting rope strung between two rusty cleats prevented our boarding. I stared at the island. It was long and narrow with an old dock peeking from the waves on the other side. Brick buildings rose behind mature leafless trees and the grounds were eerily quiet. We were held to the side by the freight operator as men loaded fifty pine boxes onto the front of the ferry.

"Excuse me, what are the boxes filled with? Supplies for the women?" Sara asked a laborer.

The man laughed. "No ma'am. Not supplies for the insane. Boxes filled with bodies. Destitutes. Unclaimed dead from the city. Gotta do something with 'em. Potters field out there beside the insane. If that ain't enough to make anyone crazy."

We were eventually guided to the back of the ferry and grasped the railing as we crossed the rough waters to the dock on the other side. When I peered over the edge of the ferry, I was sick to my stomach and desperately wanted off the boat. Beside the dock stood an unimpressive sign which said, "Convalescent Hospital" in bright blue paint. I knew what it should say, "Women's Lunatic Asylum."

A tall, lean man in his early 30's, wearing a dark blue guard uniform waited on the island's dock and offered his hand to Sara for balance as she stepped to solid ground. His right hand was missing the last two fingers. He stood confidently with broad

143

shoulders and a serious expression which only partially hid his handsome Italian features and deep olive skin. The man glanced around quickly and saw the other men watching, yet with only a slight hesitation he offered his arm to me and remarked at the intricate detail on my cane.

"Good day, I would like to speak to the superintendent, please," Sara requested.

"The Supe? Does he know you're coming? Let me tell you something. You gotta write ahead with a request," he said with an edge to his voice.

"But this is a rather sudden development and I could use your help."

"Gotta make an appointment thirty days in advance and be a relative of the deceased."

"She's not deceased. She's insane."

"Better to be deceased," the man mumbled. "Okay, forget it. Follow me."

The guard walked us to a stone building with a view back toward the mainland of New York. He thumped three times on the wooden door and a frumpy man eventually peered out.

"Yes?"

"A woman here to see you."

"Did she make a written request?" The man stroked the side of his bald head as he lecherously scrutinized Sara. The buttons on his wrinkled shirt were misaligned.

Sara ignored the man's clear indiscretion and redirected, "Sir, if I may, my name is Charlotte Zito and my mother is here. I have been sent by my father to retrieve her."

"Why didn't he come himself?"

"He is in the Army fighting the Indians in Dakota Territory," Sara lied.

"Ah. He dumped her here. She's the ward of the state until he picks her up. Families never comes back, though, you're the first," he smirked.

"May I see her?" Sara asked.

"As long as you have her number. I need thirty minutes." He shut the narrow gap and I heard a female giggle through the door.

"More like three minutes. Trust me," the guard muttered, rolling his eyes. "We can walk while we wait. Not quite sure what to do with you, actually. We don't get visitors here."

Perfectly spaced locust trees lined both sides of the trail. Some type of bug was making a high-pitched call, similar to a cricket but stronger, as if it was agitated. A group of twenty guarded women approached, slowly shuffling toward us. It reminded me of the blistering hot days in the fields, bent at the waist, picking cotton side by side.

145

The guard said, "Don't worry. They know to keep a distance from us. The other guards constantly warn them, 'If I can reach you with a rock, you're too close.' After a few bruises, they stay away."

"I find that repulsive," Sara said, stopping him in his tracks.

He turned, "My apology, I just tell it like it is and the truth is, this place gets to me." He led Sara to a bench and offered her a seat. I stood to the side, shaded by a moss-covered tree.

"How long have you been working here, mister? Mister?" Sara asked.

"Ricci. Tony Ricci. Three, almost four years now."

I glanced at the group of women who had been directed to line up on their knees and pick rocks from the grass at the edge of the wagon trail.

"I need the work but the memories are tough."

"What memories?" Sara asked.

"Probably more than you care to hear. Lost my mom out here, that's all. Now with two young boys and a sick wife, I have to keep drawing wages. Used to work fishing from the other shore. Still have a rowboat tied up there. Go out once in a while. Anyway, when I fished for a living, I watched the men over here, burying bodies like they were rubbish. Let me tell you something. Sometimes they wouldn't get them in the ground before a storm blew them into the water. I can't tell you how many times my fishing net pulled up an arm or a leg. Got the job out here initially, looking for my mom. Couldn't ever find her. When fishing went bad, I took the job moving the bodies from the ferry to the mass grave. The longer I'm here, the easier it gets, except for the babies. They still get to me. Forget it."

Sara and I had agreed I would not speak unless absolutely necessary. She did not want me to correct her when she was in the middle of a big lie. "Do you have a list of who is buried?" I blurted out from behind the bench where the two sat.

"Supposed to, but who knows. An unclaimed body found on the street is just another burden for the city to bury. Why keep track when nobody cares? Why do you ask?"

"My sister might be here," I said.

"Hmm. Might be. Couldn't say. If I put her in the ground, I did it with dignity if it eases your mind at all."

"Thank you, Mr. Ricci," I replied calmly, staring toward the open field beyond the cluster of asylum buildings.

"My honor," he replied, "Please, ladies, call me Tony,"

It was quiet for some time. Translucent orange and worn-out rust-colored leaves blew across my feet.

"Boss man got tired of me working carefully in the pit. My thought was it should be done right; each body placed carefully before we shoveled over 'em all. He said dead was dead. He didn't like how I said a little prayer at the end of each day. So they moved me over to the insane as a guard. Not sure which is worse 'cause that's where I lost my mom."

"Do you know my mother, Rose Zito?" Sara asked.

"Maybe know her face, if she's a fighter that is. They use me to shackle 'em. I don't bother with names," Mr. Ricci muttered. I glanced at his thick strong hands and arms.

"What's it like inside the buildings?" I blurted.

"Good thing you're taking her home. I didn't say it, but conditions are terrible. Things happen that never should. Not enough willing to work over here, mostly at night. So, we shackle them to pipes and beds 'till morning. The coal furnace makes everything black. Forget it. The furnaces break down and I'm expected to fix 'em. Dangerous work and minimal pay. That's how I lost my fingers. So, the walls are black. Their clothes are black. They cough up black. The chamber pots run over before they carry 'em out to dump on the shore. The craziest ones scream all night, fightin' off demons in their heads. Food's not bad, with cows and goats and chickens out here. Caring for 'em seems like the only thing that settles them down. Slaughter day is a bad, bad day 'cause they think of 'em as pets. Never should let them name 'em."

"I could use a stretch after the long buggy ride. Do you mind if we stroll?" Sara asked, glancing at a group of women who worked their way toward us.

"Suit yourself."

Tony walked close to Sara and I followed behind, invisible. I noticed she did not create more distance between her and Tony. She had changed her ways while in Dakota Territory. Tony guided us off the trail as a horse-drawn freight cart passed, loaded with wooden boxes, stacked three high and balanced by two men leaning against them. The women did not look up as the bodies passed. Ten feet from the women, we stopped and a few glanced up, enamored with my dress. The women were instructed by their guard to continue picking rocks, and they immediately complied.

Each woman seemed identical to the next. Faded, worn out clothing covered thin, meaningless bodies. No dignity remained. Only one woman caught my attention because she held something in her right hand, rotating it over and over in her palm. Occasionally, she appeased the guard by picking a rock from the grass with her left hand and pitching it toward the trail ruts.

I walked over to the woman and crouched in front of her, at the distress of Tony. He told me to step back and continued to nervously look over his shoulder at the superintendent's brick building. I ignored him.

"Good day. Can I see what's in your hand?" I gently asked.

She refused with a slight shake of her head, not making eye contact. The woman's long, dull brown hair blew in the breeze. Her skeletal face showed signs of starvation and melancholy, yet after a moment, her deep-set green eyes peeked from behind her hair.

"Step back," Tony repeated. "This ain't such a good idea." The woman cowered at his raised voice.

"I won't take it from you, but please show me," I asked the woman again.

She kept her head down, with her fist tightly clenched. She placed her other hand over her eyes, shutting me out; shutting her whole world out.

Sara stepped over and kneeled beside us. "Mama, it's me, Charlotte," she whispered under her breath.

Lines of grief were etched across the woman's forehead. Her hand dropped from her face and her shadowed eyes raised to Sara's face, searching for something.

"I said step back," the guard's voice held more urgency. "The supe is coming."

Tony physically pulled Sara to her feet and yanked my arm. His callused hand scratched my skin as I tried to pull away. "Be damned if I'll lose this job over you," he mumbled.

I glanced back as he led us away from the women. Pale and silent, Rose opened her fingers. A heart-shaped rock rested in her palm.

Rose's guard yelled, "204 get back to work." He raised his arm, preparing to backhand her, but was halted by the sight of the superintendent.

"Back away from the patients!" the superintendent hollered, briskly marching toward us, perfectly centered on the wagon trail to avoid twisting an ankle in the worn ruts. "Not a good decision, Ricci."

"Yes, sir," Tony replied.

"Ah, now Miss Zito, is it? Follow me." His penetrating eyes nearly groped Sara and his tone had an undercurrent like an open pocketknife, ready to cut us into shreds. The superintendent escorted us to another brick building with scattered boxes of water-damaged files awkwardly stacked along the walls. The man sat at a makeshift desk and left Tony, Sara, and me standing before him like the blindfolded on a firing line.

As he thumbed through files he pulled from his desk, he inquired, "Now tell me again. You are Charlotte Zito?"

"Yes. My mother is Rose," Sara answered, squaring her shoulders.

"And your father sent you, you say?"

"Yes. I can now care for my mother until his return."

"And what is your father's name?"

"Thomas."

He opened a folder, and from it, letters and two sheets of paper fell to the floor. He retrieved the papers. "Here it is. Zito. Very good. And what is your mother's patient number?"

"I believe it is 204."

"Just 204?"

"I believe so."

"And what is your address of record?" he asked, looking down at his sheet.

"I am not certain where they were last. I was attending a university down south and had not been home for quite some time. They move frequently with the Army."

151

"I see," he replied. His smirk widening on his scarlet face. He scanned the second paper before him, shielding it from Sara's view. "Well, well. Seems we have a problem. As I look at her forms, I see her number is 2204, not 204."

"My apology, Sir," Sara answered. "I must have forgotten the other 2."

"And it seems we have another problem. As I look here, I see forwarded mail from the war department. Says here your father is dead, and intake records say you, Charlotte, died from the fever as a child."

"Must be a mistake. I can promise you that I am Charlotte Zito."

"Only leaves one more issue now, which will need lawyers if you press it. See, the Zito estate had no heirs before you showed up today. Do you know what that means?"

Sara shook her head. My hands sweat.

"Means the estate was placed in my asylum account, to cover Mrs. Zito's expenses, of course, as long as she continues to breathe on this island."

"How much is in the estate?" Sara asked with bewilderment.

"Well, well, I think you already know of its great magnitude. To act out this scheme as an imposter, which I respect in some odd way, means you are well aware of the large estate that rests in my hands. Ricci, do you think I should call the police?"

"Not for me to say, Sir. I'm happy to simply escort them off the island since my shift is long over. Sir, you're a busy man, and your female company is waiting at your quarters," Tony replied, running his remaining fingers through his hair.

"Ah, yes. I do have that. Escort the thieves from the island and be done with it. I hope you learned your lesson, young lady. If no police are called, I am confident you'll never set foot on this island again?" With that, our eyes locked and when he did not receive a response, he threw the papers back into the desk, stood up, and stormed out of the room.

Tony relaxed after his boss departed and he escorted Sara out of the building. I lagged behind, grabbing Mrs. Zito's paperwork from the superintendent's top drawer. I slid the folder into my dress which would not likely be noticed, given I was invisible to those with light skin. It took great effort, limping along with my cane, but I caught up to Sara and Tony before they reached the dock. We waited as the ferry was still loading on the other side. Silence got the best of Tony.

"Is that true? You both seem like good people. Are you tryin' to steal her money or not?" he asked.

"At this point, Tony, you wouldn't believe the truth if I told you. And I don't blame you for that," Sara said, defeated by the result of the afternoon.

"Try me. The truth is the truth."

"Rose's husband was an Army sergeant under my dad's command. My dad was killed by Indians in Dakota Territory. Mrs. Zito's husband and I were caught in a blizzard. He froze to death because he covered me with his coat. I owe it to him to rescue his wife. He loved her deeply and it is my responsibility to care for her now," Sara said.

"But you understand, she's crazy."

"Aren't we all?" Sara replied.

The ferry arrived and Tony helped Sara and me on board. We were speechless as we pulled from the island, looking back as the locus trees shrunk into the distance. Again, Tony offered his arm as balance to both of us as we stepped from the ferry, docked back on the mainland.

"Sorry it didn't work out. I wish the best for you. I'll keep an eye on Mrs. Zito, now that I know the circumstances. Are you sure she doesn't have anyone?"

"She's completely alone now. Her husband is dead and she lost her daughter to the fever. That's why she went crazy," Sara said.

We turned and walked down the street, looking for our hired buggy driver. He was not at the drop location. Tony saw us milling around and asked the dock workers about our ride. They informed him that the driver was robbed of my fare shortly after dropping us off. He rushed away before the bandits stole his horse and carriage.

"It's getting dark and this is a bad area. My family lives down the path. You're welcome in our home and I'll find you a ride back to the city. Suppose I could get your true names? Not Charlotte Zito, but?"

"Sara. Sara Taylor."

"And?" he asked.

"Miss Bee. Just Miss Bee," I said.

"Very well then. Glad we got the name issue straight. Feel like I'm dealing with trouble," Tony joked, escorting us through a few blocks of shacks and worn-out wood-framed houses. He explained how he worked eight or nine shifts a week on Hart Island, every day and some overnights. In between, he worked nights as a manual laborer on odd jobs around the neighborhood. Through part-time jobs, he became a skilled carpenter, but still could not find reliable work in his poor neighborhood. Since Tony did not have a horse, his family was trapped in a two-room rental in the basement of a home which housed another family above.

"We have our own entrance, though. I dug out a staircase to reach the basement. Gotta make it work, right?"

We walked to the back of the dilapidated house and navigated down the crude steps. Sara said they reminded her of an opium den.

"We are home, my Sweetness," Tony called as he entered.

His wife came out of the other room and I was shocked that her skeleton legs could support herself.

"Babe, I brought two ladies, until they can find a ride back to the city."

We stood at the door and smiled.

"Of course, of course," she said, "Please, come in. Not every day this happens. You are welcome here and I'm sorry for the mess. I had a rough day or two. Not well at all."

Tony introduced us. His wife's name was Maria. Her arms were frail and she was well along with a child. Her beautiful, long black hair was a stark contrast from her white skin and delicate features. She pulled Tony into the other room, offering me a moment to take in the furnishings. A compact, crafted table, notched with carved scrolling on each corner offered dining space. The top was smooth as silk, reflecting light from the single candle. Tony and Maria whispered for a moment around the corner and then returned. Maria offered us seats on the mismatched chairs and stool. Tony dug into a jar from their open shelf above an icebox and headed out the door.

"Whatever is on your stove smells delicious," I said, trying to ease Maria's mind.

"A little soup is all. Tony will bring back more when he picks up the boys from their teacher. School isn't safe here. So, the boys do their lessons with a neighbor down the way."

"Are you not well?" Sara asked.

"Not well at all. Doctors are scarce 'round here. Almost left Tony a widower a year ago. But the good Lord wasn't ready to call me up. Now, with another baby on the way, I'm worried."

"Things get complicated very quickly, don't they?" I interjected. My sympathetic words immediately released Maria's tears.

"You have no idea. My Tony works like a horse to provide the best he can. Still, it's hard. We want a better life for our boys. If only Tony could move us to the city where schools are good. I could be seen by a real doctor and Tony could be a carpenter. He loves working with his hands. Look at this table, isn't it a masterpiece? Look at the grain. He saved for weeks to buy the walnut boards. The wealthy would pay one month's wage for a table like this, but the rich aren't here. We need to be where they live, in the city. Since rent is too high, we are stuck here with another baby on the way."

Two young boys pushed through the door and ran to greet their mom. They were so focused on hugging her that they did not notice the tears she quickly dried on her sleeve.

"Ah, my boys, my pride and joy," Maria said.

"Love you, Mama," they answered in unison.

Tony stepped through the door with a loaf of bread, prosciutto and olives to go with the vegetable and potato soup already bubbling at a low boil on the wood-burning stove. The boys sat on the floor, drinking from their bowls without using spoons. We sat around the table as if we had been friends for life. While the boys listened intently, the adults spoke of hardships, blessings, and the twists and turns of life which were impossible to anticipate. Tony spoke with pessimism.

Toward the end of the evening, Tony borrowed two horses and a rickety wagon from his neighbor. Sara paid the neighbor in advance and thanked him for his kind gesture to facilitate our return to the city. On the long ride back, I chatted with Tony on the buckboard while Sara slumped, dozing on a quilt in the back of the wagon.

Tony spoke of what it felt like to bury people with no identity. He said the nameless people had numbered metal toe tags. I asked if he ever buried a woman with a number branded on her flesh. He said he rarely saw the women in such a compromised state. I was relieved.

Finally, there seemed nothing left to say. We rode in silence, taking in the surroundings. Out of nowhere, long after my eyes had closed and my mind wandered to empty places, Tony raised his voice in excitement and said, "Sara, wake up. I think I have an idea to get Rose out of the asylum."

CHAPTER 11

SARA

NOVEMBER, 1876

HART ISLAND, NEW YORK

"DO WE INDEED DESIRE THE DEAD SHOULD STILL BE NEAR US AT OUR SIDE?"
~Alfred Tennyson, In Memoriam A.H.H., 1849

Miss Bee apprehensively walked beside me to the shoreline. The humid wind blew right through my dad's old military issued coats which were oversized for me and undersized in the waistline for Miss Bee. Tony's old rowboat was found tied to the base of a tree, just as he promised. The moonlight was bright enough to see the outline of Hart Island.

"I can't swim," Miss Bee professed, staring at the open span of water. The whites around her brown eyes reflected off the lantern light.

"Would have been good to know before now," I snapped nervously. "Just wait here. Hide in the brush and wait."

"No, I'm coming with you," she sternly replied and quickly changed her mind when we peered into the boat. It was compact, perhaps eight feet long, with one set of oars attached in the middle.

"Mrs. Zito will never fit with the two of us," she rationalized. "Looks like I need to stay here whether I can swim or not."

Miss Bee pushed me off the shore and I braced myself on the bench with my back to the island. Fumbling with the oars, frigid water splashed onto my lap until my clumsy strokes became more coordinated. I maneuvered to the southeast side of the island, rowing with the wind, as Tony directed. He was working a nightshift at the asylum and would bring Rose to me at midnight.

Once on Hart Island, I stood in cold, shin-deep water, turning the bow toward the other shore and balancing the boat with each wave. I waited. And waited. And waited.

My feet were numb, so I pulled the back edge of the boat onto the island shore to secure it from the lapping waves. Self-doubt enveloped me as I possibly misunderstood our meeting location. I walked invisibly along the shore because the moon had fallen behind clouds and only a shimmer gleamed off the growing waves. I prayed to see Tony and Rose approaching through the trees.

A branch snapped under my foot, reminding me of how Ohanzee taught me to walk quietly with my toes straight ahead, rolling my feet as I stepped. Bending over to grab the broken stick and throw it into the water, I realized it was actually a bone. A human bone. A tibia.

Initially stoic, I went into a doctor's frame of mind, staring at the break I caused. "Quite brittle and no marrow," I hypothesized, "Perhaps an elderly destitute." While examining the bone, my hand shook as I contemplated how it once belonged to a living, breathing human. How did it end up here? I spun in a circle, recognizing other bones exposed on the shoreline. And then it hit me and I pondered whether this was the final resting ground for Miss Bee's sister. I scooped up two handfuls of sand and dropped them into my dad's coat pocket.

The wind picked up, smothering the sound of lapping waves. I walked toward the tree line as Tony emerged holding a rope with the other end tied around Rose's waist.

"All good," Tony said. "Let me tell you something. Wasn't easy. Once I unchained her from the pipe, she didn't want to follow me. She fought the whole way across the island. Forget it. Finally, I figured it out, she doesn't want me touching her. So, I tied the rope around her and she followed like a dog. She'll fight less if you call her Rose, not Mrs. Zito. Figure that."

"Hello, Rose," I said calmly. She seemed all consumed, staring down at her leather shoes. The tops of the toes were worn through, probably from kneeling on the hard ground as she picked rocks. She never raised her eyes.

"Okay, let's get you out of here. I need to get back before they notice I'm gone. This has taken too long," Tony said. Even with the cold wind, beads of sweat collected on his forehead.

Tony handed me Rose's rope and he yanked the light boat off the coarse shore, back to knee deep water. Rose refused to step in. Tony coaxed. I watched. No progress. Tony kept looking over his shoulder.

"I need to get back, Sara. Can't lose my job. I have three other mouths to feed, four before I blink again," Tony explained.

Pulling the chain with my Saint Michael medal over my head, I said, "Mama, remember this? Daddy told me to bring his medal to you so you can be safe. You know it's safe now, right? I'll take you to Daddy. I promise."

Rose looked up at the pewter medal swinging on a silver chain in front of her face: an angel with a sword stood victoriously over the dragon of evil. Unexpectedly, her eyes met mine.

"You remember, right, Mama? I'm Charlotte," I lied.

I slipped the chain over her head as she stared at the medal. Tony lifted each of her feet into the boat while I balanced Rose by the arm, pressuring her to sit down in the bottom. Tony and I waded a bit deeper into the dark water before I slung my leg over the side of the boat. He balanced me as I sat on the bench, facing the island. Tony started us on our journey with one last forceful push out into the open water. I forgot to thank him.

I rowed and rowed toward the lights of the city, since the sky had turned overcast and concealed the moon. With gusts blowing against the boat, we made limited progress. Waves occasionally broke over the bow and drenched Rose, but she stayed low as I had instructed. As the waves grew, my arms tired. I could not imagine floating back to Hart Island or worse, out to sea. The current fought my progress but finally, the resistance eased and I rowed us closer to the correct shore where Miss Bee stood with the lantern, calling us toward her. About twenty feet from shore, a wave crashed into the side of our rowboat, knocking Rose to the other side. Panicked, she stood up, only to lose balance and fall over the edge into the icy water without a whimper.

I reached for the rope Tony had tied around her waist and held on as it burned through my hands. When it neared the end, I refused to let go and the knotted end jerked me into the water. I surfaced, still clutching the rope and held the side of the boat while trying to pull Rose to air. She was drowning without a struggle, suspended in the water without a fight. Rose was too heavy to pull up, so I secured the end of the rope around the cleat holding the oar and took a deep breath, following the rope down to her waist. My lungs stung as I grabbed frantically for something to pull; her limp shoulder perhaps. Instead, I snagged the Saint Michael medal chain and her hair, making a fist and kicking for air with Rose in tow. We surfaced and gasped simultaneously, at the edge of where black water met black sky. Somehow, I managed to rotate Rose's body so she was floating on her back. She breathed deeply and I wedged her against the side of the boat so I could tie off the rope.

Gripping the edge of the boat, I inched my way to the other side. I tried unsuccessfully to kick my legs and crawl back in the boat, using Rose as a balance on the opposite side. Dad's coat was heavy and my shoes pulled at my legs like anchors.

With arms spent from rowing, I submerged with little energy left. My legs stretched down, toes extending in hopes of pushing against sand to propel myself back to the surface. Instead, I felt nothing and kicked one last time. I reached through the surface and sucked another breath, only to be met by a wave collapsing over my head. My lungs pulsed fire and the water suddenly seemed warmer. I quit fighting. I saw Dad immersed beside me with a proud smile on his face. I saw Sergeant Zito, mouthing "thank you" with bubbles flowing from his mouth. Drowning was similar to freezing to death, I thought.

My senses returned in a strange order. First, I heard someone straining and the hull of the boat grinding against the rocky shoreline. Then I heard coughs and gasps. Next came a flickering light from the lantern which lay overturned a few feet from my reach, caught in the sea grasses. Finally, my body ached and shivered uncontrollably. Raising my head, I saw Miss Bee releasing the rope from the boat. Rose sat upright on the shore, legs extended, staring at the lapping waves.

"How did you do it?" I asked weakly. "You can't swim."

"My sister's voice insisted I could," Miss Bee answered.

CHAPTER 12

SARA

DECEMBER, 1876

NEW YORK CITY

"A GENEROUS PERSON WILL PROSPER; WHOEVER REFRESHES OTHERS WILL BE REFRESHED."~ Proverbs 11:25

Each month passed like a day while I tried to settle business in New York before returning to Deadwood Gulch. Avoiding travel in the worst winter months, I felt no pressure to rush back with two women lacking experience out west. I took time digging through Dad's desk and found the house deed tacked to the underside of his desk drawer. I was thrilled and announced at dinner that I would transfer the home into my name at the City Registrar.

"How do you prove your folks are dead?" Miss Bee asked.

"The letter from the War Department." I answered.

"But it says you are dead also," she replied.

"Oh. Right."

Miss Bee dropped her voice after glancing over at Rose, who kneeled silently in the corner, rubbing her Saint Michael medal between her fingers. "If you need me to stay to take care of your house, and Rose for that matter, until it's all sorted out, I'll stay."

"Oh no, I'm not leaving you again. We are a team now. And that goes for Rose, too. We are a team of three," I said, surprised by Miss Bee's offer. "As long as you want to come back with me and Rose, I want you with us, even if it means letting this house sit empty. You do want to come, don't you?"

"I do, but this has been home for years. I have waited and waited for my sister. If I leave, I give up. Don't 'spect you to understand. All I have of my sister is memories. You have this house. Rose has her Saint Michael medal. I have nothing," Miss Bee said solemnly.

I walked into my room and retrieved a glass canning jar that had been carefully wrapped in my belongings. I handed Miss Bee the jar and she stared at the sand inside, perplexed.

"It's the shore of Hart Island. The sand represents your sister. I collected it in my pocket the night we rescued Rose. I know it's not much, but – "

Miss Bee interrupted, "It's perfect."

The next day, Miss Bee stood in the kitchen, carefully pouring the sand into a tiny vial. Its black metal cap was the diameter of her smallest finger. She lovingly slipped it into the side pocket of her paisley printed cotton skirt.

As Miss Bee and I planned our departure, I wrote to Rebekah and Jake about the details of returning in March. I walked through the house and could not envision the furniture at my claim, even if I eventually hired someone to build a cabin for us. Miss Bee suggested I touch each item and contemplate if the object gave me joy. If it did, she suggested I freight it to Deadwood. If it didn't, she said it was best to let it go even if it ended up as fuel in a fireplace.

Rose offered no input, staring blankly at the wall as I touched each item and sadly went to the next. When I was finished, Miss Bee said, "Well, Sara, we better plan for one big bonfire." Rose didn't even crack a smile. Thankfully, she ate on her own, which eased Miss Bee's burden. I did not have time to address her nearly catatonic state since I had a long list of things to complete.

On one of my errands, I purchased a newspaper from a man calling out from a busy corner. On the third page was an inconspicuous article about another battle against the Indians. "On November 25, Colonel Ranald S. Mackenzie, with his 1,400 troops and scouts, defeated some of the last savage holdouts who just months ago declared victory at the Custer Massacre. With only seven brave soldier casualties, 200 tipis full of hostiles were eliminated, opening the door to the settlement of the west." I doubted the accuracy of the article.

Something nagged and nudged me to take a carriage ride to Tony Ricci. He had risked greatly to help with Rose's escape and I had not thanked him properly. But it was more than that because I wanted to check on his wife's health in case I could offer assistance. Four hours later, the hired driver dropped me a few streets from their home. When I walked down the grungy alley, someone stirred from a wooden shelter, not unlike what prospectors made for their first nights in Deadwood Gulch. I increased my pace and did not look back. Descending Tony's staircase, I found only a padlocked door waiting for me. The Ricci family was gone.

I walked around to the main level of the house and rapped on the front door. A sloppy woman answered and explained Tony lost his job on Hart Island.

"Where did they go?"

"No idea," she said. "The landlord traded the unpaid month's rent for Tony's table. It was like murdering his wife when the men made the deal. It had been a present for Maria. And then the landlord kicked 'em out, just like that. Tony left with what he and the boys could carry. The landlord padlocked the rest."

"Which way did they head?"

"No idea. If you find him, tell 'em he's missed. Kept trouble away," she said.

I retraced my steps down the alley past the same man in his shelter. This time he was sitting up, balancing on one arm. His ruddy face was wrinkled and his eyes clung to the sockets. He had a gash over one eye which oozed from an infection and it leaked down into what should have been the white of his eye, but it was actually yellow.

"Excuse me. Do you know where Tony Ricci and his family went?"

"Can't say," he mumbled.

"He used to live in the basement, a few houses down," I continued, pointing backwards down the alley.

"Can't say," he repeated.

"I see. Very well then," I started to walk away, but stopped. "If you don't mind me asking, how long have you had the cut above your eye?"

"Weeks, what's it to you?"

"You are going to lose your eye to infection if we don't get it cleaned up. You can't let that wound drain straight into your eye."

"Who do you think you are? A nurse?"

"Something like that. Let me help you."

I kneeled beside the man, using his canteen of water and the bottom edge of my skirt to clean the wound. When I stood up to walk away, he told me that Tony and his family were living by the water where he tied up his boat.

I found the spot easily. Without summer foliage, the brush created little privacy between the town and Tony's lean-to. He had used the boat, tipped up on its side, to shield his family from gusty winds. A canvas tarp covered a frame of boards which had washed ashore. The entire structure was the size of two carriages and stood only five feet tall at its peak.

"Hello," I called, not wanting to startle them.

Tony crawled out first, with a knife in his hand.

"Tony, it's me, Sara."

"Lucky your throat ain't cut," he responded. "What are you doing here?"

"I heard you lost your job. I'm deeply sorry. What happened?"

Tony stepped away from the structure and talked in a low voice, "The Supe found out a few days after the escape that I worked the night shift when Rose disappeared. He blamed me. Didn't care if she drowned, but couldn't risk her showing up alive somewhere, demanding her estate. He had me search along the shoreline. A few days later, he called me in and accused me of stealing the Zito records. How'd that happen, huh? It's the one thing I didn't do, but he kicked me off the island for it. Didn't even pay my last week's wages. Just like that. I do something good for someone and end up getting burned at the stake every time."

"Oh, I'm sorry," I said. "So what are you doing now?"

"Forget it. Lost all my tools when we were kicked out of the basement. Landlord claimed 'em. So now I'm asking around every morning for work doing anything for anyone."

Bitterness permeated him. We were quiet for a moment and I heard Maria cough and whimper from inside the lean-to, "Who is it, Tony?"

"Nobody. It's nothing Babe," he responded calmly. He whispered to me, "She's sick. Can't get around anymore. I can't afford a

170

doctor. The boys are down at the docks trying to make a few pennies filleting fish for market. I can't leave her like this. It's bad."

"Can I see her? I can help."

"Ah, let me tell you something. You've caused enough problems. Leave us alone. Best if you move on," he said.

"I didn't intend to cause you problems."

"Well, you did. It always happens like this."

"Like how?"

"People ask for favors and I get nothing in return. Just thrown out. Nobody ever there for me."

"That's not true. I'm here to check on you."

"Forget it. Just go. Nothing personal. I can handle it," Tony replied.

"Sounds personal to me. Maybe people are afraid to help because you don't see things any way but your own."

"That's not true."

"Then let me check on your wife. Please, let me see her," I pleaded.

He reluctantly stepped aside and I entered the flimsy enclosure.

"Maria, tell me where it hurts."

Weakly, she pointed to her distended lower abdomen. I felt her belly and it was tight.

"I need to examine you," I said.

"My water broke a while ago," she confessed.

I lifted her skirt and placed my hands where I could feel the head of the baby.

"Tony," I said calmly, "Boil water on your fire. Boil your knife in the water. Your baby is on its way."

Maria became more uncomfortable and agitated as her labor increased. I distracted her by rubbing her arms until Tony brought the water. He poured it into my dirty hands, scalding me as I scrubbed to my elbows with their lye soap. I wished I had chloroform to ease her pain. Tony crouched beside Maria, unsure of himself. The baby progressed quickly and crowned while Maria wailed for it to be over. Maria weakened and drifted off. We waited. Nothing happened.

"Maria, you need to push hard," I instructed firmly. Her eyes fluttered open for a moment. "Now is the time for this baby to come out," I said, demanding her to focus. The top of the baby's head was stuck. I slid my fingers around the edge of exposed scalp, trying to release the child. "Push, Maria!" I urged. "You need to take deep breaths. Stay with me, Maria." At first, she seemed to listen, then after a few deep breaths, she turned her head to the side and vomited. I glared up at Tony to do something.

"For goodness sake, Babe, push. Don't give up, do it for our boys. You need to be strong for our boys," Tony begged. "And me," he added with a quaking voice.

Maria's eyes opened wide and she pushed. My hands shook as I pulled the baby's shoulders from the binds of its mother. The rest of the limp body followed. No crying. Blue skin. I recalled the childbirth section of the medical journal from Doc and wiped away mucus from the baby's mouth and nose. Still nothing. I noticed she was a girl. Turning the baby over, I cradled her face in the palm of my hand and gave her a swat on her rear. A shrill wheezing sound followed and then the high-pitched cry which came from deep within the baby's core.

"I believe you have a healthy baby girl," I announced, holding the messy baby in my arms. "Do you have a blanket?"

Tony pulled off his shirt and handed it to me. I tied off the umbilical cord with a piece of twine and used his sterilized knife to cut the cord above the knot. The air was biting, so I placed the bloody baby against Maria's chest and covered her with Tony's shirt. Maria was conscious enough to instinctually direct the baby to nurse. Tony, shivering from the cold, looked on in awe.

"Love you. You are beautiful and strong," he said to his exhausted wife, "You did it. I'll never forget this moment, as long as air fills my lungs."

Maria cried. She was physically and emotionally spent. Within a few minutes, her placenta followed. I confirmed it was intact, carried it like a dripping sacrifice to the water's edge and slung it into the waves.

When I returned to the lean-to, I stood outside as a stranger. "Please, don't cry, Babe. Save your energy. This world can't keep beating us up like it has," Tony assured Maria.

"Yes, it can," I thought. A few days later, I forged Dad's signature on the house deed and presented it to the Treasurer's Office. I asked to change the owner on record to my name and requested paying five years ahead on the house's property tax. The cashier was distracted with the stack of bills on the counter and he called over a shady looking manager who overlooked the deed transfer and quickly took my cash. With the receipt in hand, I could only wonder where the funds would end up.

The Ricci family's transition from their lean-to to my home was easy, given they only had a few belongings to tote along. I gave their family my bedroom and my grandmother's room. Miss Bee insisted on staying in her room, the servant quarters behind the kitchen. Rose and I shared the master bedroom.

Late into each night I gently spoke to Rose, as she remained silent. I decided she was not benefitting by the illusion I had created, that I was her daughter and her husband was still alive. Not a word had slipped from her lips. If she wasn't engaging and improving, then I was deceiving her to no avail. So, I let the truth come out, a bit each night, as we lay in the dark. I told what I first learned of her husband; how Dad told me that Sergeant Zito was a smart and good man who naturally improved troop morale and would never let Dad down. I told Rose how her husband wrote to her every chance he had and planned their reunion as soon as his assignment was over. I told her how he saved me in the Dakota Territory blizzard.

Rose did not respond and I doubted if I could actually help her recover. Dad's words permeated my heavy heart. He had warned me about trying to save my mother, explaining you cannot give someone else the will to survive because it must come from within. Night after night was wasted reviewing the past and making no sense of it.

So, I flipped our conversations and focused on the future. I told Rose about the beauty of the Black Hills and how excited I was to take her to my claim. I told her we would wait a bit for the weather to lift. I did not elaborate that I could not risk another blizzard with two women under my care.

Miss Bee exuded positive energy in our crowded house. She routinely exhaled audible sighs of stress and suggested that Tony do the same. "It'll make you feel better," she told Tony. "Looks like you been robbed of your joy. You really want to go through life like this? It'll rub off on Maria and your kids. And the good Lord doesn't wish your darkness on any of us."

Maria did not harbor the same burden as her husband. Her mood improved daily and she was thankful I decided to leave the furniture behind. The mahogany-and-ivory clock, which hung on sage-green flocked wallpaper only reminded me of my oppressed childhood. The white, Italian marble mantel was too heavy to move. Even the crystal vase, which sat on top, did not belong in Deadwood Gulch. They were Grandmother's treasures, not mine.

175

Tony's family could use them and create good memories where I had mostly bad. The boys were excited to have a bedroom of their own and their new school was walking distance from the house, offering early independence for the boys and convenience for Maria and the baby.

I replenished the woodworking tools which Tony forfeited. He could start his new carpentry trade in the city. Miss Bee offered to sleep on the floor in front of the fire so Tony converted her quarters into a simple, clean workshop. Within days, he had orders for high-end furniture and offers for general carpentry work on five-story buildings erupting from ground previously occupied by shanty neighborhoods. Within two weeks, Tony was earning three times his Hart Island wages, vigorously pursuing his passion.

Maria's color returned and her minor ailments improved as they were related to simple malnutrition. She quickly settled into the house and relaxed. Perhaps the sense of security would allow her to heal. Once we were gone, my house would be perfect for Tony's family.

When the worst of winter was behind us, Tony escorted Miss Bee, Rose and me to the train. He asked if there was anything else he needed to know about the house until we returned.

"Don't dig too deeply in the garden," Miss Bee offered. He nodded but didn't ask.

I continued, "Now don't forget to write and let us know how things are going, okay? And one more thing, Tony. It's important.

I'm known in Deadwood Gulch as 'Sara Capable' so don't put 'Sara Taylor' on the envelope. 'Sara Capable', Deadwood Gulch, Dakota Territory, okay?"

Tony shook his head and replied, "Oh Sara, not another alias."

CHAPTER 13

SARA

APRIL, 1877

DAKOTA TERRITORY

"LIFE MUST BE UNDERSTOOD BACKWARDS. BUT THEN ONE FORGETS THAT IT MUST BE LIVED FORWARD."~ Soren Kierkegaard

Our train was initially crowded. I sat facing Miss Bee and Rose, who bounced along, shoulder to shoulder, weighted with melancholy. I expected excitement and joy about the adventure before us. Instead, they ignored the wooded hills of New Jersey and the forested Pennsylvania mountains. I was frustrated and focused on the scenery rolling past the window, glancing back to wonder why Miss Bee became quiet with self-reflection. Rose only accompanied us in body as she had still not spoken a word. She remained a detached, damaged woman; something clearly was not right in her head.

As we progressed west, more open seats appeared and we were each able to claim a bench intended for two. The occasional tar paper shacks near the tracks caught Miss Bee's attention and she said they reminded her of the Georgia plantation where she was a slave child. One evening, when Rose seemed to be dozing, and Miss Bee contemplatively stared out the dark window, I moved beside her and asked if she was having second thoughts about moving west. She sadly explained it was hard to leave her sister behind.

"When I heard her voice as you were drowning, I finally accepted she was dead and buried on Hart Island. Before that night, I had faith our paths would cross again. I had convinced myself that she would somehow come find me."

"Tom will come for me," Rose blurted over the of the train from across the aisle. With her eyes still closed, she repeated. "Tom will come for me."

Miss Bee slid from her seat and knelt in front of Rose, hugging her as only Miss Bee could do. She pulled Rose close against her ample bosom, rocking back and forth with her eyes clenched shut. Neither cried.

When our late arriving train's metal-on-metal brakes screeched into the Cheyenne station, I told the women to wait while I fetched Blue. Wearing my New York dress, I walked as fast as the impractical skirt allowed to the livery stable. Anxiety crept through me of what I might find. Assuming Blue would be waiting for me, I peered into the dark stable. Six horses stood side by side, sleeping. I did not see Blue and so I walked between the dozing horses, confident Blue was hidden by another. He was not there.

I panicked and paced through the stable, looking for the owner and then looking again for Blue. A drunken man walked up to one of the horses and tightened his saddle girth.

"What do you know? Where ya headed?" he asked when he saw me. "Lookin' to buy a horse? This one will get you down the trail. He's for sale. Everything's for sale in Cheyenne."

"Is the owner of the stable here?"

"He ain't here."

"Excuse me? A woman owned the stable a few months ago."

"She sold it. Couldn't take it anymore."

"Where did she go?" I asked, afraid of what I would hear.

"Just down the road a few blocks." He pointed north. "It's on the left, can't miss it. The stone house with scrub oaks lining the trail."

I thanked the man and headed as he directed. After walking past a few tar paper shacks, more substantial homes emerged, each on small pieces of property. The stone house stood just beyond. I took a deep breath and entered the front yard through a whitewashed garden gate. The house was dark, so I walked around to the side and found another fence, with a rectangular pasture stretching behind. Three horses stood in the back corner. Although it was dark, I thought I spotted Blue.

Instead of searching for the gate, I hiked my dress and straddled the smooth wire to cross the fence. The horses spooked as I approached, still one stood firm and alert. It was Blue.

I wanted to run to him and wrap my arms around his neck, but I knew he would not understand. Instead, I called to him gently. He did not move as the other two horses snorted and spun in circles, pawing at the ground. I called again and he walked straight to me, sniffing my neck. He calmly followed me to the house as though I had never deserted him.

After knocking again and again on the front door, a lantern finally illuminated the windows. A man answered the door, with the woman standing behind. I explained I was fetching Blue. The woman invited me in and offered me tea. She explained that after her husband died in the Custer Massacre, she took their savings and built a livery stable because she needed to support herself. After I had boarded Blue with her, she met a man who helped her maintain the stables and they eventually fell in love, marrying and moving to the stone house. They sold the stable and she brought Blue with her, caring for him as she had promised and wondering if I would ever return.

Satisfied with the charges, I gave her an additional month of board for her efforts. She asked if I was interested in selling Blue. She said he had something special about him, which is why Blue was not for sale.

When I rode up to the train station, Miss Bee and Rose were sitting against the side of the building, not saying a word. Miss Bee was relieved to see me and asked why I was delayed. Rose did not speak that night. Or the next. Or the next. It was a week later, while she was on Blue's back, that her lips parted again.

Miss Bee and I limped along beside Blue, slowly venturing to the Black Hills. The trail was well-traveled, with occasional drifts of spring snow creating slight obstacles. I encouraged Rose to walk occasionally, but she meagerly covered ground as she shuffled along. Out of frustration, we hoisted Rose onto Blue in hopes that we could hurry through hostile Indian country. It seemed to be the first time Rose had been on a horse, at least bareback. She grabbed his mane and her legs stiffened against his sides. Within a few hours though, she was as relaxed and balanced as if she had been raised on a pony.

Spring brought forth the sweet smell of buffalo grass. The melody of invisible birds rejoiced over the warm weather and when the breeze was just right, I could hear Rose whispering to Blue. In deep conversation, she asked if Blue thought I would return when he was left at the boarding stable. She paused, as if he was answering her. Then she asked if he ever lost faith.

A few moments later, after Rose nodded her head and reached down to rub his shoulder, I asked, "What did he say?"

Rose responded, "He knew you would return."

When Miss Bee's awkward gait caused blisters on her left foot, she joined Rose on Blue's back. He had shed his winter coat and filled out nicely at the stable, not wavering with the additional load. Halfway through the twelve-day journey, I doubted my decision to take an insane woman and a limping former slave back to Deadwood Gulch on horseback. Crazy, Black and Blue.

Deciding where to set up camp each night was stressful because I knew we needed to stay close to other travelers. One evening, as the sun dropped from the horizon, the Deadwood Stage, full of passengers, passed us at twice our pace. The driver hollered he would offer protection for $15 if we could keep up with the difficult terrain as we approached the Black Hills. Since Miss Bee chatted less, I knew she was tiring and so I declined his offer.

The stage and five wagons following close behind left us struggling, Others occasionally passed us, hoping to find safety in numbers before nightfall. A hefty man driving a horse-drawn wagon with crates stacked on top came up on us. His crates were filled with agitated cats.

"Eighty-two," the man claimed roughly. "Workin' girls in Deadwood want 'em for company. Everyone else wants 'em for mice." He introduced himself as Phatty Thompson and kept talking, excited about his venture. "Paid twenty-five cents apiece. Gonna sell 'em for ten, fifteen, maybe even twenty-five dollars each. Look at that one in the corner, a beauty, isn't she?"

I urged Blue forward, trying to keep up with the cat wagon, yet we fell behind and purple shadows of twilight settled on the surrounding familiar hills. We did not reach the group until long past nightfall, and I breathed a sigh of relief when we spotted the smoke from their fire on the other side of Spring Creek. Camping beside them offered a degree of protection and a less edgy night of restless sleep.

When we arrived, the camp was in utter chaos, as Phatty Thompson's wagon had flipped while crossing the creek and his cat crates broke open. Men were laughing and chasing dozens of the escaped cats as Phatty Thompson hollered out a promised twenty-five cent reward for each returned feline. Most of the frantic cats were eventually returned and the embarrassed man left the next morning before daybreak, cats meowing furiously as the wagon bounced out of sight.

We lingered behind the stage, only glimpsing the group when a long, straight stretch of trail was before us. Snow started to fall from the sky. Even so, I was reassured by the smell of spring escaping the thawing earth. A few miles from Deadwood, as I lowered my guard and quit scanning the horizon, we caught up to the stage.

"We were just robbed!" the driver proclaimed.

The customers were standing in small groups, some in a daze, others looking into the thick trees, fearful of what lurked within.

"Was anyone hurt? What happened?" I asked.

"They charged down, trapped us in the draw, some on horseback, some on foot."

"Did you recognize anyone?"

"Not a one. Just one fella had quite a limp. Steady and calm, like he'd robbed stages all his life. Thank the good Lord, though. Nobody was shot. They got off with a few thousand dollars, by golly."

"What did the man with the limp look like?"

Shaking his head, the driver replied, "No idea, just a blue cloth over his face and dark, lifeless eyes."

With the havoc of the stage robbery and the exhausted women beside me, I decided to head directly to my claim, skipping a food resupply in town. Mentally planning for an uncomfortably cold night, I would light a campfire and we could squeeze under my tent for extra warmth. I second-guessed my assumption that winter would be over in the Black Hills by April. The high altitude proved me wrong.

Dusty and footsore, we came to the clear, rushing stream where I left my tent months earlier. What stood before me was a dream - a log cabin, a barn, and a privy, nestled along the hillside. I glanced back down the path to verify I had not taken the wrong trail.

We stepped inside the rough-cut door with heavy iron hinges into a spotless one-room cabin. A ladder tipped against the wall to a partial loft. Split wood was stacked beside a stone fireplace. A straw-filled mattress rested on the floor against the far wall, with quilts folded at the foot. A long shelf was loaded with provisions. A note tucked under a spent candle rested on top of a rustic table with three stools pushed underneath. Miss Bee carefully read the note out loud, "Welcome home. We missed you. Jake and Rebekah." I nearly collapsed on the plank floor.

I ran past a corral made from young pines to the barn. Its open
sliding door hung from heavy black iron rollers. The barn's metal
roof was made of cyanide can lids, likely from the mill in
Terraville. Thankful to see that the entire interior was open, I
knew Blue would appreciate moving about the whole area. On
one wall hung a metal bucket full of water. Dry hay filled the
corner.

I rushed back toward the cabin where Blue waited patiently with
Miss Bee and Rose. I snatched his reins and led him to the barn,
with the women following behind. Blue sniffed around the bottom
edge of his new stable, lingering in the corners where the logs met
the ground. He pawed at the dirt before settling in and focusing
on the hay.

186

I closed Blue in his new space and walked with Miss Bee and Rose down the well-worn trail to Jake and Rebekah's claim. Where nothing stood before, a similar log cabin was nestled in their trees. Smoke from the chimney teased the brisk air. I knocked on the door and a pack of dogs barked from inside. The door flew open before I took another breath. Rebekah squealed and hugged me. Jake embraced me quickly and then pulled back with a smirk on his clean-shaven face. Shadow was no longer a puppy. She stood politely in front of me, sniffing my knees and wagging her tail. I introduced Miss Bee and Rose, which was a bit awkward when Rebekah's eyes grew big as she fixated on Miss Bee for quite some time before eventually turning to me.

"The cabin was entirely Jake's idea. I simply encouraged him," Rebekah exclaimed. "Winter beat us with a vengeance, but Jake never gave up. First, he focused on the fireplace. He had already started the chimney when I realized your loft needed a window. So, leave it to my Jake, he just curved the chimney to accommodate the window. I hope you like it."

The couple was giddy as they followed us back to my claim to show us what they had accomplished.

"Look at this, Sara," Rebekah gloated. "Jake angled your cabin so you might get sun earlier in the day. We worked from sunrise to sunset, with scarcely a break for a midday meal. No matter, though, for most of the time Jake was too tired to eat. And the barn, Jake wanted a place to protect Blue from the Indians. How was your journey?"

Jake lit a fire while we exchanged highlights of our last five months. Jake and Rebekah had married the day after I departed for New York, partly because Rebekah refused to sleep at their new claim until it was official. Jake continued working in town for a mining company and Rebekah was not afraid to stay alone in the woods because she had the dogs. On days when work was scarce, Jake and Rebekah cut trees and raised the cabins as snow blanketed the ground. While Jake was working at the Old Abe Mine, Rebekah initially tried panning for gold, but gave up and spent her time piecing together quilts.

"I can't tell you how much this means," I whispered, dizzy on my feet.

"You don't need to. We know," Jake said and they edged toward the door. "We need to be going so you can rest. Tomorrow night I'll work on two more mattresses."

"The purple quilt is yours," Rebekah gleamed. "And extras are in the corner.

When Jake and Rebekah left, I latched the door, overhearing Rebekah say, "Miss Bee is all too familiar. It's as if I have seen her before." Jake laughed and replied, "Dark as night is dark as night. Can't tell one from another." Rebekah said something else, but they were too far down the path for me to understand.

Shadow curled up in front of the fire like she had always been there. Miss Bee claimed her quilt, inspecting it for bedbugs. Rose wrapped up in an old sky-blue blanket beside Shadow. I wandered around, treasuring the gift from Jake and Rebekah. The cabin was perfectly simple and scrupulously clean.

Underneath my pillow, I found a bundle of envelopes tied with a purple ribbon. I took the bundle to the fire and sat on the floor. Through the flickering flames, I stared at the top envelope with a return address of Fred Schwatka. I shuffled through the stack. My cheeks flushed when I saw his name again and again. Ten letters from Fred awaited my arrival. The eleventh was from Mr. Ellis Whiting, Rochester, Minnesota.

I chose to read them in order of how Rebekah received them. I opened the first letter from Fred, dated October 14, 1876. Mail delivery was so slow I did not receive it before leaving for New York. Fred started out explaining how he missed me immediately upon saying goodbye. He focused on his new Army assignment of tracking down resistant Indians and forcing them onto reservations. "I have to say, Sara. I don't want you to feel I am on the side of the Indians but something in my heart churns when I see them restricted from their nomadic lives. They are not familiar with our ways of claiming land as our own and making improvements for personal comforts."

I slid Fred's letter back into its envelope and pulled out the letter from Ellis Whiting. "Dear Sara, thank you for notifying us of Chance's loss. We are particularly sensitive to Chance's difficult situation because Charlie, our own grandson, lost his mother during childbirth. We raise Charlie here in Rochester so he has more opportunities and good schools. Charlie's father and our son, Ammi, is busy on his farm and cannot properly school

Charlie. Chance was our neighbor and he also lost his mother at childbirth. We never cared for his father and since the boys were friends, we did our best to keep Chance fed and clothed. If Chance needs a stable place to finish growing up, he can stay with us, but he will be required to conform to the rules of our house and attend school. We will likely keep Charlie until he graduates from high school. We are old and it would be nice to have another boy around our place to help with chores. Sincerely, Ellis and Laura Whiting."

I placed the letter in the envelope and retied the entire bundle with the ribbon Rebekah must have carefully chosen before sliding it under my pillow. As I rested on my bed, I decided to read the rest of Fred's letters, one each evening, according to the date. Then once each was read, I would start again at the beginning.

Sleep did not follow so I quietly opened the next letter. Fred wrote late at night by the light of the fire, after spending each day with his regiment, still searching for stray Indians. "You are my sanity in this unjust situation. As I pass the time learning their language, you are my cool drink of water, Sara. I long for you every moment of my day."

The sun appeared as a dusty orange sliver peeking over the eastern ridge. Shadow and I snuck out of the cabin without waking the others. As if hearing of my arrival, the golden eagle skimmed over the top of the ridge and stalled, catching the updraft from below. His static wingspan gracefully floated him to a tree overhead, attaching effortlessly to an arched branch. He peered down, welcoming me home.

I walked the perimeter of my claim, as if to announce my return. Shadow ran ahead, sniffing the ground. A squirrel scampered nearby, searching for food. The faint scent of smoky sage crossed my path, but the recent snowfall made the morning crisp and I was distracted by shimmering trees with the sun nicking the rim of my claim. Shadow stopped occasionally to chew the ice accumulating between the pads of her paws.

With burning thighs from climbing hillsides, I kicked off my shoes at the cabin door and propped them against a stool by the fire to dry by the heat. Miss Bee stood at the table with Rose observing over her sturdy shoulder.

"Best we start our sourdough yeast if we want bread. Do you remember how, Rose? We take the flour and add lukewarm water to make our sponge. Three cups or so," Miss Bee said. "We'll put it on the shelf above the fireplace 'till morning. Can't be drafty."

I told Miss Bee and Rose that I was riding to town to see how Doc was faring. Miss Bee assured me that they would be fine as she had collected enough water from the stream and they had enough food to last a week. I told them not to worry if I did not make it home for a few days.

"You left me for a year in New York. I'm sure we'll get by for a few days. But Sara, hurry back or you'll miss our fresh baked bread with a drizzle of warm syrup," Miss Bee teased.

191

Blue whinnied as I approached the barn and seemed energized as we rode toward Doc's place. A string of false-fronted businesses terraced the sides of the forest where a few placer miners had been last summer. The noisy clatter of heavy iron stamps crushing rock at different gold mills echoed between the ridgelines where I used to ride Blue in tranquility. I second-guessed the route to Doc's cabin and then hesitated at his door because the magical music of a fiddle came from the other side. When I finally knocked and his door swung open, Doc wrapped his arms around me like he never expected my return. I handed him the medical journal and smiled.

"Hope you read the whole darned thing, 'cause it'll come in handy. Lots been going on in these hills since you been gone. Flipped wagons, gunfights, more attacks on prospectors, some even minding their own business."

"What about the ones that weren't?" I asked.

"Well, you know Seth Bullock is now Sheriff Bullock? Yes, sir. He has his hands full but chased out Wyatt and Morgan Earp when they showed up for a few weeks, nosing around about being hired as the law. Sheriff Bullock had none of it and ran them out of town. He hired Dillon McFoley as his deputy."

"What's happening with the Indians?"

"Well, the sheriff upped the bounty to $50 so some drunks were out looking for Injuns. Heard they were camping in the trees not far from your claim as a matter of fact. But no heads that night and the drunks rode back to town with an arrow in one man's chest. He ain't dead yet, staying here at my place. Infection setting in. Serves him right in some ways. You go out looking for trouble and it might come back on you."

"When did that happen?"

"A few nights ago. Whisky was flowing at the saloon and a group of men acted up on the news. They threatened to mount up and storm the hills for revenge, but the chairs never emptied around the poker table."

"What else did I miss?" I asked.

"Justice, finally justice. Jack McCall was retried for murdering Wild Bill. He was found guilty as a fox in a chicken coop. Hanged in Yankton a week ago."

"What about Sheriff Bullock. Is he doing a good job?"

"I don't know, Sara. You know, it's truly each man for himself out here. Can't expect much more. And you might best be careful around your place. Injuns could still be up in the woods. And I don't want to alarm you, but a prospector was asking about you a few weeks ago."

"What do you mean?"

"You shouldn't worry 'cause I told him you went to New York and probably wouldn't be back. He said he was a friend of yours from town, still didn't seem right. Pretty rough. Seemed like trouble. So I didn't tell him a thing."

"What was his name?"

"Didn't mention it, I guess. Just came up to me on Main Street, with his mule with a pack on its back."

"What did the mule look like?" I asked, with fear creeping into my voice.

"What kind of a question is that?" he laughed. "He looked like a mule. Ah. So glad to have you back. Much has changed since you been gone. Sure could use your help tending to this man tonight, if you don't mind. I've been up for the last two nights and need rest."

I told Doc that I would stay but needed to run to town for supplies. Deadwood Gulch was abuzz, equally excited about news of the stage robbery and of the supply of cats up for sale on one of the side streets. One man hollered, "Phatty sure got it right this time! Yes sir. Selling 'em by the pound, yes sir."[33]

I spotted Sheriff Bullock watching the cat sale from the edge of the crowd. I knew what I had to do.

"Sheriff Bullock?" I asked. He spun around and stared down at me with arms folded.

"Sara, good to see you. Welcome back to the world where you are outnumbered a hundred to one! I know one handsome young man who will be happy to see you. Not to name names, but I made him my deputy."

I knew he was referring to Dillon McFoley.

"How can I help you?"

"I wanted to congratulate you for becoming sheriff. And, if you ever need a lead on yesterday's stage robbery, I might be of assistance."

"Oh, might you? Usually, the best information comes from the shadiest characters, but I'm all ears."

I quietly told the sheriff about the similarities between Rusty Reynolds and the masked stage robber from the previous day. I told him of the possibility that his injury was the result of a botched stage robbery. Sheriff Bullock chuckled and discounted my claim.

"Ain't a man in town who doesn't have beady eyes, a blue cloth, and a limp."

Frustrated, I headed up the street to quickly shop for a few basic goods at the Big Horn Store. Loaded with supplies, Blue seemed content returning to Doc's barn and I put him in the fourth stall, where he spontaneously relieved himself with a pungent grass-infused pile of manure, directly on top of my buried bag of gold.

I walked to Doc's porch and we discussed the letter from the Whitings and Chance's future with them. Doc said there was little probability of Chance stumbling upon a mother figure to raise him in Deadwood Gulch. "Shoot, I can't even find an eligible woman within 400 miles to show me respectable attention," Doc laughed. He took me inside and taught me what needed to be done for the injured prospector. Then, exhausted, he fell asleep on a feather bed in the corner.

I returned to the barn with blankets and when it seemed quiet, I grabbed the shovel which leaned against the stall wall. I dug up the bag of gold I had buried nine months earlier. Blue sniffed my treasure and pawed at the freshly turned soil. I moved to the next stall and curled up in the blanket, resting my head on the bag which made me wealthy.

I woke three times throughout the night to go back in Doc's cabin and clean the man's wound, which consistently filled with white mucus. He was delirious most of the night and came to his senses at only one point during a treatment. He mumbled, "Two Injuns out in the woods. One warrior. One squaw. Shot me for no reason."

"What did the warrior look like?" I asked.

"All look the same to me. All savages. Better off dead."

By the time I returned home, weighted with the supplies and gold, I had angered at how the man's mind was more repulsive than the infected wound in his chest. After dropping the supplies on the front porch of the cabin and putting up Blue, I took the bag of gold to where the other bag was buried along the bank of the creek. I scouted for eyes in the trees before I dug to the other bag, placed the second on top and shoveled soil over my treasure.

When I walked into our cabin, Miss Bee was encouraging Rose to engage with daily life.

"Rose. Can you smell it? The yeast? Can you smell it?" Miss Bee repeated over and over. She carefully pulled down the bowl from the shelf and smiled at the bubbles on top. "Ah, look at it, Rose.

We did it! We'll use half in our loaf today. The other half will keep bubblin' till we need another loaf."

Fred's letters continued arriving and I answered most. His words were thoughtful and gave me hope that someday I would be loved fully. The more he wrote, the more I cared. His latest letter said:

"Sara, your letters strip emptiness from me. You rescue me from the darkest nights when I am reminded I am not drawn to this work. I love the adventure, the nights out under the constellations. But I am not cut out to be a soldier, at least not for this cause, which is particularly depressing. I secretly hope I will not cross paths with the Indians. Why do we deserve to be here more than they? Why, when a group of them give in to our newest rules, do we try to change everything about them? We cut their hair. We tell them to believe what we believe: in the one Son of God and not in the wind that lifts the wings of an eagle. I believe our Creator made us all in his likeness, and He simply gave us individual perspectives. Why can't God be a silver-haired old man to one and the Milky Way's path of stars to another? Well, enough philosophy for one letter. Sara, know my thoughts are on you day and night. I know you are healing the injured and raising hope simply with your smile. For me, the thought of you is like whisky in my coffee cup. With each sip, you take away my pain and I look for your words at each mail call. Please write soon. Fred"

I wrote back that evening, after the chores were done and Rose was tucked into bed. I asked what Fred wished for the rest of his life. I asked what spoke to his heart. A part of me hoped he would want to move to the Black Hills and live in a cabin with a strong-willed loving wife, a few children and more animals than any reasonable person could fathom. Not wanting to duplicate my parents' relationship which was full of business and empty of passion, I sought adventure with a man who I knew had my back, who could cry and laugh with me without holding my weaknesses against me. I fell asleep while convincing myself that I likely craved something that could never be found.

We were stir-crazy in the cabin, so I invited Miss Bee and Rose to walk to Deadwood Gulch with me to mail my letter to Fred. Our trail cast off the scent of snapped sagebrush and drew my eyes into the thick timber surrounding us. I did not spot anyone. Disinterested in conversation, I only offered murmurs of acknowledgement toward Miss Bee's joyful observations of the season before us: chirping birds, the musty smell of mushrooms and pine bark, the trickle of snow-fed streams, and between the pines, a glimpse of sandhill cranes migrating north. As we approached the Grand Central Hotel, I decided to treat the women.

I had not been in the hotel's dining room since having dinner with Fred. I glanced at the table where we sat and chose the same one. The dining room was empty and not as magical without Fred across from me. Miss Bee and I sat politely and Rose sat stiff as a board against the back of her chair. Toward the end of our legendary meal, Aunt Lou peeked from the kitchen and saw Miss Bee. She was at our tableside in moments with plum pudding in hand. Aunt Lou and Miss Bee introduced themselves with slight southern drawls as if I was not there. Both women had been slaves - Aunt Lou on a plantation in Tennessee and Miss Bee on a Georgia plantation near Savannah. Both had been trained to cook and clean. Their instant familiarity could have been mistaken as coming from long-lost sisters.

Just as Aunt Lou was offering Miss Bee a job in the kitchen, a disheveled man boisterously entered the dining room. Clearly inebriated, he raged about what he called "savages" and the high price of supplies at the Big Horn Store. I wished I wore my revolver but I had left it at the cabin. Aunt Lou retreated to the kitchen and quickly returned with a shiny butcher knife. The man swung his arms and ranted about an Indian he had killed. Strong and stern, Aunt Lou maneuvered between the man and our table, calmly requesting him to leave. He glanced at the knife in her hand and took heed of her demand.

CHAPTER 14

MISS BEE

APRIL, 1877

DAKOTA TERRITORY

"THERE WAS ONE OF TWO THINGS I HAD A RIGHT TO, LIBERTY OR DEATH; IF I COULD NOT HAVE ONE, I WOULD HAVE THE OTHER."
~ Harriet Tubman[34]

I almost gained a job and lost my life within a matter of minutes. The day started as any other but Sara finally noticed the cabin shrinking day by day from unspoken stress between us, and she insisted we go to town. Then, she lifted our spirits with a meal at the hotel.

I felt I knew Aunt Lou from the moment our brown eyes met. It was as if I were staring into a mirror. We talked of recipes and Aunt Lou offered me a job, an actual job, where I could use my skills and be paid, not as a servant, but as a cook.

Before we discussed the wages, a drunk prospector charged into the dining room, hollering about how he killed a savage and how merchants charged too much for their goods. I was not afraid of him, as drunk angry men had been scattered throughout my life and most had authority over me. Here, I knew the man would either kill me or not, and he seemed more upset about red skin than the chestnut hue of mine. His brown skin and black hair made me wonder where he came from. I knew one thing for sure, he would not take my body for his own pleasure. I was not afraid. Neither was Aunt Lou. She challenged him with her butcher knife and he made the decision to leave, which eased my lingering question of why I agreed to come to this unsettled territory.

Aunt Lou said we could talk about the kitchen work later and Sara paid the bill. We wandered down to the Big Horn Store and Sara introduced us to Mr. Gushurst. I bit my lip in anticipation, but he was quite cordial to me and tolerant of Rose's passivity, which was a relief. Irony surrounded Deadwood Gulch, where backgrounds and skin color were typically overlooked, unless you were an Indian.[35]

I wandered from aisle to aisle, whispering prices to Rose.

"That crazy prospector was a bit right. Look, Rose, the flour is eleven cents a pound. Outrageous! Beans are eighteen cents a pound. Look, Rose, the bacon is twenty-two cents a pound. Eggs, good Lord, seventy-five cents a dozen. Rose, are you listening to me? When have you ever paid seventy-five cents for a chicken or twenty-seven cents a pound for sugar?"

"Never," Rose said, startling us.

As Sara purchased a few supplies, Mr. Gushurst advised that Annie and her new baby were living in a shed behind a shop at the end of Main Street. Mr. Gushurst said Annie was struggling to keep working in her profession while tending to her extremely agitated infant.

We walked down the alley past sheds and a one-story framed building as Mr. Gushurst had directed, easily approaching the shrieking baby. The cracked shed door offered a sliver of light to a dark figure rolled on her side, unconscious. A baby, bound in a blanket, cried beside her. Sara stepped inside and kneeled beside Annie. Rose pushed past me and quickly picked up the baby, who stopped fussing within moments.

I curled my fingers and dug my nails into my palms of my hands. Sara shook Annie awake and I gazed down at the blood trickling from my left palm. Annie belligerently claimed she had not slept all night because she tended to the fussy baby. Sara asked if she had taken Laudanum or been to the opium den. Annie denied both.

Annie said Calamity Jane had purchased supplies for the baby and dropped them off the day before. She ignored me in the doorway and did not seem to mind Rose holding the baby. There was no reason to bother with formal introductions.

"I told you Calamity is a good person, Sara. Maybe she ain't no doctor, but she gives all she has when she sees a need. Who would have guessed, in a year's time I would end up in a mess like this? I came here to make money. Now I have a cranky baby and nothing else."

Sara asked Annie if she would move in with us at the cabin, where we could help with the baby and get Annie back on her feet. I wondered how we would all fit if she agreed. Annie refused. Sara asked what she did with her baby while she worked. Annie thought for a moment and slurred, "None of your business." Annie pried the baby from Rose's arms and demanded we leave.

I told Sara that I wanted to stay in town to talk with Aunt Lou about the kitchen work and I would return later to the cabin. Sara's jaw dropped in shock at the suggestion. I thought she was only worried for my safety but there was more.

"Miss Bee," Sara said quietly, "I can take care of you. I have the ability to pay for all your needs. Is it another dress you desire? Tell me what you want and I'll find a way to give it to you. I just don't see why you would want to tie yourself down with a job. We need you at the claim."

I did not have the heart to tell her that I desired something she would never understand. I desired to be with someone who looked like me. Someone who understood what it felt like to be a slave. Someone who could show me how to pull myself up and make something of myself. I saw the elevated white scars running across the back of Aunt Lou's arms. Sara had not noticed. She never even asked about the deep scars across my back, symbols for all to see, silently revealing a time when evil tried to break me, but failed.

"I can't let you walk home alone. It's too dangerous," Sara blurted.

Her words imprisoned me. "I'll take my chances, Sara. I'll be fine."

After she walked away with Rose, I became nervous. I was familiar with New York City, not Deadwood Gulch. I had no feel of what was safe and what was not.

Distracted, I did not hear the jingling harness as I stepped blindly into the street and was struck by one of two perfectly matched palomino horses pulling a wagon. I simply bumped off the passing horse which kept me safely away from the wagon wheel. As I crawled to my feet, I heard the driver halt his horses. The tall, handsomely dressed man jumped from his seat to retrieve my cane.

"I'm terribly sorry, ma'am," he said. The man wore a long mustache and a narrow-pointed beard. "Are you hurt?" He offered his arm.

"No, sir. It was my fault. I wasn't looking," I said, leaning heavily upon my cane. I was a bit dizzy.

"I fear you'll bruise from the fall. Let me help you. Where are you heading?"

"I'm fine, thank you. I'm heading to the hotel."

"Likewise. I'm in the hotel business and always taking note of my competition."

"From the look of your horses and wagon, I guess you're a success story?" I asked, interested in how he acquired his financial means.

"Well, it wasn't easy until I learned to pursue my gifts. Started as a hotel desk clerk. Worked up to manager. Hotel after hotel around the country. I made a big mistake and thought I could become rich prospecting out here. Couldn't pull an ounce from the stream, so I decided to fall back to what I know. Hotels. Set up the town of Rapid City with friends. Then, I rented my cabin to settlers and prospectors as they passed through. Just a little room. I saved every penny that came my way. My investment grew into the America House. Ever heard of it?"

"No, sir."

"It's the first hotel in Rapid City. You should visit. We can always use help cleaning rooms if you're looking for employment."

"Do you have a kitchen? I love to cook."

"No kitchen, at least not yet. But please, take my information. If I can ever be of assistance."

He handed me a small rectangular piece of paper which read, "John Richard Brennan, Owner – America House, Rapid City, Dakota Territory.

"Are you sure you aren't hurt?" Mr. Brennan asked again.

"No, sir. I had a bum foot long before I stepped into your horse."

"Very well. It was a pleasure bumping into you," he chuckled. "Take care now."

Once inside the hotel's dining room, I realized my skirt had a tear from my fall. Still, I did not regret lingering behind on my own.

Aunt Lou was sitting at a dining table, working through her daily receipts, carefully recording the day's income and expenses on a ledger. She wore a clean, starched blouse with hidden buttons up the front. The pattern of the cotton had subtle specks of pink thread shimmering around a blue background. Her skirt was deep blue with no obvious grease stains. She earlier used an apron in the kitchen, but her role had changed to bookkeeper for the moment and the apron was nowhere to be seen.

Aunt Lou invited me to sit across from her and as I gazed at her dark skin, I missed my sister. Aunt Lou asked question after question and was most surprised I knew how to read and write.

"I draft letters for Rose since she is compromised. Rebekah decides most of the formal words but I help where I can."

"Don't need any private details. This town has enough gossip to drop a mama grizzly in her tracks," Aunt Lou replied. "I'm proud of you. It's that simple. Not easy for our skin color to have the gumption to educate when others try to hold us down."

I told Aunt Lou that I did not know how to add numbers on her slips of paper. She promised to teach me. We talked about how my sister and I were born into slavery in Georgia and emancipated when we were barely more than girls. Aunt Lou was born in Tennessee and was also a slave child.

"Blessing was, I was assigned to my owner's daughter. I traveled with her out west before the Civil War," Aunt Lou explained. "Got the gold fever I guess, or more like travel fever. Love to travel about."

"Now that you put it that way, Sara's parents assigned me to her, I suppose."

"So, you're still in bondage. Still a product of their whims. Still a slave of sorts 'cause all they do is take care of you in exchange for your service?" Aunt Lou asked, challenging my perspective. I had not thought of it like that.

As I stepped outside, I nearly tripped over a crouched man who was sweeping the mud from the restaurant steps. With skin as dark as mine, he stood up humbly and grinned with a smile as white as fresh snow.

"Excuse me, beautiful lady. If I might say, you're a sight for sore eyes."

Heat rose in my neck and cheeks.

"Old Frenchie is my name. You must be new in town."

The handsome man casually chatted with me for a few minutes and then offered to walk me home. I cautiously declined, although I yearned for more time with him. Pushing as fast as my legs could carry me, I disappeared into the deepening dusk. The entire way home I wondered if I would always be a servant in Sara's eyes. Could I break free and find a way to support myself? And as Mr. Brennan said, how could I pursue my gifts?

The dark forest closed in on me and it was easy to see why the Indians rarely ventured into the trees at night since they believed the Black Hills held the spirits of their dead.[36] I heard a noise back along the way I had come and was certain I was being watched.

When I reached the cabin, Sara said it was likely my imagination and she quickly changed the topic, asking my thoughts of Deadwood.

"Seems each man has a spark of adventure, not like the men in New York," I answered. "And with all the men covered in mud, I won't create a stir with my dark skin."

Sara laughed and said, "Good or bad, two things motivate out here. Striking it rich and running from something. Brings out the best and the worst in us all."

CHAPTER 15

SARA

MAY, 1877

DAKOTA TERRITORY

*"THE HOLIEST OF ALL HOLIDAYS ARE THOSE
KEPT BY OURSELVES IN SILENCE AND APART;
THE SECRET ANNIVERSARIES OF THE HEART." –
Henry Wadsworth Longfellow, Holidays*

Day was breaking earlier and earlier, lighting the west ridge of my claim. Drifts of snow were slow to melt on the north hillside, yet pasque flowers emerged around the white edges. The delicate lavender petals bravely endured the cold nights, claiming victory over winter. Enormous wolf prints crossing the drifts melted in the afternoon sun, evidence of activity hidden in the cover of darkness.

The seasons came and went differently in the wilderness, with more vulnerability to each storm and to the animals lurking in the trees. My last year had been unimaginable. Significant change and loss overwhelmed me at unexpected moments. I could not put words to the feeling of an empty abyss in my stomach, and I feigned happiness to those surrounding me. Still, Miss Bee noticed my true somber mood beneath my smile. "We all got scars, Sara. Mine are right across my back. Yours are on the inside." I felt guilty for my occasional moodiness. Years before, I saw Miss Bee's scars which she carefully hid beneath clothes - five or six wide streaks across her back and one across the side of her face. I never asked her about them, not because I didn't care, but out of respect in case she did not want to be reminded.

I took Rose and Miss Bee to town whenever the trail was dry and I had extra time to stroll at Miss Bee's unsteady gait. Rose's mood was clearly lifted by fresh air and exercise. The lines of turmoil magically disappeared from her face. Miss Bee seemed less affected by the benefits of exercise, however, she craved the social interaction with people in town. We stopped by Doc's cabin and I introduced him to the women. Doc's eyes lingered for a moment on Rose and he asked playfully why I had been hiding my friends in the woods.

After a morning in town, when we returned to our cabin, I saw a figure crouch behind a tree downstream. I ran to the barn, afraid Blue had been stolen. He was resting comfortably in his stall and nickered as I entered. I snuck out the back of the barn and crouched between the cover of trees, working my way downstream. Within fifty feet of the figure, I recognized the physique of Rebekah, peeking toward our cabin, not aware that I had snuck up behind her.

"Rebekah, what on earth?"

Startled, she uncomfortably stammered to legitimize her position. "Just hunting for wild mushrooms for our rabbit sauce tonight."

"You were not. You were spying on us."

"No I wasn't," she insisted.

"Yes, you were."

"No, I wasn't."

"Why wouldn't you come up to visit?"

She screamed, "Because you don't include me in anything you do."

"What are you talking about?"

"I saw you take Miss Bee and Rose to town. What about me? Am I some sort of untouchable because I am a lousy mail order bride?"

"I never thought that, Rebekah."

"I don't believe you. You befriend a slave, yet you don't befriend me? Why?"

"She is not a slave," I said, under my breath, which drew anger from Rebekah.

"You, Sara, are ignorant of proper social etiquette and for that matter, you are oblivious as to what character exudes from a good friend."

She paused. Shame tightened my stomach.

"Have you not for just one moment thought of how lonely it is for me to be stuck in a one-room cabin in the middle of nowhere with a husband who works long hours and comes home from the mine exhausted? Have you not considered how I walked away from the guaranteed riches of a coddled life in the arms of a well-to-do southern plantation owner? All to follow love, Sara. The real thing. And now I am dropped into a sea of the lowest possible financial ebb of existence."

She wasn't done.

"Am I just a menace to you? Or maybe you don't even care enough to notice how I fight my melancholy? Nearly every day since I stepped off the stage. I pretend to need nothing other than Jake. But in reality, it hurts that you don't include me. It hurts that you don't wonder what makes me happy or sad. I profoundly care about you and Rose, and even Miss Bee. Still, you fail to include me in your circle."

"I'm sorry, Rebekah. I didn't realize."

"Of course you didn't. You are too busy trying to heal everyone. Too busy trying to be everything to everyone, except to me. All I want is to be your friend."

Jake came running up the trail toward us. Out of breath, he gasped, "Sara, we need you. Come quick. The Old Abe Mine."

"What happened?" I asked.

"They were drinking and bein' boys. Tucked in an ore car and released the brake, taking a ride down the track. Hit the end of the ore chute and sprawled through the air when the car hit the end. It's bad, Sara. They're piled in a bloody heap at the bottom of a ridge against trees. One can't feel a thing below his neck."

I turned back to Rebekah, whose fists were no longer clenched.

"I'm sorry, Rebekah. I'm truly sorry."

Jake looked on in confusion. "Best get going," he suggested.

I snatched my black bag of dressings from the cabin and ran down to the barn, hopping on Blue. By the time we reached the Old Abe Mine, one of the three men, with an obvious depression in his skull, had taken his last breath. The other two were unconscious with broken bones and bleeding head wounds. I told the gathered men to cut boards to the length of the mangled legs and arms. Splinting them with torn shirts from the prospectors, I immobilized what I could, relieved in a twisted sort of way that the men were not aware of their condition. I was exhausted from dealing with the arduous fallout of avoidable tragedy.

The driver of the loaded buckboard wagon raised his lines and slapped the worn-out sorrel smartly on the horse's rump. I followed behind to Doc's cabin and watched the dead man limply bounce beside the injured as the wagon slid in and out of the wheel ruts on the trail. Chance and Doc were standing on the porch as we arrived. The men were moved into Doc's cabin and after I consulted with him, I stepped outside with Chance.

"Did you hear the news, Miss Sara? I'm moving back home. Doc is taking me to the stage tomorrow, then I'll ride a train, and then another stage."

"That's great news, Chance."

"Charlie is going to help me catch up in school. I can live with him and go to school and be like his brother. Thank you for finding him."

"You're welcome. This is an important step for you. It's a time to become whatever you want to be. You can forget about school and fall into trouble like your dad did. Or you can focus on your studies and helping Charlie's family. You can become someone who makes an honest living for yourself. But the choice is yours."

"I might even come back some day and be the mayor of Deadwood."

"You might, Chance. You just might."

I pulled my dad's pocketknife from my makeshift doctor's bag and handed it to Chance.

"This was my dad's knife. I want you to keep it until you come back to Deadwood to be mayor. Dad was honest and good, so every time you reach your hand in your pocket and you feel the knife, think about the kind of man you want to become."

"Is this all you have left from your dad, though? I can't take it from you."

"You aren't taking it from me. I'm giving it to you."

Chance reached for the knife, opening the short blade and testing the sharpness on the edge of his finger, drawing a sliver of garnet-colored blood. He winced and exclaimed, "Holy smoke, it's sharp. You sure know how to keep a cuttin' blade, for a girl."

The sky was full of stars by the time we said our goodbyes. I was thankful for the peacefulness I still experienced on the back of Blue and rode home in solitude. Blue's bright eyes scanned the trees and when he disregarded his footing, there was the occasional click of his hoof on a rock. The snap of a downed branch in the distance no longer troubled me. I had learned to accept not knowing what exactly caused the sound, whether it was the wind, an animal, or human. When I approached the cabin, a faint scent of sage brought me to my senses. I searched the dense pines but saw nothing.

I opened the door to the cabin. Miss Bee and Rose were crouched over a body in front of the fire.

"I'm afraid you aren't going to like this," Miss Bee said.

A frightened Indian woman was propped listlessly against the edge of the fireplace. Her brown skin had fever blemishes and her eyes were despondent. Her long, black hair was kept in two messy braids, extending to the middle of her ribcage. She wore a plain caramel-colored deerskin dress with no embellishment and her feet were bare. She startled me with a weak-rattled cough that brought up blood.

"Where did she come from?"

"An Indian carried her here. We thought it was Rebekah or Jake when he knocked. We opened the door and there they were. Buckskin and all. Red horse standing behind them, not even a piece of steel in his mouth. Just a rope around his neck. The Indian asked for you."

"What do you mean, he asked for me?"

"He said, 'Sara doctor' and I said I was not Sara and you were gone. He carried her over here and set her by the fire. He left without another word. That was that," Miss Bee explained.

"Stay back. I don't want you to be sickened with whatever she has," I said, noticing the skeletal frailness of the ill woman. Miss Bee and Rose backed away quickly. The illness drove the breath from the woman's lungs and she gasped, pleading for more air.

"Han maske," I said, trying to ease her stress.

"What did you just say?" Miss Bee asked.

"Hello, lady friend."

When Jake came to our cabin to check on us the next morning, he saw my new patient and shook his head, "Deadwood ain't gonna like this, Sara."

"Deadwood doesn't need to know, Jake."

CHAPTER 16

SARA

JUNE, 1877

BLACK HILLS

"THE CIVILIZATION OF THE WHITE AND THE CIVILIZATION OF THE INDIAN IS JUST AS FAR APART AS THE SUN AND THE MOON" ~Words of Crazy Horse, To Kill An Eagle by Matthew H. King

The mornings remained chilly and cold drafts crept into the cabin. The Indian continuously shivered even though she was curled up near the fire. To the rest of us, the welcomed breeze rushed through, freshening the stagnate air that my queasy patient exhaled. Scarcely a word was spoken as I carefully maneuvered the feverish, aching woman throughout the day. I was most focused on tending to her hygiene, wiping vomit from the side of her face and dumping containers of excrement. She was too sick to feel humiliated and I repositioned her enough to prevent bedsores.

Each morning, as I bathed her and treated her cough, I asked the same simple question with no response. Fairly confident that the woman could understand English, I did not give up. Weeks later, after trust grew and her fever subsided, I asked once again.

"What is your name?"

No answer. I dampened a washcloth and wiped her face and neck. Miss Bee quietly delivered two cups of honey tea, hoping to soothe the woman's stomach.

"You know my name. Sara. What is your name?" I asked, raising my voice a bit out of frustration.

"Dyani."

"Oh, Dyani. Deer. Who brought you here?"

"My people," she coughed.

"No, who?"

"Our brave one, who beat Yellow Hair."

"Crazy Horse?"

She nodded.

"How did he find me?"

"We watch you. We see skinny white medicine girl. We talk of you. Black Elk's vision you healed me. Crazy Horse carry me to you."[37]

"Black Elk? From the battle?" I remembered him taking Shadow from the tipi.

"Our spiritual one. He go between earth and sky."

"Why didn't he heal you?"

"He said Sara heal me. Wasicu."

"How did you become ill?"

"Rotten food at fort. Me Waglukhe.[38] I now follow Crazy Horse. Crazy Horse medicine bag," she said, weakly reaching toward the pouch that I had removed from around her neck weeks before. After daily therapy, a bit of purple coneflower and wild licorice remained. Her voice grew weak and her eyes closed.

"Do you know Ohanzee?" I asked, secretly pleading for a positive response. "Ohanzee, a Lakota, a Minniconjou?"

I knew what to do with the purple coneflower. I had watched the medicine man pack Ohanzee's deteriorating wound with the medicinal flower. So I had crushed the petals and roots, mashing it into water for a strong potion I forced her to drink. Dyani's face dripped in sweat. The fever was persistent. She closed her eyes and drifted off with Shadow curled up against her, panting in double-cadence to the woman's breath as she heated the dog with her fever.

A few hours later, she woke delirious, mumbling, "Omakiya. Omakiya," which meant help me, help me. Then, she dreamed and spoke in words which I partially grasped. She said something about a white buffalo escorting her to the other side.

I rode Blue to town for supplies, intending to collect mail and check on Annie in the same trip. Beside the trail, delicate white

219

blossoms peeked through the green grass, and I noted their location. I intended to dig up the wild strawberries on my way home and replant them next to the cabin. Sheltered in thriving timber, I was certain something, or someone, was watching me. Chills ran down my spine. As the trail turned from thick timber to dense prospector shacks, the sensation disappeared.

When I reached the store, I asked Mr. Gushurst for the latest news. He shared that three horse thieves were strung up in Rapid City on Hangman's Hill. I asked about Annie and he estimated he had not seen her in a week.

The wind blew across the street, kicking up dust and forcing an unproductive cough as I walked down Main Street toward Annie's shed. Sheriff Bullock sat on a wooden crate in front of his store, with one leg crossed over the other.

"Hello, Sara. Missed my deputy by a minute or two. He'll be disappointed," the sheriff said, lacing his fingers together in front of him.

"Please give Mr. McFoley my regards," I answered, intentionally formal as I passed without pause.

"He would rather you called him Dillon; I'm certain. He's fond of you, Sara. Just a little shy."

"I'm flattered, but things have been quite busy."

"So I hear. But you might benefit from an honest man. Might quiet the talk around town."

"Appreciate the thought, but I'll be fine."

"Of course you will, Sara. You are strong-willed and beautiful. Plus, with all these men, your odds are healthy. Just hope you'll consider Dillon."

"I'm certain he appreciates your endorsement."

"Oh, Sara. By the way," Sheriff Bullock added after I was a few paces away, "That Reynolds man you mentioned? Well, he was found this morning, dangling from a branch of a tree. Seems that someone made a pinecone out of him."

"I'd be a liar if I said he'll be missed. Guessing a posse did your work for you? Maybe you owe them one, as you seem to keep track."

"Not sure who owes who, Sara. When I spoke to Reynolds last week, 'course I didn't mention your name, but he denied robbing stages. Said I should concentrate my efforts on you."

"I beg your pardon?"

"Yep. He said you sympathize with Indians, talk to them in the trees."

"That's nonsense," I replied, turning back toward the man.

"That's what I said," Sheriff Bullock replied. "But with all this talk around, consider what I said about Dillon. Might be a good choice if you want to shine up that tarnished reputation of yours."

I continued on. Annie's shed door was ajar, creaking with the strong breeze of fresh spring air. She lay with her back to me, curled up in the corner, holding her still baby.

"Annie," I whispered.

"Leave us alone," she answered.

"Is your baby okay? Do you need help?"

"I said leave us alone."

The baby whimpered and I sighed with relief.

"Annie, how can I help you?"

She rolled over and faced me. The ray of sunlight through the door revealed bruises and cuts covering her face and neck. The rest of her skin was not exposed and I imagined the purple bruises that likely lay beneath her clothes.

"Annie. What happened?" I gasped.

"A customer."

"Why didn't your madam protect you?"

"Nobody protects me now. I lost my job. The Gem Theatre won't even hire me. With this baby, I'm only in business on my own. A predicament since I'm at the end of the line. But I refuse to work at a hog ranch.[39] No man will come to my shed with a crying baby unless he wants something nobody else will give."

"Who did this to you?"

"Joe. A prospector."

"What's his last name?"

"Didn't ask."

"Why did he do this?"

Annie started to cry.

"Annie, why did he do this to you?" I repeated, wiping the tears from her blood-crusted face.

"He wanted to know where you lived."

"What?"

"He asked where the doctor girl with all the gold lived. I didn't tell him at first. Then he beat me harder and harder. When he threatened to kill the baby, I told him where your claim is," she cried. "I'm sorry. Sara, I had no choice."

"I understand. You have to protect your baby. That man needs to pay. Did you tell Sheriff Bullock?"

"What, that a lady of the evening had a rough customer? He doesn't care. I'm invisible. You know that."

Annie was right. Her profession was a present and real part of life in Deadwood Gulch but nobody acknowledged the pain and inequity it caused. Whether he was bribed or saw the taxation and fines as economic necessity, the sheriff obviously looked the other way.

"Tell me about Joe."

"Tall, skinny, foul smelling. Rotting teeth."

"That could be a thousand prospectors in town. Think hard, Annie. What else?"

"Rolled a cigarette over me, calm as day, smoked the whole thing towering over me. He tapped the hot ashes on my bloody head. Didn't leave payment for what he took, that's for sure."

Annie adamantly refused to move to my cabin. I gently used my fingers to comb through her knotted locks and pull them into a loose bun. Mites and fleas dropped from her scalp. I left my pouch of gold at her feet, unsure if she would use it to feed herself and the baby. I suspected the worst. She would do whatever she could to make herself more comfortable.

I checked the rounds in my revolver. The original seven were in the cylinder. Storming down the street, I intended to confront Sheriff Bullock but he was gone. Furious, I blinded myself by stepping from daylight to darkness within the saloon walls. In the smoke-filled room, gamblers sat on stools at round tables with their savings piled in the center. Men raised their voices only when they threw in their cards, as wealth moved from one player to the next. Other customers bellied up to the long walnut bar, drinking away their cares.

I did not recognize the man I was looking for so I asked the bartender if he knew a man named Joe. He rolled his eyes and ventured there were dozens in town, but one was sitting at the end of the bar.

"Hey, Joe. You know this young lady?"

The man turned toward me and our eyes locked. I nearly vomited from the lump in my throat. Swallowing hard, I did not drop my eyes as the man grinned with his black smile. He was as I remembered: tall, skinny, and filthy. He wore the same canvas pants held up with suspenders over a disgusting unbuttoned white shirt. Brown armpit stains stretched half-way to his elbows.

"Well that was easy. I didn't even have to track you," Joe said.

"You attacked me months ago and now you beat up a woman. You should be hung from a tree," I said.

"Annie? She ain't no woman," he said, hacking into the cast iron spittoon at his feet. His volume grew as he spoke. "Hey men," Joe hollered. "Take a look at this doctor girl. She's an Injun lover. One now, at her place. She heals them so they can scalp us in the dark of the night."

"You're a liar," I shouted back.

"Am I? Maybe we should empty this saloon and ride out to your claim? Let's see who should actually be strung up with a noose. It's you girl and you know it for more reasons than this."

The men stopped playing their card games, riled with escalating words of prejudice.

"Easy way to get a head bounty if we follow Sara to the Injuns," one man exclaimed.

I nervously made eye contact with the bartender who fidgeted with the pocket of his vest as if picking a fiddle. He met my glance.

"Injun lovers not served here," the bartender chimed in. He winked and tipped his head toward the door, silently encouraging me to leave the saloon.

Swill Barrel Jimmy, wedged in the corner with his mud-encrusted frock coat, kept his head low until he stole a shot of whiskey from the distracted man at the table to the right. After gulping it down, he stood boldly, slamming the shot glass onto the table and hollered over the agitated crowd, "What's the point here?"

Most men ignored him.

He tried again, this time louder. "Now listen, I got somethin' to say and when I do, it's good."

Only a few men around him turned and paused.

Swill Barrel Jimmy pulled a revolver from under his coat and squeezed off a round straight into the ceiling. Silence fell over the saloon. He had each man's attention.

"People killing people, for the sport of revenge. That's all it is. Ya'll can end up like me with ghosts haunting you day and night. You can stay awake waiting for someone to slit your throat just like you did to the man before. Then you can wait so long that you wish someone would finish you off."

"Just 'cause she's a young lady doesn't mean she shouldn't hang," Joe countered. "If it was me housing Injuns, I'd already be swinging in the wind."

Methodically, Swill Barrel Jimmy dropped tobacco along a half-creased cigarette paper. He rolled it, licking the edge, reshaping it, and tapping it on his dirty thigh before he continued. "So, what's she guilty of? Helping someone with the wrong-colored skin? I already fought that war so when will this ever stop? This Sara girl, she's got plenty a sand in her crop. [40] More than any of you. She's a healer. She sews up us drunks. True or not, this ain't worth killing her over."

The men went back to their poker games. Those standing at the bar turned away and ordered more drinks. As I walked out of the saloon, Joe hollered, "I ain't done with you yet, Injun lover. Next time I'll get all of you."

"Yes, you will," I thought. I would fight with all I had, with all the pent-up fury I could muster. Yes, he would get all of me.

A strong headwind pounded against me as it blew through Main Street. The Deadwood stage was unloading and I waited for the mailbags, relieved to see the familiar handwriting of Fred.

"My dearest Sara. I breathe in your words over and over again. You mean the world to me. I must confess of other women who have interest in me, perhaps because of my stable Army wages, perhaps because I am a free bird they long to cage. Still, no woman has ever cared about what I yearn for, what I am drawn to. The Army fails to speak to my heart or drive my soul. Sara, you are the first to hear my deepest desires only because you have asked. I dream of the Arctic. Please do not find humor in this. I am quite intent on determining the fate of Sir John Franklin[41] and his companions after studying his expedition for years. Seems England can forget, but I am one to never forget and I believe the mystery can be solved. Likewise, as for you, I cannot place you behind me. You are constantly in my thoughts. I deeply wish I could propose to you and hear a yes and have you beside me, to explore the fire in your eyes as we cross the icy Arctic together.

227

Yet I know it is not reasonable to ask such a thing from a lovely young woman void of the same dream. I wish I could promise to return safely to you and take you in my arms as your dutiful husband but an explorer's promise easily spoken may be impossible to keep. Longingly, Fred."

I stopped, breathless. Had he just proposed and then taken it back? All in one letter? I folded up the pages, sure to analyze it once I was safely home.

I opened my cabin door to Miss Bee and Rose sitting against the opposite wall, staring straight at me. My eyes scanned the room and froze on the Indian woman, still laying in front of the fire. Now, another body lay beside her.

"It was almost like last time," Miss Bee whispered. "We heard a knock, opened the door, and there she lay."

"Who brought her here?"

"We have no idea. She was crumpled right where you stand, wrapped in that deerskin blanket with these tucked inside," she said, holding up a beaded pair of moccasins. "We didn't see anyone else," Miss Bee said, sliding her stiff feet into the gift left behind. "Sure are beautiful, but they fit terrible. How can Indians bear to wear these? Can't even get my right foot in, too short on the side and pinch my little toes."

"Maybe they'll stretch out for you," I answered, stepping across the threshold and approaching the woman. Her brown skin was smooth and her eyes held fear and pain. Her black hair was kept in two messy braids as Dyani's had been when she arrived. She wore a deerskin cover over leggings with beaded designs on the bottom. Intricately needled moccasins with the detail of dainty yellow roses protected her feet. They seemed too fancy. The Indian was fully conscious and she seemed miserable. Her arm was wrapped tight with strips of tanned rabbit hide. Pain filled her face. She only gritted her teeth, making no sound when I moved her.

"Han maske," I said. "What is your name?" I asked, knowing I would receive no response. "Well, let's see what we have here." I unwound the rabbit dressing and found a sharp white bone protruding from gray infected flesh.

"How did this happen?" I asked.

Dyani answered for her, "Sun Dance at Beaver Mountain. With Crazy Horse. Great Spirit was pleased but no food or water, No sleep for days. She fell. Bone broke."

A great dilemma stood before me because if I succeeded in resetting the compound fracture, the infection I exposed back in her body would likely spread and kill her. If I treated the infection first, she would face weeks of intense pain while the bone protruded from her skin. Finally, if I amputated her arm, her culture would reject her if she happened to survive. She needed all her limbs as she left this world and began anew on her next spiritual walk.

"Do you understand me?" I asked. Her eyes cast down, which I knew was out of respect. Delirium had set in. I tried to explain the dilemma, through simple words and pointing at her arm. When I gestured a slicing motion to amputate, her eyes filled with panic.

Dyani spoke for her. "She go to next world whole. Through the path of stars."

"Yes, the path of the Milky Way," I answered, honoring her and knowing the potential excruciating recovery. My treatment would be to minimize the infection with compression bandages and frequent cleaning before I reset the bones.

"Run and check on Rebekah. Bring her here if she is alone," I instructed Miss Bee and Rose.

"Do you think the Injuns got her?" asked Miss Bee.

"No. Of course not. But a prospector has shown bad intent and he's been watching us from the trees."

Even with Miss Bee's encouragement, Rose remained frozen in time so Miss Bee snatched her cane from the corner. "Don't fret about it, Rose. I'm sure Rebekah is fine. She only went to Deadwood with your letter, not something worth being killed for."

"What letter?" I asked.

"Wrote it up for Rose. Nothing for you to worry about," Miss Bee said, shutting the door behind her.

Ten minutes later, Rebekah, Jake, and Miss Bee rushed into the cabin. After explaining the situation, Jake shook his head side to side and said, "Well, girls, looks like we need to add another room to your cabin."

With sunny warm days and the help of Blue, Jake swung his sharp ax against dead standing pines and Blue skidded them toward our cabin. By the end of each day, Blue was lathered and extremely fatigued. Nonetheless, the work could hardly be done without him. Rebekah and Miss Bee cut the branches from the trunk of each tree and stripped the bark. Jake used a notching ax to stack each course which grew from the dirt floor. Rebekah and Miss Bee chinked with mud from the stream, jamming the barrier between the logs. As they waited for the next assignment, they gained confidence and personal strength.

"Jake put in a window on the back wall for summer ventilation. It slides open, see?" Rebekah proudly proclaimed as she wedged herself between two bunkbed platforms. The new room was tight but would sleep four.

At the end of each day, we gathered around our campfire. Meals became a community gathering. I consistently purchased the food as my gold would likely hold out forever. Jake and Rebekah were living within their narrow means and Jake did not earn enough at the mine to feed five additional women. He hunted when he could and shared the meat when he was successful.

Our meals were simple and sufficient. We never went hungry. Miss Bee did most of the cooking since her natural talent outpaced the rest of our ambition. She started a garden on the sunny side of the claim, adamant she could improve upon the limited variety of fresh produce offered at the Big Horn Store. Each evening, when the Dutch oven finished simmering on the open fire, Miss Bee let

231

out a holler and Rebekah ladled the stew into our individual bowls.

"I made you something special for dessert," Rebekah whispered to Jake as she stood beside him, drawing a smile. "Chicory coffee cake!"

"Oh, my dear princess, you know me too well," Jake said, hugging her so her feet came off the ground.

As the weeks went by, we lingered by the campfire long after cleaning and chores. It was by the glowing embers that a calm and sense of peace emerged. We joked that Jake was the only man in the gulch who was outnumbered by women. Leaning a shoulder against the new room of our cabin, Jake smiled at the women scurrying before him.

The Indian women chose to sit in the cabin while we ate around the fire. Dyani said it was not right for them to eat while their people starved, repeating each night, "You kill buffalo. You kill my people."[43] On nights when Jake used his charm and lured them out to the fire, we stared into the orange flickering flame, restlessly moving around the fire as the breeze changed directions and sent smoke into our faces.

Dyani's fever was gone but her face was still swollen, mostly around her bloodshot eyes. I was not certain of what still battled within her body but she gained strength daily, which gave me hope. The other Indian refused to disclose her name so Miss Bee nicknamed her "Mystery." When she quit hallucinating, I assumed Mystery's infection had diminished so I reset her arm.

232

When she fainted from the pain of the procedure, I bound her arm tightly which helped her heal. She no longer vomited from the agony.

One evening, Miss Bee walked straight to Mystery and started brushing the knots from her hair.

"They could use a hair washing before they infest our whole cabin," Miss Bee said.

I warmed a pot of water over the fire. Miss Bee told me to fetch lard from the house because she saw fleas. We bent their heads over the pot and dropped their hair into the water, scrubbing the filth away with soap. Then, after rinsing, we massaged lard onto their scalps and through their long black locks. We waited patiently and then rinsed again with fresh water.

CHAPTER 17

SARA

AUGUST, 1877

BLACK HILLS

"SOMETIMES DREAMS ARE WISER THAN WAKINGS." ~Black Elk

I woke, drenched in sweat. Not from the sultry August night, but from a dream where Joe shot at me from the trees. My heart pounded from my nightshirt. Regaining my bearings, I pulled the quilt aside and took deep breaths. Late night thunder energized the air. Through the window, I stared at blackness until bolts of lightning flashed through sheets of rain across the starless sky. Unable to fall back asleep, I rose and stood at the groaning cabin door, swaying to the gusts which swooped down from the dark of night. I saw nothing but felt someone.

Dyani stirred and I motioned for her to join me. We shut the door and sat under the covered porch, watching the storm before us. She had gained weight over the last few months and her cough no longer brought up blood.

I asked about what she had seen with her eyes. She told me in broken English how she had been married to a Cheyenne. As she spoke, I slowly pieced together her personal details, nudging her with a string of questions. Moons ago, they prepared for the winter in a village tucked away from the wind at the edge of the Big Horn Mountains. She followed Dull Knife as her peaceful leader. They were resting with their elderly and babies curled beneath buffalo robes to ward off the cold.

Dyani woke one morning to bullets cutting through her tipi. Her husband forced her to lay low and they peeked through their tipi door at storming white man troops, shooting into the camp. She knew they were outnumbered and her husband told Dyani to pretend to be dead as he rushed out to defend their village. Before the flap on her door had time to swing shut, she saw her husband struck through the back with a rifle slug. He collapsed near the door, whispered "run" and then died. Instead, she crawled from under the back of her tipi. In the thick of gun smoke and her burning village, she somehow slipped alone through the chaos and hid against the hillside, hoping other survivors would join her. Some did and they fled to Crazy Horse and Black Elk's camp. Most froze to death along the way. The few who reached Crazy Horse's camp were only given clothing since the camp was already eating starving ponies and food rations were depleted.

Dyani's group agreed to surrender at a fort, but when they arrived, promised food was not shared with her people. She heard lies that her people attacked a white soldier, Colonel MacKenzie. She said MacKenzie actually attacked her village as they slept. Hungry, waiting beside the fort, Dyani decided to flee to her

Lakota people led by Crazy Horse since she would rather starve with him than wait for rotten meat from the fort.[42]

While in New York, I read a significantly different version of the battle. My blood boiled beside the humid summer night which caused dark clouds to burst wide open and feed the desperate grass.

Shadow usually chose to sleep beside the porch, spinning in circles to pack down the grass before claiming a bed for the night. Once comfortable, she usually rubbed dirt and pollen from her eyes with the sides of her paws before dozing off. Somehow, she remained on guard and occasionally growled at the darkness.

The weather drew invisible gnats into our cabin, biting us throughout the night. Miss Bee had been working more and more evenings for Aunt Lou and sometimes she did not bother coming home, which gave us more room. I longed for cold nights around the fire and reminded myself to ask Jake to start cutting trees for a winter's worth of firewood.

One evening, as we settled in for bed, a knock at the door startled us. All four women turned toward me, waiting for guidance. I glanced at my revolver on a shelf beside the door before cracking it open. Annie stood before me in her tattered and faded red shimmering dress with a low-cut, black laced bodice. She held her baby. I urged Annie to step inside, yet she refused. I lightly touched her arm and she pulled away, taking three steps back and stumbling off the porch.

"Don't touch me," she growled, regaining her footing.

"Okay, Annie, what can I do for you? Come inside? You can rest for the night."

"I'm not tired and I don't want to live in your prison," she slurred.

"What do you want, Annie? Let me help you."

"Take this baby. Give her what I can't. No use ruining two lives since I can't even take care of myself."

"Stay here," I pleaded.

"No. I'd rather die."

"No, you wouldn't Annie. It's not the end of the world. I know you'll find your way."

"I said take the baby. Please?" Annie cried.

"Of course," I answered as she thrust the stinky bundle toward me. I stepped onto the porch and met her reach.

Rose stepped behind me and touched my shoulder lightly. I passed the baby to her without looking back.

"What happened, Annie? How has it come to this?"

"Lost my mind," she said. "Been down to China Town earlier and I wanted to sleep, but the baby wouldn't stop crying. She was waking up the whole town. I took my dress and pressed it against her mouth and nose. Tried to stop the crying. She squirmed at first, then stopped moving. Everything fell silent and if it wasn't for my racing heart, telling me I'm a monster, I would have killed her. When I pulled my hand away and puffed air back into her lungs, her precious eyes looked up at the devil and I knew. I just knew."

"What did you know?"

"That the baby needs to be with you, not me. You're the only one who won't worry about where this baby's been, or that the father could be any man in the damn gulch. You take in anyone and don't judge, so please raise her to be someone like you and not me."

"Everyone can change, Annie. Come on, step inside with me. We can take it slow. You don't need to drink whiskey and smoke opium to take the pain away. You have this baby to live for."

"I can't change. I tried. I'm too far gone. I'll rot in hell for the things I've done."

"Nobody is too far gone. You can stay away from town, here with us. Stay away from the temptations that make you into something you weren't ever meant to be."

"I'll make up some buckwheat cakes and fry some eggs in the morning if you stay," Miss Bee added. "Everything looks better on a full stomach and in the light of day."

"Ain't hungry. Just take the baby. If you come to town tomorrow, Sara, let's talk. I promise. I need to sleep, but I ain't staying here."

Annie turned from the cabin and disappeared down the trail into the darkness.

"Annie!" I hollered after her. "Annie, what's your baby's name?"

"Ain't got one yet, called her the baby," her voice called back.

I stepped inside the cabin. Rose rocked back and forth on the floor with the bundle in her arms. Miss Bee watched for a moment and said, "What will we name her then? It ought to stand for something. A fine name, something to cherish."

"Charlotte. Her name is Charlotte," Rose answered.

At daybreak, dark clouds collected in the morning sky. I sat with coffee, watching Rose cooing with Charlotte. She spoke softly to the baby and both occasionally smiled. "My dear Charlotte, do you think we can convince Jake to craft us a rocker?" she asked the baby. Before Rose became too attached, I knew I needed to check on Annie.

I spent time with Blue, brushing his mane and tail until the comb slid effortlessly through the sleek hair. I picked each hoof as he voluntarily lifted them when I moved to the respective leg. He was a special gift. I pulled my hair back into a loose bun, hopped on Blue and headed toward Deadwood.

Not far down the trail, Blue alerted, with nostrils flared, ears tucked, and a proud lift to his head. I scanned the trees but saw nothing alarming. As the trail curved, I saw what he smelled. Annie was crumpled in a heap on the side of the road. Her worn red dress partially covered gray skin and meatless bones. Flies were already accumulating on her legs. I rolled Annie over, attempting to give the disturbing scene a bit of dignity. Empty bottles of laudanum and whisky rolled out from under her corpse.

I grabbed the bottles, and with a roar of frustration, launched them into the trees.

Rebekah and I spent the entire day digging Annie's grave. The pickaxe was heavy and with each strike, my neck spoke a language of fire. How could one malady hold on when others came and went? I hit impenetrable black clay at four feet and decided the hole was sufficient, especially for such a petite woman. Rebekah donated a pink and white quilt to suffice for a coffin.

We wrapped Annie carefully and I took one side while Rebekah and Miss Bee shared the other. Where I wished for a delicate placement into the resting place, we instead struggled with the cumbersome bundle and dropped her into the hole with a thud. Rose gasped as the rest of us pretended to not notice. Then, we covered her with dirt and talked of how someday Charlotte would be told of the tragedy.

Hosting a funeral would be considered appropriate, yet we quickly decided that as a whole, Deadwood Gulch only took from Annie and had no right to say goodbye. Perhaps Annie's family would come searching for her one day but it was unlikely. So, we waited for Jake to return from the mine and then gathered around the mound of fresh dirt. Miss Bee and I stood shoulder to shoulder at the edge of the grave. The Indians watched curiously from a short distance. Rose held Charlotte against her chest, patting her back. Rebekah stood quietly beside Jake as he said a few words of how Annie lost her way and finally did the right thing when she placed Charlotte in safe hands. Fresh wildflowers adorned one end of the grave, but we were uncertain which way we placed her below. Jake said he would build a cross made from pine when he had the chance.

That night after everyone was asleep, I snuck out of the cabin with Shadow, grabbed the shovel and walked the worn path beside the stream, searching for my mark in the soil along the bank. Fresh growth had concealed the location but knowing now Joe had watched me from the trees, I needed to move the gold to a place few would dare dig. I stood steady, leaning against my shovel, and listened. There was nothing but Shadow panting as she searched for a squirrel or a mouse.

A few shovels of dirt uncovered the top of my treasure. After pulling out the bags, I covered the hole again, certain the fresh dirt would draw attention if someone stumbled upon it. Returning with the gold to Annie's grave, I spent ten minutes and quietly shoveled away half of the dirt that covered her. After resupplying my gold pouch with a handful of gold flakes and storing another year's worth in a large jar, I carefully sealed the bags and placed them in the grave above Annie. Then, I shoveled the remaining dirt over the top of the bags.

By the time I went to town, a few days later, rumors had circulated and recirculated. Sheriff Bullock caught sight of me walking into the Big Horn Store and although a bit stoved up, he strut toward me.

"Heard you been having some trouble out at your claim," he said.

"No trouble," I answered.

"Heard Annie went out to visit. Some people in town noticed she never came back."

"Exactly who is so concerned? The men who paid her for what should never be bought? The Chinese man who sold her opium while she was pregnant? The man who beat her face bloody?"

"Once things are reported to me, I take action," the sheriff said.

"Well, it's a little late now, isn't it?"

"Maybe it is, maybe it isn't. I've been hearing stories about your claim out there. First, that it can't be as productive as you say. Then, I hear that you're hosting hostiles. And now, a valued citizen turns up dead at your place. Deems looking into."

"A valued citizen? To you perhaps as you take such an interest? Truth is, Annie was an addict. No offense, but you aren't worth a grain of salt as a sheriff if you don't agree. Annie drank herself to death on her way from my claim. I did not kill her."

"Not what I hear."

"What did you hear?"

"That you shot her after she threatened to reveal your big red secrets out there. That you mend the hostiles so they live another day to scalp us."

"That is a lie," I answered, involuntarily clearing my throat.

"Is it?"

"Yes."

"You know, the Lawrence County Board approved a higher bounty for each Indian captured, dead or alive. Heads are worth $250 now. And we all know you already got a darkie out there. Sara, you are walking on very thin ice if any of these rumors are true."

"They aren't."

"Well, let's just say, for the sake of argument, Annie did come to your place and you did have Indians there and you did put a bullet in her to keep her quiet. How would you prove me wrong?" Sheriff Bullock asked.

"You want me to dig her back up to show you there are no bullet holes?"

"Maybe it's the best thing."

"You insult me. She was my friend and I wanted the best for her. I buried her. I'll raise her baby. But I sure as hell am not going to dig her back up so you can count how many holes are in her."

He stared at me. I stared back.

"Sheriff, you know Annie was a regular at the opium den. You know her profession and how she drank too much."

"I know. You know. But the town is stirring it up. I need proof and the town expects me to look into it."

He did not drop his stare, searching for a defect in my story. I scrambled for a solution, knowing what was on the line.

"Follow me up the trail to where I found Annie's body. I can show you the bottles that I threw into the woods. The bottles of laudanum and whiskey that were under her when I rolled her over."

"That's a start," he replied, grinning slightly. "Better yet, how about we fetch my deputy and the two of you can clear this up. Just the two of you."

Sheriff Bullock located his deputy within a few minutes and sent us on our way. Dillon had obviously been briefed and did not ask a single personal question. I focused our conversation on him to minimize disclosing information about me as we rode side by side to the song of his creaking saddle leather.

As we came around a bend in the trail, I immediately identified the exact place where Annie took her last breath. The grass was pressed flat, still reflecting the shape of her collapsed body. I walked between the trees and searched for the bottles while Dillon waited on his horse, watching a rusty-red coated squirrel voice his alarm at my invasion of his territory. I reached under a tangled mass of a wild raspberry bush. The thorns snagged my skirt and scratched my face. A month late to harvest the berries but with the usual good intention, I mentally noted the location, knowing the squirrel had nothing to worry about.

Impatient, or out of guilt when he saw me wince in pain, Dillon finally assisted me, pacing off the area with his spurs jingling as he stepped in a methodical grid, well beyond where I desperately searched. He found the bottles further from the trail than I ever envisioned.

"Didn't know you had such strength, did you?"

"How did you know?"

"Grief of a lost friend, anger over the pointless tragedy, it all made you stronger in the moment. I knew to look deeper in the woods if you really cared about Annie as you said you did." He flashed a painfully shy smile, remounting his horse and spinning in a full circle before turning his horse's head back toward Deadwood. "I think I have seen all I need to see. No need to head up to your empty cabin, or to waste our time digging up the corpse, if you get my point."

"No. No need. Nothing to see there," I replied.

"I hope to see you soon, Sara."

"It would be my pleasure," I answered, cringing at the lie.

As he rode away, Dillon energetically hollered the obligatory words of Sheriff Bullock, "Remember, Sara, you owe me one."

When and why did Dillon accept the role of Sheriff Bullock's puppet? Why was it always about keeping score? As I turned Blue toward my claim, I took a deep breath and felt a huge sense of relief, well aware of the ramifications of what I nearly lost. I rubbed Blue's neck and mentally disappeared into a different world as we plodded along. Dropping my guard, I forgot about my surroundings, focusing instead on the dread of what my future held if Joe continued to cast a dark shadow over me. That night, in a deep sleep, I saw the sinister grin of black-toothed Joe as he whispered, "I still ain't done with you, Injun lover."

245

CHAPTER 18

SARA

SEPTEMBER, 1877

BLACK HILLS

"MOST OBSTACLES MELT AWAY WHEN WE MAKE UP OUR MINDS TO WALK BOLDLY THROUGH THEM." ~Orison Swett Marden

Men were bellied up to the bar and did not notice me as I walked to the back of the saloon and asked Swill Barrel Jimmy questions about Joe. He knew more than anyone what each man in the gulch was capable of because he lurked in the shadows of the saloon, day after day. He was invisible, listening to the drunks rant and rave. With me, Swill Barrel Jimmy was cautious with his words but seemed flattered I trusted him. The longer I sat beside him, the more forthcoming he became, admitting that Joe had been watching me for months.

"Be careful, Sara. Desperate men do desperate things."

I thanked him with a shot of whiskey from the bar. He lifted his shot glass with a toast. "May the angels of mercy protect your heart," he offered quietly, "Might think 'bout carrying a muff gun, if you don't already have one. Here, take mine. I have an extra."[44]

"I have my Colt," I answered, raising the blouse over my hip so he could see the holster.

"Lordie, where'd you get your hands on that?"

I dropped my blouse.

Swill Barrel Jimmy slid a gun from his coat pocket into my hand. "Never hurts to have a backup. Might get Calamity to teach you how to shoot the thing straight. A bit tricky with the stubby muzzle when your hands a shakin' 'cause the enemy is standing there staring at your soul. Don't care how evil he is. Your hand is gonna shake. No doubt, you'll come out okay, but sure as hell different than when you started."

I tucked his gun into my blouse and promised to return it as soon as I purchased my own.

"No hurry, I got a few more where that came from. Take my word for it. Calamity hits right where she aims. Just ask for help, girl. You'll never regret it."

How had it come to this? How did Joe infiltrate my life? He even spoke to me as I slept, which annoyed me since I could not fight back in my dreams. As Joe became more obsessed, I became more imprisoned by his sickness. I left the saloon as disturbed as when I entered and was thankful the stage arrived with mail.

Returning home, I passed Miss Bee's garden, which had sprouted weeks before. The rows were bare. She stood to the side of the cabin, skinning rabbits and harvesting the breasts and thighs. Blood and animal innards filled a bucket beside her. Nearby, Rose blended pepper, salt, and flour together in a dish. Charlotte was swaddled against Rose's torso, freeing her hands.

"What's going on?" I asked.

Miss Bee stormed past me with the cast iron skillet, full of cubed meat. Over the open fire, she pan-fried her concoction.

Rose replied, "The rabbits ate Miss Bee's garden so she said it's time for rabbit stew."

The Indians picked wild greens from the ground and watercress from the stream as Miss Bee and Rose cooked the meat. The nearly healed women were unusually enthusiastic about the rabbit meal. After our first few bites, as they squatted by the fire, Mystery made a contorted face and urgently spoke to Dyani in Lakota. Dyani interpreted and explained how Mystery said her people made tastier rabbit stew. She said Miss Bee needed to use dried timpsila, which I knew were prairie turnips. She said Miss Bee needed to add wild onion, buffalo fat, and water to the fresh rabbit meat. "Then," Dyani said, "Then, wohan."

"What is wohan?" Miss Bee asked.

"Wohan means cook them," Dyani answered.

Somehow, through Miss Bee's deep, dark skin, she still flushed in anger. "You wohan them!" she yelled, throwing down her plate. "If I had a little help around here, maybe I could spend more time on recipes. You can get off your sorry rumps and forage for what you want, and wohan whatever you please. Last I checked, we won the war and I ain't nobody's slave."

That night, I waited until the others slept and I read the letter Chance sent. The lone candle flickered against the pages of clean, creamy paper.

"Dear Sara, I am doing good in school so I don't know why father always said I was stupid. Charlie's grandparents are strict, but they tell me I can grow up to be respectable. When I miss Deadwood, I feel your dad's knife and know how I need to be strong. I showed the knife to Charlie. He said all he has in his pocket is a stupid old rock. You see, Charlie was mad about having to do chores and so he threw the rock at his father's favorite horse. His father whipped him and picked up the exact rock and put it in Charlie's pocket. Said it was his burden to carry until his dad said he could take it out. Problem is, Charlie's father is mean as an old bull so Charlie keeps carrying the rock around every day, afraid he might be punished again.[45] I wonder how long he will carry it. I need to go split firewood now. I will write soon. Sincerely, Chance."

I lingered in the cabin the next morning. In a makeshift rocking chair that Jake built one evening by the fire, Rose continued to hold the baby as she did from the first moment. They were engaged, cooing and giggling at the faces Rose made. When she was on her feet, Rose completed her chores with one arm as the other held Charlotte tight to her side, balancing on her hip. Where the baby had earlier shown signs of colic, she now was well-nourished and loved. Rose moved about the cabin with ease and

249

fed Charlotte at our bare, rough-hewn tabletop. They took walks along the claim and touched things as she told Charlotte the names. "Touch this, my dear. It's a rock. Can you say rock? Oh, and how about this, Charlotte? Put your hand in the stream. Isn't the water refreshing? Burrrrr. It's cold. Can you say, burrrr?"

The warm summer days and disappointing rabbit stew encouraged the Indian women to forage for their traditional food. They went to the edge of the creek and dug for breadroot bulbs they called timpsila. The size of duck eggs, the root was dried in the sun and crushed into flour. Then, the women handed their flour over to Miss Bee.

"What exactly do you want me to do with this?" Miss Bee asked, unimpressed.

When Miss Bee was away, the Indians took over and scavenged for wild asparagus or lambs quarter to simmer over the fire with wild herb water or fat from Jake's recent deer kill. Sometimes they buried chunks of the carcass under a bed of coals even when I suggested they use the Dutch oven.

 The women's ailments were history and I waited for them to somehow return to their people. Without Rusty Reynolds spreading Joe's rumors, the town gossip about me was easing. Still, our cabin was crowded, even with the room addition full of beds. Since the Indian women did not need our care, I hoped they would leave.

Calamity Jane heartily agreed to teach me to shoot, so I showed up where she lived, exactly as she directed. Her one-room shack suggested the habitation of a bachelor. One plate and cup on the wooden counter. No furniture, other than a single chair and a barrel for a table which sat adjacent to a bedroll. Mining tools stood by the door against the wall. A wash basin rested on a stand with a bar of mushy soap in the center and a towel hanging over the edge to dry. Calamity had swept and the floor was reasonably clean. She appeared less disheveled with her hair pulled back and her buckskin leathers covering her lean body.

"Guess how old I am, Sara?"

"I have never been good at determining ages."

"Would you say 20? 25? 30?"

I noticed her rough, sun-aged skin, and the grooves across her forehead from drinking whisky. Thinking she was at least 30, but not seeing a reason to verbalize it, I remained silent. Life in the gulch was tough and for someone like Calamity, who chose a difficult lifestyle, she might look well beyond her years.

"I'm 25. Just look older. Lost both parents by the time I was 15."

"I lost mine also."

"Hard to be tough as a man, sweet as a girl and tender as an orphan all at the same time, huh? I decided, no use crying about it. I decided to get mighty, bullwacking for a living. So anyway, let's get some shootin' done. That's what you're here for, not to listen to me talk. So, whacha wanna know?"

"How to hit what I need to hit."

"You afraid of someone?"

251

"No, I want to be ready if I need to be."

"Well, do what I do. Just like I tell you, okay?" She pulled her gun from her brown leather holster and aimed it at a tree beside her shack. "See how I pulled it out? Just like it's an extension of my arm. Now you do it."

I reached inside my blouse and pulled out the muff gun.

"Now, first of all, you need a holster that hides in your skirt band. Too tough to reach it in a coat or blouse." She walked back inside and came out with a worn leather holster and wide belt. "Might work if we cinch it up real tight. I can punch an extra hole in it for you. Would be more stable if you wore trousers. Shouldn't care what others think."

The belt fit on the tightest hole and Calamity Jane suspended the holster on my right hip.

"For now, keep it on the outside. When you go to town, you can hide it in your skirt. So, put that little piece of metal in your holster. Always keep it pointed away from me. Keep your finger off the trigger till I tell you. Understand?"

I nodded, concentrating.

"Okay, so slowly pull it out and aim for that tree over there."

I did exactly as she instructed.

"Now Sara, you gotta hold it like it's a bird in your hand. Strong but don't break it. Cover all the grip with both palms, like this. Don't stick your trigger finger too deep, just the first pad."

I placed my finger on the trigger.

"Now keep your elbows in and pull the trigger real slow. You should be surprised when it goes off."

I did as she said and the gunshot rocked me on my heels and startled me as I took a step back to regain my balance.

"Okay," Calamity said. "You got that first one over with. Now you know what it feels like. Ain't nothing like the smell of burnin' gun powder in a shootout. Bet you never smelled nothing like it."

I did not want to tell her that as soon as the smoke filled my nose, I was back at Custer's last battlefield with death surrounding me.

"Try it again, aim for that knot in the tree."

I jerked the trigger, anticipating the blast.

Calamity laughed. "I got no idea where that piece of lead flew."

I tried again and again, each time gaining more confidence with Calamity's instruction. Finally, I was immobilized by all the tips she offered. I stared at the target through the sights and I tried to squeeze carefully as my breath released, still the sights would not stay on the target and my arms fatigued.

"You ain't out here shootin' legs off damn bedbugs, girl. Don't take too much time to aim. Point in the right direction. That's why you have more than one bullet in the gun."

After my first lesson, we went back into Calamity's shack and she gave me extra tips as she gulped down a few shots of whiskey. "You need to be quick on the trigger. Don't necessarily need to be provoked. If someone wants you bad enough, they'll find a way to get to you. Stand your ground and you'll likely live to talk about it 'cause they won't expect you to pull the trigger."

"I'm not looking for trouble."

"Of course not, most of us ain't. But do what you gotta do. You need to stand up out of cover and shoot without flinching. I'll help you if you want to practice over here. I can give you a few more tips, not that I'm perfect," she chuckled. "You already have gumption and a steady hand. Anyone who can stitch up a hole in someone's gut should be able to shoot a gun."

Calamity Jane offered me a handful of bullets and reloaded my gun with "heavy loads." I thanked her, intending to return the next day.

Back in town, Dillon approached me and asked, "Sara, have you heard? The Keets mine hasn't paid the miners for weeks and $3.50 a day adds up fast."

"Where is the money? Did the bank go under?"

"Nope. The owners wasted the money away. You know, on all the sins around here. So, the miners said enough is enough. They shut down production and took everything they need into the mine with them: their bed mats, food, even their cook stoves. They said they'll strike till the owners pay up."

"Is that legal?"

"Sheriff says he wants to wait it out and see where it goes. Might be some mighty big favors in the works."

CHAPTER 19

ROSE

SEPTEMBER, 1877

BLACK HILLS

"WHAT LANGUAGE CAN BE MORE EXPRESSIVE THAN THE EARS OF A HORSE OR THE TAIL OF A DOG? IF AWARE, ONE CAN SEE THE MANIFESTION OF JOY, FEAR, SORROW, APPREHENSION, AND COURAGE."
~Rose Zito

Shadow growled and stared across the meadow when Doc approached unannounced to check on my dear Charlotte. The young dog seemed to instinctively guard as she quickly sized up the lack of threat. Doc spoke to her softly and won her over, rubbing the tips of her fly-harassed ears. She relaxed in front of the cabin door, yet blocked him from the Indian women inside, who had the good sense to remain silent throughout his visit.

"Good day, Rose. Seems like a fine dog you have here," Doc said as his introduction. He stepped close enough for me to smell fresh soap and a touch of cologne. His full head of sun-kissed buckskin hair was combed back behind his ears, still damp from a bath. Doc stood tall, almost puffing out his chest in a white pressed shirt and clean canvas pants. I suddenly became self-conscious, wondering if he noticed the few strands of gray in my loosely braided hair.

"Shadow isn't mine, but she's nice to have around."

"I agree, with all the unrest in the hills. She looks a bit like a coyote or a young wolf?"[46]

I shrugged.

"Rose, I came to check on the baby. How's she doing?" he asked.

"She's fine," I answered, nervously rocking back and forth.

For shade and a butterscotch scented breeze, Jake had moved my chair from the cabin porch to a flat spot under a mature pine tree. Doc asked to hold the baby and he checked on her, stretching out her limbs, feeling her grip, and looking in her eyes, ears, and mouth.

"Any concerns?" he asked.

"Just her eyes. They don't seem to follow me in a coordinated fashion. The left one seems to have a mind of its own."

Doc grinned at my comment and handed Charlotte back to me. He suggested it was not unusual for a baby to have a lazy eye. "She'll probably grow out of it, don't worry. We can keep watch and if need be, we can try something like taping over the strong one. Might force her to exercise the lazy one. Golly, she has beautiful green eyes," Doc said, examining them more carefully.

256

"Well, I know Sara is quite competent and has your best interest at heart, but I felt it necessary to pay a visit to see for myself that you're fine," Doc said perceptively.

"We're fine," I said shyly.

"Yes, yes you are," he affirmed quietly, never taking his gentle eyes off of me. "You have been through a great deal, Rose. Sara has shared you lost your daughter and your husband."

I simply nodded, drawn to his kindness.

"So, Rose. I'm checking on you 'cause I want to be sure you're okay in your mind. Clearly, you are a survivor and I'm confident you'll get through it all, but we need to talk about this baby."

Compelled to ease Doc's concerns, my voice trembled ever so slightly as I responded, "If you are worried about my sanity, I must set you straight, no offense. I know Charlotte isn't my first Charlotte. I am not crazy. It's that this is my second chance. My chance to be a mother again. To love this baby like I wanted to love my first Charlotte."

Doc smiled at me, seeming relieved I had all my senses. "Sara says you rarely speak. I was a bit concerned, until now. Can you tell me more?"

"Tom always said I didn't speak often, but when I did, it was worth listening to," I said.

"I'm listening," Doc replied, sitting on the ground beside the rocker.

"The night the fever stole Charlotte, I rocked her, thinking if I kept moving all night, she would reciprocate and keep breathing. She died just before daylight. Tom tried to take her from me, but I couldn't let go. I continued rocking my stiff, cold baby. When I eventually fell asleep, Tom pulled our lifeless girl from my arms. I unconsciously released her. When I woke up, I glanced at Tom with unbearable pain. He tried to hold me, but I refused. I lost my mind when I lost my girl."

"I'm deeply sorry, Rose."

"Thank you. I had to work through blame. Maybe if I had forced her to take longer ice baths. Maybe if I had given her more water. Maybe this. Maybe that. But in the end, the Lord took her."

Tears welled in my eyes and I wept for the first time since the day we covered her grave.

"So, I quit speaking because I found nothing worth saying. Something snapped in my head. It made no sense why our good Lord gifted me something so precious and then ripped her away. Tom and I loved Charlotte with our whole hearts. We poured everything into her. And then she was gone. So, I stared at walls, with nothing left inside me. I dreamt of her joyful brown eyes. They were the exact color of Sara's."

I sighed and dried my tears, though my voice quaked. "I'm sorry, I don't mean to burden you."

"No burden at all, Rose. I have watched you for months and knew there was something very complex inside you."

"Have you ever lost someone you loved?" I inquired, unconcerned the question may be too personal.

"Not a child or a wife, if that's what you are asking."

"Well, God has blessed you then."

"Actually, He has protected me from the pain of loss, yet I have missed out on deeply loving someone. You are stronger and more whole than I am from all you have been through and how you have loved."

"If that is true, I wish I wasn't as strong," I smiled. "It wasn't nearly as difficult to lose Tom, because he chose to be a soldier and put himself in harm's way. He fought in the Civil War with Sara's dad. He was a loyal husband and friend to the end, so that story rests easy in my heart. My only regret is I wasn't strong enough in my mind to follow Tom out west to Fort Randall. Before he took me to the asylum, he kept telling me that I had a reason to live. The reason was him. I regret that I couldn't hear him because I had stepped off a cliff."

"So, when did it all start to make sense, Rose?"

"It never did, not to this day. I prayed and prayed for answers, rubbing my heart shaped rock with my fingers. I finally decided it was never going to make sense and I needed to make peace with my soul and claw my way back up the cliff. That's before Annie dropped off her baby and I had another chance, to give this baby another mother."

"I understand," he said, smiling as I swayed back and forth to put Charlotte down for her nap.

Doc stayed longer than a house call check-up. He drew closer to me and told me about doctoring in Deadwood Gulch. He said Miss Bee's apple pie was selling out every day at Aunt Lou's restaurant and she was making a bundle on the side selling her wild raspberry jams to the prospectors. He told me a mine owner was growing impatient with the striking miners, and he was pressuring Sheriff Bullock to act. Doc even shared more personal matters and said that when he settled in at night, alone in his cabin, he was empty and missing out on an important part of life. He loved being a doctor, yet wished it was balanced with a family. He winked at me and my cheeks flushed.

"Welcome back, Rose," he said, kissing the baby on her forehead and turning to leave.

"Welcome back?" I questioned.

"Welcome back, just welcome back from wherever you were."

A few days later, I walked to Deadwood with Sara, which was the first time I had left Charlotte with Rebekah. We stopped by Doc's cabin, which was quite a sight. Thick goldenrod swayed in the wind as bumblebees balanced on the flower heads, doing their work. Doc already had long six-foot high stacks of firewood, neatly braced between strong pines shielding each side of his cabin. Sara mentioned he was already prepared for the whole winter.

Three moaning men were lying on blankets across his porch. Doc told us the patients were striking at the Keets mine when the owner demanded that Sheriff Bullock do something because he was losing $10,000 a week with no gold coming out. So, the sheriff dropped burning sulfur down the mine's air shaft, ending the strike on the spot. The men high-tailed it out of the mine, coughing and rubbing their swollen eyes. Doc's patients had red rashes on their faces and hands. One miner's cough would not cease and he complained his lungs were on fire.

"I need to save a little money to build another cabin for my patients," Doc said. "I need to get them off my porch if I don't want to be a bachelor for the rest of my life."

"You won't be a bachelor forever," Sara said, full of encouragement. "Not someone who plays a fiddle like you."

"I'm not the best, never had the courage to have an audience," he answered.

"Oh, I have heard you from those nights that I slept in your barn. You make the air dance," Sara said.

"Oh, to be serenaded by something other than the melancholy cries of the wolf who watches us from the ridge," I said.

Doc's mouth relaxed. His lips slightly parted, but no words gathered on his tongue.

CHAPTER 20

SARA

SEPTEMBER, 1877

BLACK HILLS

"WHAT IS LIFE? IT IS THE FLASH OF A FIREFLY IN THE NIGHT. IT IS THE BREATH OF A BUFFALO IN THE WINTERTIME. IT IS THE LITTLE SHADOW WHICH RUNS ACROSS THE GRASS AND LOSES ITSELF IN THE SUNSET." ~Crowfoot, Last Words

One morning, Miss Bee said she was tired of fetching the water, fixing the meals, cleaning the cabin, and tending to the Indians. Defensively, I reminded her that she had free room and board in exchange for her work. Just like that, Miss Bee gathered up her dress, skirt, blouses, shoes, moccasins, and cooking utensils as she mumbled to herself. Placing them into a knapsack, she announced she was moving out and said she would be back to pick up the rest of her things when she had a day off work. From what I could see, she took everything that belonged to her.

Rebekah groaned when she heard Miss Bee left. She said Jake would be no help in picking up the extra slack because he had agreed to double shifts at the mine and would sleep in town for the next few days. When Miss Bee did not return within a few hours, I rode into town, searching for her and planning to apologize for not appreciating her more. Mr. Gushurst had not seen her. I asked Aunt Lou, and she said it was not any of my business as Miss Bee was not my slave.

"I know she isn't, but she's my friend," I replied. As I walked along the street, looking for Miss Bee, a desperate man approached and explained his wife was having a difficult labor and needed help. I walked beside him for thirty minutes and then followed him up a steep slope to a small dugout against the base of a limestone cliff. The couple was basically living in a cave, like wild animals. I immediately sensed death when I stepped into the space which was concealed by a gigantic boulder. The woman was curled under a blanket and did not move. I walked over, squatted beside her and held her cold hand, feeling her wrist. She had no pulse. I placed my ear near her gray lips. She had no breath. Her eyes were peacefully closed as if she was sleeping. I rested her hands on her belly.

"I'm sorry. She's gone."

"She can't be. She promised to stay here with me. She said she wasn't feeling well. But she didn't say she was dying," the man whispered in disbelief. He crumpled to the ground and struggled to cradle his wife in his sun-bronzed arms. I waited for the man's shock to wear off. He wept inconsolably in a hopeless pit of emptiness. I understood.

"She was so excited to see if the baby was a boy or girl. She thought she carried a boy. I didn't care and just wanted to start our family," he professed. "It doesn't make sense. We came to the gulch to get ahead and build something together. How did this go so wrong?"

I helped the broken-hearted man dig a grave near his dugout.

"I can't see doing this without her. There's nothing left for me now," he cried. "I'll head back east in the morning. Please, take my mule as pay for your services."

I refused the offer, gave the man my condolences, and walked away. Deadwood was quiet when I passed through, still with no sign of Miss Bee. I decided to stop and ask Doc if he had heard anything. When I approached the house, I heard Rose talking inside. I peeked through the window beside his front door. There on the floor was Rose, with her legs delicately folded back, resting more on one hip than the other. Charlotte was trying to crawl, lifting herself up on all fours and moving like a worm. Doc was sitting in a chair, smiling at the sight. I turned and walked away with a tinge of envy.

It was nearly dark by the time I reached my claim. The scent of snapped sagebrush was strong and drew me to the trees. I reined Blue off the trail toward the cabin and focused on the top edge of the ridgeline, near where the headless remains of the Indian rested beneath the pile of rocks. The golden eagle floated above me as a gray wolf silently paced to and fro. Perhaps he had brought down his dinner, likely a whitetail deer. Although curious, I did not scale the ridge and disturb him. Unlike bears, the wolf's work would be wasted since he would never return to a cold kill. Then I heard a screech owl.

Motion at the cabin caught Blue's attention moments before mine. His nostrils flared and his ears tipped back, touching his mane. I don't know what blinded me, but I didn't hear the voice of caution from my soul until it was too late. A man waited there, sitting in Rose's rocker, boisterously swinging a lantern in each hand. Smoke from the cabin's chimney rose through the deepening dusk and melted into the sky.

"Stop right there, Sara, if you know what's good for ya," a man's voice growled. It was Joe.

I sank into Blue's back and he immediately halted. Blue whinnied to Joe's mule, tied to a tree away from the cabin. The mule called back.

"Shut up, you stupid beast," Joe hollered, throwing a rock at the mule from the rocking chair. He struck the animal on its side, causing it to pull back and snort, resisting the rope but not breaking free.

"Got yur red savage friends tied up inside with that damn dog of yours. Dynamite sticks against your front door. Seems you got yourself a dilemma now, don't you," Joe's sinister voice echoed across the clearing.

"No dilemma," I answered. "What do you want?"

"I want my gold back, you sleazy little thief." He puffed from a cigarette, wedged between his lips.

"Fine, you can have it," I hollered back.

"No silly stuff, girl, or I'll set your red Injuns ablaze. Blow 'em all to bits." Joe picked up a metal container and started pouring kerosene around the base of the cabin.

"Wait," I projected, confident he would listen. "I'll give you whatever you want. Don't do this."

"I want the gold. I want to finish what we started when you worked your womanly ways on me."

"I don't know what you're talking about. You threw a rock on my head and knocked me out."

"Not how I remember it. Not how all the men in Deadwood have heard it." He snickered as he continued pouring kerosene.

"Wait. I'll give you what you want," I said, starting to panic. He stopped and grinned.

I slid from Blue and let him free, but he stood at attention, sensing my stress.

"If ya know what's good for ya, you'll drop that revolver of yours right there."

I slowly placed my holster and Dad's revolver on the ground.

"Now that's a good little girl. Just do what I tell ya."

I walked toward Joe, knowing the small gun was inside my skirt waistband.

"Easy now, ya hear. Just give me the gold."

"I need to dig it up."

"Where is it?"

"Over on the other side of the cabin," I uttered, pointing.

"Go ahead. Dig. If you make a wrong move, you'll be sorry."

I walked toward Annie's grave and then turned toward the cabin and explained, "I need the shovel." It stood against the side of the cabin and as I retrieved it, I glanced at the three sticks of dynamite wedged against the front door.

The soil was surprisingly soft as I pitched out the top level of Annie's grave.

"Can't believe you," Joe scoffed. "You're crazier than I thought. Knew you weren't right that first time I saw you, wearing Injun pants and moccasins. Didn't know you were so sick in the head, though, digging up bodies."

I didn't look up as I kept digging quickly, becoming winded in the process. As Joe paced back and forth like a caged animal, my hole reached the top of both bags of gold. I worked them loose from the moist earth, lifting them high into the air for Joe to see.

"Here they are. Take them. Leave us alone," I said.

"You think I'm gonna believe you? Bring them over," Joe taunted.

I walked toward him and could smell his stench from five feet away.

"Open the bags," Joe demanded.

I complied, holding one open for inspection. He kept his distance and raised his chin, stretching over the bag and momentarily losing his balance. Not wanting to forfeit my chance, I drew my muff gun from my skirt and pointed it at Joe, who was quickly regaining his footing. Following his movements with my gun's sights aimed at his chest, my fingertip gently touched the metal trigger, warm from being against my belly.

"Go away, Joe. Just back away and go home. You'll get a bullet in your heart if you light this cabin on fire." I heard Shadow snarling inside.

Joe smirked. "You don't have it in you girl," he said, lighting the lanterns in slow motion, one at a time. His face was gaunt. "Ya know, I should have taken you when I had the chance. Been waiting so long to hear you scream. Better late than never."

"I'm giving you what you want. The gold. Me. Whatever you want. Just put down the lanterns and I'll put down my gun." My hands shook as Swill Barrel Jimmy warned.

"Didn't nobody tell ya? Once you draw it, you can't put it away less you're a coward."

"You are the coward," I retorted, cocking back the hammer with my thumb.

With that, Joe threw one lantern against the wall of the cabin and ignited the logs.

I drew a bead on Joe's forehead and pulled the trigger. The kick I braced for and the sound I anticipated were reduced to a mere click as the gun misfired. I pulled the trigger again and nothing happened other than Joe laughing at the other end of my sights and a screech owl calling again in the distance.

Joe drew his own pistol. "Guess it's time for dancing, Sara. If you don't dance for me, I'll shoot your damn foot off. You'll howl like those coyotes and I'll sit here and laugh."

I stood still.

"Last chance, Sara. Dance," he said, cocking the hammer of his revolver.

I refused. I'd rather die. He smirked at my stubbornness and threw the second lantern through the window of the cabin, which immediately burst into flames.

In slow motion, he aimed at my feet and pulled the trigger. Instinctually, I jumped to the side. I did not hear the bang, yet I saw the circle of smoke puff out and surround his gun. Simultaneously, we looked down at my right foot, where his shot had blown off the end of my shoe. Joe looked back up at my face. I did not wince. He looked back at my foot. No blood gushed from the hole.

"Well hell's bells, you're a witch!" he huffed in exasperation.

With nothing other than my left fist and my right hand wrapped around the gun, which was now only a club, I rushed him before he could pull his trigger again. I knew this time I would fight to the end.

The blaze gained momentum and was close to burning us alive as Joe wrestled me on the ground. I hit him as hard as I could, over and over again, still his strength and leverage were overpowering. He rolled on top of me, pinning me as he caught his breath and decided what to do next. I dug my fingernails into his eyes and he screamed out in pain, beating his fists against my face. Then he rested, distracted by the flames, glancing back and forth between the sticks of dynamite and the bags of gold. He cast me aside, crawled to the bags and maneuvered them farther from the fire, protecting what meant the most to him.

By the time he turned back around, I was on my feet, struggling to run as blood poured from my face. He would have to chase me down. As I ran past the cabin, I did not hear screaming from within and thought of the stoic women inside burning to death. The blaze was scorching, so I moved up the hill into the woods and hid behind a lone aspen like a hunted animal. From narrow cover, I peeked around without spotting Joe.

Assuming he was stalking me, I stayed low and silent, resting patiently for a few precious minutes. The smoke filled the meadow offering the benefit of concealment. I waited, crouched, thinking through my options. Shadow nudged me from behind and electrified my already pounding heart. Patches of her fur were burned off, yet somehow, she survived the fire and found me. I quietly ordered Shadow to stay and she complied with a faint whine. I traced my way back toward the cabin, conscious of staying downwind so the smoke would cover my movement. When I rounded the corner, I staggered from a breath of smoke, billowing from each broken window. The door remained intact and I refused to think of what was crumpled on the other side.

I crept closer and closer to where Joe likely waited, beside the gold. Crouched over with the butt of my gun ready for battle, I peered through the smoke, and slowly placed my remaining toes down first, followed by my heels. After a few steps, I stopped behind the next tree, camouflaged long enough to fill my lungs with more smoky air. The crackling embers were excruciatingly hot as they landed on my skin.

When I was close to where Joe last stood, I carefully dropped to my knees, staying below the scorching heat, still concealed in the smoke. I crawled, immediately stopping when I saw Joe, inches from my face. He was crumpled on his side with an arrow perfectly piercing his evil heart. His wide-open eyes still sparked with hatred as the flames flickered in his fully dilated pupils.

I pulled back and sat on my heels, taking a deep breath that ended in a smoky cough. Shadow had followed and cautiously sniffed the air before backing away, disinterested. Surprisingly, minimal blood dripped from where the arrow entered his chest, and where it did, the small pool was nearly black. Light red blood oozed through a thin layer of pink translucent tissue where his scalp was laid open from front to back. The fluid formed a stream which ran down around the back of his ear, past his chin and stained the brown soil beneath his contorted head. As death set in, his eyes faded to a blank gaze.

Tipping back on my rear, I pondered where dark spirits travel once their body lies motionless. I studied the arrow protruding from the dead man. It had scored a direct hit and almost traveled completely through Joe's body. Then, I finally focused on the design on the shaft of the arrow. In red, a line swirled around the circumference three times, slowly turning to yellow. The wavy line extended into tiny hearts on each end, both in blue paint. It was the identifiable mark of Ohanzee.

I froze. Ohanzee was alive. He was here. I pulled myself to my feet, determined he would not disappear into the trees forever. I charged up the hillside, through the thick smoke, gasping and hacking as I ran. "Ohanzee!" I hollered, over and over again. Then I heard the screech owl and followed his call. *Screech!* One, two, three, four, *Screech!* One, two, three, *Screech!* One, two, three, four, five, six, seven, eight, nine, ten, eleven, twelve, thirteen, fourteen … *Screech!* Clearly not the right cadence for an owl, but exactly as Ohanzee had taught me months before. I quit calling out, and instead, followed his sounds, which led me to a thickly covered area where pine and aspens lived in unison. Ohanzee stood with Dyani and Mystery.

"Sara," Ohanzee said. I ran to him and hugged his frail body. He stood tall by bracing against his strong leg and leaving the other weight-free. Ohanzee's cheekbones stuck out from his rutted flesh but he remained dignified as his hair drifted with the breeze, decorated with one eagle feather. At his feet rested his bow and quiver of arrows. A bloody scalp was jammed into the top of the quiver. "How did you save them?" I breathlessly asked.

"The window in the back of your tree tipi. I watched."

"It's a cabin, not a tipi," I whispered. "For how long? How long have you been around me?" I asked.

"For many moons," Ohanzee replied. In noble patience, he had waited; He was half-starved, yet not weary from his watchfulness. Wearing buckskin pants, he looked leaner but his copper-colored skin tone had replaced the gray cast from a year before. His sleek black hair still extended past his shoulders, and the front of his neck showed the scar he received after being dragged behind a cavalry horse.

"You are our medicine wasicu. You heal us. You heal me. Thank you." The prominence of his chiseled cheeks and nose reminded me of the days when I lived among his people.

"You saved me, Ohanzee. Thank you," I said.

"I want to talk. To tell you my story."

"I want to hear your story, Ohanzee. But it isn't safe for you, not here. Deadwood will see the smoke and come. They'll see the

273

274

arrow through Joe. They'll track you down. They'll kill you and Dyani and Mystery for the bounty."

"Bounty?" he asked. His eyes, blacker than dark coffee, assessed the wounds on my bloody face.

"For your head. They pay money for your head."

Ohanzee looked confused and mystified.

"Your head, cut off your body. Just go. I beg you. Just go."

In a low, gentle voice, Ohanzee said, "I'm not afraid, Sara. They can take nothing more away from me and my people."

"But they can. Believe me. They want to take your life."

"It matters no more. They killed Crazy Horse. They can kill me."

"What do you mean, Crazy Horse? Who killed Crazy Horse?" I asked. My throat tightened.

"They stabbed him and killed him. They called him to the fort and they killed him."[47]

"I'm sorry. I don't know anything about that. I do know I cannot bear to see you killed. Please, just go. They'll be here soon."

Ohanzee wrapped his arms around me and we clung to each other for more than a moment, absorbing the other.

He pulled back and said, "I was with you, in your heart. Did you feel me?" I nodded. "You are never far. You are in my heart, forever. I give you my word."

275

I believed his promise because they were rare and only offered when he was certain to fulfill them. Ohanzee's black and white Pinto stood beside the women. The horse was lean and strong but could still only carry two on his back. I ran down the hill and untied Joe's mule from the tree and he eagerly trotted with me back up the ridge.

"I knew he sensed good from evil," Ohanzee said, stroking the face of the mule before lifting the lighter woman onto his splotchy, wire-haired back. Then, Ohanzee lifted Dyani onto his Pinto.

Dyani thanked me and Mystery simply offered a faint smile. Ohanzee opened the bag hanging from his hip and pulled out herbal salve. "Come here," he said, gently rubbing it over a gash in my cheek and scrapes on my chin. I could smell the mixture of spearmint and oregano, certain he had infused the salve with crushed monarda, used by his people to treat skin infections.

Then, he took a pinch of powder from his pouch, placing a bit of his medicine in the nostrils of his Pinto and the mule, to make them invisible and strong on their journey. He took another pinch of medicine and sprinkled it over each woman. Finally, he offered the open pouch to me and I complied, dusting him for protection.

Ohanzee closed the pouch and focused on me, reaching for another hug, "Goodbye Sara," he whispered in my ear.

"Goodbye Ohanzee."

He jumped on his horse in front of Dyani and nudged him forward with the mule in tow. Ohanzee guided the women up the ridgeline to an unknown fate. And then, the smoke rendered them invisible.

I raced down the hill, plotting as I ran. Grabbing the shovel, I stumbled to Annie's gravesite which was partially dug from retrieving the gold. I knew the locals would ride out, if not to check on me, then perhaps only out of curiosity for what was burning. The eerie, thick smoke saturated my claim as I furiously dug up Annie's grave, glancing over my shoulder at each crack of something collapsing in the cabin. I looked back at Shadow who was wagging her tail, greeting Rebekah as she appeared out of the smoke.

"Oh my dear Lord. What on earth has happened?"

"No time, Rebekah. Help me dig."

She dropped to her knees and used her hands to desperately pull back soil since we only had one shovel. "Why are we digging up Annie?" she asked. Without hesitating for me to reply, she continued to furiously dig. We were winded and choking up smoke before we had the grave re-opened only two feet deep.

"This will have to do," I gasped, out of breath.

Rebekah stood up. "What is going on?" she asked. I grabbed her hand and led her through the grey haze to the nearby corpse of Joe.

"Oh, my gosh. Oh, my gosh," Rebekah sputtered. "I must have almost stepped on him when I came up to check on you."

I gripped under his shoulders and raised his torso, directing Rebekah to grab ahold anywhere. She scanned his body quickly and thought about pulling on his arm but changed her mind as she took in the scalped corpse.

"I can't touch him," she said and settled on pulling from the side of his shirt. We drug the dead man ten feet before Rebekah lost her grip. Suddenly undeterred, she latched onto the arrow and threw her weight into the task.

"Keep going, Sara. Pull."

We dragged him another five feet until the arrow snapped and impaled Rebekah's palm. She yanked the shaft from her hand and threw the feathered end piece into the trees. Rebekah moved to Joe's feet, lifting his shabby brown boots as I pulled from the opposite end. My hands wore out and I dropped his shoulders. Rebekah's pushing momentum continued and she fell directly on top of the dead man. Amid a sincere howl of disgust, she rolled off his warm body and quickly regained her composure.

We continued dragging Joe until he finally stretched beside the grave. Rebekah and I sat side-by-side on the ground and pushed against his torso with our feet until he rolled into the hole with a thud, face down, on top of Annie.

We quickly covered the grave with dirt. I shoveled and Rebekah used her feet like an oxen-pulled road blade. Then, Rebekah ran to the barn, retrieving old hay to scatter across the disturbed, moist soil.

The cabin still burned and the smoke was thicker than ever as the first locals arrived on horseback and squinted from a distance, across the meadow, straining to see the show. I told Rebekah that I would distract them while she finished camouflaging the grave.

Shadow led the way as I crossed the meadow. She smelled of scorched fur and walked stiffly, pained by her burns. I was covered in soot and bloody dirt. One prospector gasped as we approached. Another asked if there was anything he could do. I explained that nothing more could be done to save the cabin. It was useless. They did not offer to tend to our wounds.

About twenty men eventually gathered, standing with me and watching the blaze. The sides of the cabin were gone and only the corners and door remained. As the flames faded to glowing embers, Sheriff Bullock and Dillon McFoley arrived. The sheriff stepped from his horse, spurs singing as he noticeably swaggered toward me. His steel badge reflected the dying flames.

"Well, well. What do we have here?"

"I lost my cabin."

"And how did this all happen?" he asked.

"Not quite sure. I came home and it was already in flames."

"How did your face get all cut up?" he asked suspiciously.

"Fighting the fire, I suppose," I said.

His steely-eyed glare unsettled me. "Usually fighting fires doesn't include bruised and cut faces." His eyes turned back to the fire. "I suppose we best head over and check for bodies."

The whole group of men moved toward the smoldering cabin that lit the dark night with a mysterious glow through the veil of smoke. As I followed behind on foot, I realized I had left the bags of gold out in the open.

The men rode around the cabin, suspiciously scanning the area as their horses randomly spooked from the lingering heat and smoke. I approached with Shadow, trying to come up with a story about my gold because Sheriff Bullock was certainly looking for anything to take me down. When I reached the place where Joe and I struggled, the gold bags were nowhere to be seen. Neither was Rebekah.

Sheriff Bullock looked around and asked about the hay covering Annie's grave. I explained we recently planted iris bulbs over her grave and invited him to visit when they bloomed next spring.

One of the men dismounted and walked a few steps into the trees, retrieving the end of Ohanzee's broken arrow. The man studied it, and commented, "Same markings with this heart and all. Yes, sir. It's the same arrow that was sticking out of Reynolds."

"I thought you said he was hung?" I asked, turning to Sheriff Bullock and hoping to stall until I covered with another lie.

"He was hung, but he also had an arrow through his heart."

I had nothing left to say.

Dillon saw my dad's gun and holster on the ground and retrieved it before handing it back to me.

"Must have lost this while fighting your fire," he said, not looking for affirmation. "Well, this is an easy one to solve," he went on. Dillon's eyes glanced at me before the sheriff turned to listen. My heart raced.

"Well, let's hear it," the sheriff demanded.

"It's plain as day. The Indian who killed Reynolds also burned down Sara's cabin."

The sheriff thought for a moment and asked me, "You know any Indian who wants you and Reynolds dead?"

Before I could answer, the burning front door collapsed from its frame hinges onto the sticks of dynamite. I screamed, warning the men as I dove for cover. The explosion knocked me senseless.

CHAPTER 21

SARA

OCTOBER, 1877

BLACK HILLS

*"WEEPING MAY REMAIN FOR A NIGHT, BUT
REJOICING COMES IN THE MORNING."
~ Psalms 30:4*

I remember little after the blast other than everything going dark.
As I came to my senses, Rose hovered over me, sponging my
lacerated face with cool water. She had tended to my needs for
almost two days, but I couldn't recall. Immediately after the
explosion, I did not respond to Sheriff Bullock's questioning, so
the men threw me over the back of Dillon's horse and dropped me
at Doc's cabin. The concussion from the explosion was so
powerful that it knocked off my shoes and blew my skirt from my
body. Rose was told that while slumped over Dillon's horse with
my bloomers exposed, I uttered, "Dillon, let's pretend this never
happened."

As I regained my senses, Rose and Charlotte never left my side.
When Rebekah, Jake, and Shadow showed up at Doc's cabin,

Rebekah gasped at my cuts and bruises, uttering "Oh, my gosh." She regained her composure and whispered she had snatched the gold and buried it in Blue's barn, which was untouched by the fire and explosion. They said nobody ever asked why a crater was left where the front door once stood or how I knew the cabin was about to blow up. Rebekah and Jake left Shadow for my companionship, curled up at the edge of my bed. Doc cleaned Shadow's open burns and dabbed on salve to prevent infection.

Rebekah insisted Rose and I stay in their cabin until we rebuilt mine. I couldn't think that far ahead. Miss Bee visited the next afternoon after word of the fire spread throughout Deadwood. I planned to apologize for being insensitive as soon as we reunited, but she acted as though we had never had an argument.

"That fog will slowly clear from your head," Miss Bee promised, lifting her hair and exposing the old, jagged scar across her temple. "I was busted open by my owner's son when I was a slave. It takes time. Heads mend slowly."

When I told her confidentially about how Joe shot off the end of my shoe, but missed my toes since they were already gone, we laughed until we cried.

The next day, she returned with the moccasins Ohanzee had left as a gift when he dropped Mystery at our cabin. "No wonder they didn't fit me," Miss Bee said, "He had them made to fit your foot without those darned toes!"

I studied the intricate detail on the top of the moccasins. Two beaded blue hearts were quilled together with a red ribbon of color, just as Ohanzee's arrow was painted. And then below, the hearts were separated, symbolically torn apart. I tried them on. The left moccasin slid onto my foot as expected. Carefully crafted, the right moccasin formed perfectly around what was remaining of my right foot.

Back at our claims, I rested and healed while Rebekah took it upon herself to sift through the cabin's ashes. The dynamite explosion left an eight-foot-deep crater which Rebekah methodically searched. The contents from the explosion were scattered fifty feet. Everything seemed charred beyond recognition, yet Rebekah used a stick and diligently poked around. Miraculously, she found Rose's heart-shaped rock from Sergeant Zito. She picked out a tin coffee cup and one unbroken plate. Her motivation increased with each salvaged article.

"I guess it's more about the attached memories," she said. "Isn't that the whole point? It's all we have when it comes down to it."

One day, I kept Rebekah company near my cabin site as she continued to scavenge. While I rested in Rose's rocker that Jake had repaired after the blast, Rebekah dug in the crater and pulled out Sergeant Zito's Saint Michael medal that Rose had worn since her rescue. I wondered if she intentionally took it off when she spent time with Doc. Rebekah slid the chain over my head, suggesting I keep it until Rose decided if she wanted it back.[48]

"Oh, look at this pretty rock," Rebekah said, lifting it to the sun after pulling it from the crater. "It shimmers. Isn't it beautiful?"

I barely noticed the white quartz because my foggy mind was elsewhere. My head throbbed as I tried to plan my future. I thought of Fred and wondered where he was and if he was thinking of me. Then Rebekah murmured she might start a rock collection.

I slept away much of the day and night, which Doc said was good therapy. My brain lacked sharpness, yet with each passing day, the extra rest seemed to heal me. Jake and Rebekah placed two new mattresses in the corner of their cabin. Charlotte slept beside Rose and I had my own bed in the congested space. I reminded myself that the situation was temporary. Usually before daybreak, Jake slipped out the door and left for work before the rest of us stirred.

One morning, I awoke to Jake asking Rebekah, "Princess, where did you find these rocks?"

"Up in the crater at Sara's. I started a rock collection. That's why I put them on the windowsill. Is that okay or should I move them? I thought they were pretty."

"Darned right, they're pretty!" Jake hollered. "Rebekah, you found gold!"

"Fool's gold, no doubt," Rebekah said.

"No," he exclaimed, holding it to the light streaming through the window. "It's the real thing. A bonanza! You did it!"

Jake rushed the fist-sized piece of quartz to me and I saw the wide vein of muted gold running through the entire piece. It came from a significant lode.

Jake and Rebekah ran out of their cabin and up to the crater to figure which way the quartz vein ran through the ground. It took a few days for Jake to determine the depth and direction of the vein. They followed its path and dug gopher holes on their own claim to verify Jake's hunch. Tears welled in his eyes as he stared at a quartz vein filled with heavy gold streaks.

"We did it, Princess! No more working for someone else. We have prosperity right here. Gold, right here! We can afford as many dogs as you want! We can start our family!"

"Um, Jake?" Rebekah said with a grin on her face. "There's been something I've been meaning to tell you." She pressed her cupped hand against the front of her skirt, revealing the start of a pudgy belly.

Jake collapsed in tears, crying like the child he would eventually hold. "You're with child? You're with child?" he repeated over and over before lifting himself from the ground and embracing Rebekah.

"We need to celebrate," he said. Rebekah told him it was bad luck to announce it publicly until she was further along.

"Well, you can get all superstitious on me, but I want to share our blessings. This has been quite a day. I'm the luckiest man on earth. We'll have a special dinner tomorrow night, the five of us. I wouldn't mind another man around though. I'm a bit outnumbered. How about Doc?"

The next morning, Rose asked me to escort her and Charlotte to town. She said she had an errand to run and wanted to buy a baby gift. When I agreed, she confirmed that I would carry my gun to town.

We walked to make a day of it, giving Blue a rest since he seemed worn out. I let him loose in the meadow because he never wandered far and he grazed as he pleased. With the summer heat behind us, the grass was coarse so Blue pawed for the short tender growth underneath.

We bundled Charlotte into a sling that hung from Rose's neck and wrapped tight around her waist which carried the bulk of Charlotte. The child seemed to love Rose's walking motion and slept while we chatted along the way.

"I would first like to stop at the bank and then at the Big Horn Store," Rose said. "You brought your gun as I asked?"

"Yes," I confirmed again.

We entered the James W. Wood Bank, and the man greeted us by name.

"Good day, Miss Capable. Good day, Mrs. Zito. How may I help you fine ladies today?"

"I was checking on my account, to verify the funds arrived."

"Yes, ma'am, they sure did. From the state of New York. Exactly what you said, and they even added interest." The man cleared his throat and continued, "With all due respect, when someone of your wealth has accumulated as you have, you obviously don't need guidance as a proven businesswoman. I humbly ask that with your extraordinary means, you consider keeping a minimal portion of your balance with my bank."

The man swooned over Rose as she made a minimal withdrawal of her funds, leaving her satchel full of banknotes. We left while the banker continued to cast pleasantries our direction. "Now, you come visit anytime, Mrs. Zito, and bring that beautiful baby of yours along."

"I need this to be confidential, Sara. The town doesn't need to know about my financial affairs. If people know my means, they'll treat me differently. Tom and I were quite successful with an import business before your father called him back to service. We were like squirrels, storing it away for tough times."

"You have my word, Rose."

"It's ironic. Only one letter to New York and they sent my entire estate without me even needing to hire legal services. I threatened that, all right. They must have something to cover up. Maybe the superintendent of Hart Island is on the take."

Charlotte woke as we stepped inside the Big Horn Store for food and gifts. Mr. Gushurst had added more variety to his store, with a new assortment of items: more delicate fabrics, glass containers full of candy, tools, children's toys, and more men's clothing. Rose wandered, searching for the perfect baby gift and selecting food for our celebration dinner. I lingered behind with a basket, carrying all she pulled from the shelves. Personally, I was touched with the realization that Sergeant Zito was not a soldier because he needed the money. Sergeant Zito was a soldier because he chose to serve.

CHAPTER 22

SARA

OCTOBER, 1877

BLACK HILLS

"A MAN NEED NOT BE PERFECT TO BE A
GREAT MAN, BUT HE MUST LEARN FROM
ALL HIS EXPERIENCES, GOOD AND BAD, AND
DEVELOP BEYOND THEM THROUGH
THOUGHT, PRAYER, AND ACTION, OR HIS
GREATNESS WILL ONLY BE DUST UPON THE
WIND." ~Vinson Brown, Great Upon the Mountain

That afternoon, Rose, Rebekah, and I chattered like squirrels and
giggled incessantly as we prepared the celebratory meal. We
continuously bumped into each other, working in Rebekah's cabin
and at the Dutch oven, buried in the coals of their fire pit. While
Rebekah sliced the carrots, onions, potatoes, and celery, she asked
Rose what to expect during her pregnancy. Rose came alive,
describing the good and bad details and offering tips of how to
cope with morning sickness. I wished Miss Bee had been with us.

Not only because she was ten times the chef of us three put together, but because I missed her wholesome presence.

Rose cubed the venison into bitesize pieces. She seasoned the meat with chopped vegetables while I rolled out the dough. We put the mixture in the bottom of the Dutch oven and covered it with the dough. Rebekah buried the oven in the coals of the fire. We waited over the meal, entertained by the powerful colors of the sky as the sun dropped, fading into deep blues and oranges.

Shortly after the sky muted to nothing except dim purple and gray, Doc and Jake arrived on horseback. We sat around the fire with short logs on end sufficing as stools and individual tables. As I scooped from the Dutch oven, Jake kicked up the fire by adding a few more logs. We ate and then moved closer to the flames as the night chill came on. The peacefulness of the still evening surrounded us and we knew few beautiful nights remained before winter set in.

Jake was a master storyteller and started reminiscing of how he thought he wanted to be a priest, at least until he laid eyes on a beautiful young woman. We laughed. He told us how he chanced into becoming a soldier when the sign at the post office said the government was looking for brave men to serve out West.

Jake recalled, "The notice said something like 'The horse is man's most noble companion. Join the Cavalry and have a courageous friend.' So I thought, hey, I'm brave. I love horses and adventure. I can protect settlers. And just like that, I enlisted."

291

We stared at the flames in silence and waited for Jake to continue. When he did, he described how the Army betrayed him when they would not authorize a rescue party for me. Jake even requested approval to travel alone back to Whetstone to rescue us, but the officer in charge denied the request. Although he was not proud of it, Jake deserted and tracked back to Whetstone. He found the scattered remains of Sergeant Zito and my mother. After he buried the pieces he could find, he turned west since gold fever struck the Black Hills.

"And that's where I came in, right?" Rebekah chimed in.

"Yes, Princess. That's where you came in," he answered.

Doc went to his horse and pulled his fiddle from the pack. "Well, I've never done this before," he muttered.

"This is a safe place to start," encouraged Rose. Doc played like he had performed all his life. Charlotte fell asleep within minutes and Rebekah took her out of Rose's arms and into the cabin.

The music filled the valley, accompanying our heart-filled conversation. I was blessed by my friends and felt no desire for more. With so few women in Deadwood Gulch, I still doubted why any woman remained unmarried unless it was her choice to go it alone. I was young and ill-equipped to make such permanent decisions, yet Dakota Territory had the tendency to force youthful innocence from people in uncomfortable ways.

"And what about you, Sara? What's next?" Jake asked.

"I don't know, yet. Just keep moving forward till I see something worth stopping for, I suppose."

"You can be our baby's official auntie, or the baby's private doctor," Rebekah teased. "Seriously, after the struggles you've had over the last couple years, Sara, you deserve to rest."

"But I can't just sit here in the woods leading an ordinary life or one of indifference. I'll drown in regrets if my life is constant compromise, like it was for my mother. I need something exciting and worthwhile to pursue."

"Well, how about this for exciting?" said Doc. "How about taking a chance, right now, and kick up your heels? Let's see some dancing to this music."

"I'd like to see you do the same, Doc!" I said.

"Sorry, I'm playing the fiddle. Can't dance."

Jake stood up and walked over to Doc, taking the fiddle from his hands.

"Jake, you play?" asked Rebekah.

"You betcha but not in years." Jake started to play. A little rusty on the high notes, still his fingers remembered where to move.

Doc asked Rose to dance and they spun in the light of the fire. Rebekah and I danced. We laughed as we stepped on each other's feet, each trying to lead the other. I glanced over at Doc and Rose. They had slowed their pace, clearly mesmerized with each other. Doc took a step back.

"Well, I've never done this before either," he said. Doc held out his hand to Rose and when she offered hers, he dropped to one knee. "Rose, I know I don't have many earthly possessions, been pretty focused on helping people. But I wish to care for you, to protect you and Charlotte, to honor you, as my wife. Will you marry me?"

Rose stood before him, her every limb shaking. "Yes, yes, yes," she replied. Doc joyfully hugged her. Ignoring the fact that Jake had put down the fiddle, they started dancing again.

"I love you. And I promise you, Rose, I'll find a way to get patients out of my cabin and off my porch," Doc chuckled.

"That is an easy issue to fix, but let's still put it in our vows," Rose smiled, glancing at me. We both knew she could build an infirmary without even nicking her wealth.

As the conversation lulled, each of us relaxed, mesmerized by the glowing embers. Doc threw another few logs on the fire and I walked to the barn to check on Blue.

"Blue, it's me," I said quietly. He whinnied as I stepped into the barn. Blue was bedded down, flat on his side. When he saw me, he tucked his legs underneath his body but did not rise. I dropped to the stable floor beside him, appreciating him, smelling him. At times like these, when we were alone with nowhere to go, he consoled me, and I buried my face against his neck. I was blessed to be in the presence of a great animal. He had walked me through radical changes, with unrelenting effort and loyalty.

I finally stood up and pulled a brush from the shelf. Blue stood with a slight grunt of stiffness, still ready if his service was required. I brushed out his mane and tail as his eyes closed for minutes at a time. He stood perfectly still and lifted each foot for me before I even asked for it. His soles were clean but I picked them anyway. I lightly blew into his nostril and he blew back against my cheek. Then, I stood at Blue's side and scratched my short fingernails on the underside of his belly. Like every other time, he bent his neck and turned his muzzle to my shoulder, blissfully moving his lips back and forth. "I love you, Blue," I whispered.

As I walked from the barn, with my eyes fully adjusted to the dark, I spotted two figures on the opposite side of the meadow. They were both on horses, still as statues.

I rushed into Jake and Rebekah's cabin and grabbed my gun from beside my bed. By the time I was back at the fire, Doc had pulled Rose to cover behind a tree. Jake and Rebekah were holding their ground and I assumed I was the only one armed.

As the two approached, I stood tall and focused, with my gun held at my side yet ready to raise.

"Sara, it's me," Miss Bee's voice rang out over the gurgling stream and the snapping wood on the fire.

I released an audible sigh. Out of the dark and into the firelight rode Miss Bee and Fred. I dropped my gun and stood on wobbling legs.

"He was at the restaurant, asking for you. Thought it best if I brought him out so he wouldn't get lost," Miss Bee said, smiling.

Dressed in a gray shirt with the sleeves rolled up, Fred rode up to me with a charming grin across his face. His buckskin pants were neatly tucked into knee-high leather jack boots. Fred slid from his mare and quickly embraced me, raising me off my feet without reserve. My head knocked off his broad-brimmed, whitish-gray hat. Lacking any sort of composure, and not caring, I fingered through his long locks of hair that covered his vibrant eyes. He took my breath away.

"Oh, my dear Sara. I have missed you so."

Miss Bee was stunned by his forwardness and my reciprocated lack of caution. She nervously jumped in. "Sara, did you see my new horse? I earned enough at work to buy him right out. Solid black gelding. 'Bout time I take better care of this crippled leg. Enough walking with work and if I visit out here, as much as you'll have me that is, then he'll come in mighty handy."

"He's a beauty," I said, not missing the point that they were both dark as night.

I offered Miss Bee and Fred the robust black brew, coffee that Rebekah made in the morning and set on the coals until it was gone. My pulse was still fast and Fred seemed unaware of how his gaze caused my knees to tremble.

"I almost forgot, in all this excitement," Rose exclaimed. She retrieved a yellow paper box with a green satin bow on top and handed it to Rebekah. "It's for your new baby. It's all I could find;

Deadwood isn't the best place to shop for little ones. I'm excited for you. A baby changes who you are, for the better."

Rebekah carefully opened the box and found a soft yellow-and-green cap, mittens, and booties inside. "Thank you, Rose," Rebekah whispered. "They are beautiful."

Jake carried out two dollars' worth of candy in a brown paper bag and passed it around the campfire. Fudge, ginger snaps, gum balls, chocolate bites, marshmallows, Horehound candy, and red licorice.

"Wouldn't it be good if we could find a way to melt the chocolate and white fudge over the fire?" Jake suggested.

"It would melt," Rose said.

"What if we speared a marshmallow on a branch and heat it over the fire? Then we can squeeze it hot against a chocolate bite in between two ginger snaps. Come on, ladies, it's worth a try."

While Jake tried to heat his first marshmallow over the flames, Fred, without any intention of dominating the conversation, captivated us with his stories of the plains.

He spoke of the skirmishes and battles over the last year. He said the Army, for the most part, had lately been chasing the Indians across the plains to wear them out, so they would accept defeat and move permanently onto their reservations.

I asked Fred about Crazy Horse and the circumstances around his death.

"Can't recount the details since I wasn't there, but something went awry. As I see it, you can't kill a man for a different perspective. In my opinion, mind you it's only my opinion, but Crazy Horse was a good man. He protected his people. He would never accept our restrictions over his roaming ways. Freedom was everything to him. I have to say, I relate to the man's moral code more than I probably should."

Jake's second marshmallow dropped into the fire before he handed the stick to Miss Bee, who insisted she would be successful, placing the end near the bottom edge of glowing coals instead of the hot flame. She was patient and the white fluff turned golden brown.

"Quick, Jake, get the chocolate and ginger snaps," she instructed. Jake constructed the ingredients and squeezed Miss Bee's marshmallow off the stick and between the snaps.

Rebekah received the honors since she was with child. It felt as if brighter skies were ahead as we socialized throughout the evening. We were together but diverse, sharing our individual histories.

Miss Bee had not spoken much at first. She mostly stared into the flames. Then, after her first roasted sweet treat, she seemed to prophesize.

"When each of us felt stuck, like we would never heal, in time, circumstances changed. Now we share more. We look past the flames and see the whole fire and the possibilities before us. Those glowing embers are tragedies behind us. It's not about why this happened to us. It's about how we move forward."

Nobody said a word. Miss Bee continued, "I don't know why I was born a slave on a plantation in Georgia. And Rose, you don't know why Tom and your little girl were taken from you. Sara, you don't know why you have lost so many you love. Rebekah, you don't know why your family disowned you. See? God doesn't give us answers to everything while we are on earth. He just loves us and promises to love us no matter where we are in our journey."

Miss Bee was tired and her eyelids grew heavy, so I offered her my bed. Rebekah, Jake, and Rose turned in as soon as Doc headed home.

Fred and I were left at the fire. He pulled our log stools together, until they almost touched. For hours, we shared our pasts and our dreams for the future, in ways I never felt comfortable speaking of before. I don't know why, but I was confident he would not judge my past, nor would I judge his. Our conversation flourished, as if two kindred spirits were reunited.

Fred's back was aching from his long ride so we moved to the foot of a pine, where he propped against the trunk. I reclined beside him and Shadow slept with her back against my thigh. It took moments of silence gathering courage before I sighed. Unsure of the answer, I asked, "Why did you come back?"

Fred gently held my face and raised my downcast eyes to his. He dropped his voice and whispered, "Because I'm crazy about you. The first time I saw you, I knew. You buckle my knees."

"What about the Arctic expedition?"

"It'll kill me if something happens to you, but please come with me."

Shadow stood up and moved to Fred. She resettled and he rubbed her belly. Fred pulled me close and securely wrapped his arms around me, supporting my tired body. My eyelids grew heavy and his words became distant as I breathed in the night air, certain to always remember the moment.

When I opened my eyes again, it was with regret that I saw streaks of light in the eastern sky. Fred was still holding me.

"Look, Sara. It's beautiful," Fred whispered, pointing to the horizon.

High above, the silhouette of the soaring golden eagle danced with the swirling winds above the ridge.[49]

The End.

HISTORICAL TIMELINE

Pre-1800: The Great Sioux Nation, consisting of Dakota, Nakota, and Lakota speakers, unified and called themselves Oceti Sakowin, meaning "Seven Council Fires." They numbered about seven thousand people. For many generations, natives fought amongst themselves for all things provided by the Great One. The Chippewa drove the Sioux from the northern lakes and forests, into the woods, and down to the prairie. The Sioux Nation was vast, extending north from the Platte River. The western boundary was the Bighorn Mountains, and the eastern boundary was the Missouri River. Seven Lakota-speaking tribes made up the Teton Sioux Nation: the Minniconjou (Plant beside the Stream), Hunkpapa (End Village), Oglala (They Scatter Their Own), Sichangu (Brulé), Sihasapa (Black Foot), Itazipcho (San Arcs), and Oohenonpa (Two Kettles). Around 1750, horses were first obtained by the Oglala, and they transformed the daily routine of the Lakota. Approximately sixty million buffalo roamed the plains.

1803: The Louisiana Purchase was acquired for $15,000,000 which added to the United States territory from the Northwest to the Gulf of Mexico.

1804: The Lewis and Clark expedition met the Lakota.

1818: Smallpox outbreak within the Lakota.

1834: Bear Butte and Devil's Tower (Mato Tipila) represented the spiritual center for the Oglala Lakota. Trading posts were placed near the Laramie and North Platte Rivers. Beaver pelts were nearly gone and buffalo hides were anticipated to be the next substantially demanded hide.

1838: Trail of Tears. Fifteen thousand members of the Cherokee nation were pressured to give up their land east of the Mississippi River. The military forced the Cherokee to march to present-day Oklahoma, and along the way they were subjected to hunger, disease and exhaustion. Over four thousand died.

1842-1844: Birth of Crazy Horse, Oglala.

1845: Smallpox outbreak throughout the northern plains.

1847: Frederick Douglass published the North Star, an abolitionist newspaper.

1849: The United States purchased Fort Laramie from the American Fur Company and assigned troops to the fort.

1849: Harriet Tubman escaped to Pennsylvania from her slave owner and began helping others escape through the Underground Railroad.

1849–1850: Outbreaks of white-man diseases such as smallpox, cholera, and measles hit the Indian tribes. Cholera was especially prolific. The Brulés and Oglalas fled north from the southern plains in an attempt to avoid the diseases. They went to a former campsite on the White River in Dakota Territory. Soon every villager was dead inside their tipis. The cholera epidemic killed nearly half of the Cheyenne and was just as destructive to the Lakota. In 1850, the smallpox epidemic killed hundreds of additional plains Indians. The Indians believed the white-man diseases were a wicked spell placed upon their people and they sought revenge.

1850: Congress passed the Fugitive Slave Act of 1850 which required federal officials to arrest runaway slaves.

1851: Fort Laramie Treaty of 1851. The white man invited all tribes of the western plains to meet with United States government officials for the purpose of agreeing on a plan that would allow them to live in harmony. Between eight thousand and thirteen thousand natives attended the Fort Laramie Council. The eighteen-day council resulted in the first Fort Laramie Treaty, which was signed by some tribes. The treaty identified the territory reserved for the tribes and allowed the safe passage of white settlers through the territory on the Oregon Trail in exchange for payments to the tribes. The tribes who signed the treaty remained good on their word for three years and did not battle the thousands of settlers who flowed through their land. However, the United States broke the treaty when it did not make the promised payments of "$50,000 a year for ten years, or maybe five more, not for more than fifty years."

1851: Whites settled in the area now known as Minnesota. Two treaties were negotiated, Traverse des Sioux Treaty and Mendota Treaty. The white leaders purchased the woods and prairie from the Lakota. They gave the Lakota three million dollars over fifty years and promised the Lakota reservation land. Some of the agency land was fertile, and some was extremely barren. The Lakota did not know the poor quality of the land before they signed the treaty. The Lakota claimed they were cheated by the white man because they did not understand the words in the treaty. The payments were made, yet much of the money went to traders and mixed bloods.

1852: Uncle Tom's Cabin by author Harriet Beecher Stowe was published.

1854: Approximately four thousand Brulé and Oglala Lakota lived in villages near Fort Laramie, in accordance with the terms of the Treaty of 1851. A group of Mormons traveled along the Oregon Trail, and one of their injured cows lagged behind the wagon train. A visiting Minniconjou followed the cow and killed it, taking the meat home to his starving village. Conquering Bear, the chief of the Brulé camp, was concerned and rode to Fort Laramie. He offered to pay ten dollars for the cow. The Mormon settler was at the camp and demanded twenty-five dollars for the cow, which Conquering Bear did not pay. A small detachment of soldiers, led by the inexperienced and arrogant Lieutenant Grattan, went to the encampment to arrest the warrior who had killed the Mormon settler's cow. Conquering Bear refused to deliver High Forehead to the fort, still he offered a horse to repay the party for the lost cow. Tensions rose, partly due to the drunk translator who insulted the Lakota. Then, as Grattan turned to walk away from the group which included Crazy Horse, a soldier shot and killed Conquering Bear. The Brulé Lakota returned fire and killed the thirty-one-man party. This "Grattan Massacre"—as the press called it—is considered the first battle of the Great Sioux War.

1855: Colonel William S. Harney and 1,310 soldiers were sent from Fort Leavenworth to retaliate against those who killed Grattan and his men. He surrounded the camp of Little Thunder, who claimed no responsibility for the Grattan incident. Colonel Harney and his men, however, massacred the entire Brulé village before even one warrior was able to defend himself. There were 136 Indians killed, and the soldiers mutilated the bodies of the women and children. Colonel Harney was nicknamed "Squaw Killer Harney." Colonel Harney told the village that Spotted Tail, who was injured in that fight, was to surrender or he would come back in six months. Spotted Tail reported to Harney within a few weeks. The Brulé were willing to give up their freedom to protect their people from another attack. The Indian men were dressed in war clothes and sang death songs as they approached the soldiers. The soldiers did not kill the warriors but took them to Fort Leavenworth and eventually released them.

1856: During the summer, Crazy Horse made his vision quest, called a hanblecheyapi, on the top of the sacred prairie mountain, Mato Paha. (Bear Butte).

1857: The Lakota held a council and agreed if the white man attacked again, the Lakota would fight.

1857: The United States Supreme Court upheld slavery in Dred Scott v. Sandford.

1858: During the spring, Indian representatives traveled to the United States capital because traders were not dispersing the promised annuity payments. The desperate Sioux signed two more treaties to sell more land. In the end, the United States paid nearly nothing, and the Sioux Nation lost one million acres. The United States leaders created policies that instructed the Lakota to farm which was impossible in the poor soil. The Lakota no longer had enough land to feed their people in their traditional ways of hunting and fishing.

March 1861: Dakota Territory was established. To the white man, this annulled the 1851 Fort Laramie Treaty.

April 1861: The American Civil War began. During the war, more than 186,000 African Americans fought with the Union Army in segregated regiments called United States Colored Troops. The Civil War claimed 38,000 black soldiers' lives.

June 1861: Crazy Horse participated in a battle with the Shoshones which killed the son of Chief Washakie. This battle was fought in the valley of Sweetwater (Western Wyoming).

1862: The Homestead Act allowed the white man to flood in from the east to claim 160-acre plots of land surveyed in the western territory by the United States government.

1862: Santee survivors were driven west, starting the Sioux Uprising.

December 26, 1862: Thirty-eight Indians were executed in Mankato, Minnesota, for supposed crimes during the Sioux Uprising.

1862–1863: The Great Winter of 1862–1863 was one of starvation for the Indians. They tried to farm, as they had promised, yet the crop failed and left them hungry. The natives were promised annuities and goods in June 1863, but never received them. The natives felt the white man was trying to starve the natives because the food was locked up in white-man buildings. The prairie braves watched their children cry for food and decided to storm the buildings, taking the food by force. More food was promised by the white man but it never came. Hunger demoralized the Indians, and when the white man brought devil water (alcohol), their thinking was clouded. A few braves killed the first settlers and started the war.

1863: President Abraham Lincoln delivered the Emancipation Proclamation.

1864: The Bozeman Trail, which accommodated gold seekers, was opened into Montana. The Indians called it the "Road of Thieves" because it cut straight through Indian buffalo hunting grounds and broke the Fort Laramie Treaty promises. The Oglala, Brulé, Cheyenne, and Arapaho had been pushed too far and declared war along the South Platte River. They attacked and plundered white settlers, burning ranches and stage stations. They attacked wagon trains, burned railroad stations, destroyed telegraph poles, and stole cattle and horses. The Hunkpapa, led by Sitting Bull, raided the whites from the Powder River to the Missouri River.

November 29, 1864: Massacre at Sand Creek. Colonel John M. Chivington, the First Colorado Regiment, led volunteers and a troop of soldiers from the First and Third Regiment to a peaceful Indian camp in Colorado whose chief was Black Kettle. The military told the Indians in the camp that they would be safe camping there. Black Kettle flew the American flag and a white flag. In the freezing dawn, Chivington's troops attacked the sleeping village at Sand Creek. The attack lasted all day. They massacred between 152 and two-hundred Indian women and children, in addition to twenty-eight men. They scalped and mutilated the Indian bodies, cutting off fingers, noses, ears, and genitals for trophies. Many wore the chopped-off body parts as ornaments on their hats and saddles. The massacre led to more talk of revenge and less talk of peace.

Two young lieutenants, Silas Soule and Joseph Cramer, defied Chivington because they knew the Indians believed to be under the protection of Fort Lyon. They held back their men at Sand Creek and refused to participate in the massacre. Soule met an untimely death for his act of defiance, murdered on a Denver street.

April 9, 1865: The Civil War ended when Lee surrendered to Grant at Appomattox.

April 14, 1865: President Lincoln was assassinated and Andrew Johnson became president.

July 1865: Powder River Campaign. Brigadier General Patrick Conner invaded the Powder River Basin with three columns of troops, totaling one thousand troopers and 250 Pawnee scouts. They had one order from General Conner to "attack and kill every male Indian over twelve years of age." He built a fort on the Powder River to protect wagon trains on their way to the Montana gold rush. Nelson Cole, with an additional 1400 troopers, was to meet Conner as he moved north.

July 24–26, 1865: Battle of Platte Bridge. The Lakota and Cheyenne attacked the post and killed all members of a platoon that had been sent out to protect a wagon train. They also killed the wagon train drivers and escorts.

August 1865: Battle of Tongue River. General Conner's column killed over fifty Arapahoe villagers and destroyed their winter food supply, tents, and clothing.

September 1865: One of the plains greatest warriors, a Cheyenne named Woqini (Roman Nose), led hundreds of Cheyenne warriors into a fight against worn-out and starving Army mounts. They continued to harass the starving soldiers who were trying to return to Fort Laramie. The Cheyenne attacked in revenge for the Sand Creek Massacre but did not overtake the soldiers because they had limited weapons.

October 1865: The Southern Cheyenne signed a treaty giving their land to the United States.

October 1865: General Connor returned to Fort Laramie and left troops at a fort at Crazy Woman Creek and Powder River. Red Cloud isolated the fort and the soldiers were forced to survive all winter without supplies. Most died of malnutrition, scurvy and pneumonia. Colonel Carrington's company finally rescued them on June 28, 1866.

1865: Nine treaties were signed with the Indians. None of the established Lakota leaders signed the treaties.

December 18, 1865: The Thirteenth Amendment was passed, prohibiting slavery.

April 1866: Congress overrode President Andrew Johnson's veto of the Civil Rights Bill, which gave equal rights to all United States born citizens excluding Indians.

1866: The Ku Klux Klan is formed in Tennessee. The members of the white supremacy group were predominantly white Confederate veteran soldiers.

Late spring 1866: The Red Cloud War. Chief Red Cloud, Spotted Tail, Standing Elk, and Dull Knife traveled to Fort Laramie, intending to negotiate a Powder River Basin treaty. Meanwhile, Colonel Carrington marched with hundreds of infantry up the Bozeman trail to establish forts. This began the Red Cloud War, which gave Crazy Horse useful battle skills. In a council meeting before the war, Chief Little Crow told the braves they were young children drinking white-man devil water. He said they were little herds of buffalo where great herds once stood. He warned the white men were locusts of the prairie and were as thick in the sky as a snowstorm. He foresaw that if they killed one or two or ten white men, then ten times the number of white men would kill them. The younger braves convinced Chief Little Crow to lead their fight anyway because his pride was great and he did not want to appear timid like the elders who were against an uprising. The Indians killed hundreds of white men while only a few dozen brave warriors were lost. The white man lost the war and closed the Bozeman Trail in 1868.

June 13, 1866: The Fourteenth Amendment to the United States Constitution gave blacks the right to citizenship.

July 13, 1866: Colonel Carrington began building Fort Kearney. The Cheyenne were angry because the land was in the middle of their prime hunting ground. However, the colonel's forces were strong. Strategically, the Cheyenne spent the summer harassing the troops while forming stronger alliances with other plains Indians.

September 21, 1866: The Buffalo Soldiers (African American regiment) were established.

November 1866: Colonel Carrington received reinforcement from Captain William J. Fetterman and his troopers.

Early December 1866: Crazy Horse and other Lakota warriors lured soldiers out of their fort, killing several officers and wounding others.

December 21, 1866: Fetterman Massacre/Battle of the Hundred Slain. This battle occurred in north-central Wyoming. Two thousand warriors, including Red Cloud and twenty-two-year-old Crazy Horse, waited while selected decoy warriors lured troops into their trap. Indian casualties were high because they were outgunned with the new Springfield and Spencer repeating rifles. Still, the warriors killed eighty-one soldiers. Fetterman claimed earlier he could wipe out the entire Sioux Nation with one company of men. The bodies left at the Fetterman Massacre were mutilated in a similar fashion to those left at the Sand Creek Massacre.

1867: During the summer, Crazy Horse, Sitting Bull, and Red Cloud attended the Grand Council of Six Thousand Tribes at Bear Butte. They pledged to fight all encroachment by the whites.

March, 1868: Crazy Horse was part of the war party which attacked Horseshoe Station (north of Cheyenne, WY).

1868: Sioux Treaty of 1868/Treaty of Fort Laramie (1868). A group of Lakota tribal leaders signed the Fort Laramie Treaty of 1868, which required the United States to protect the lands from white intruders. The Kiowa, Crow, and Cheyenne actually had successive claims on the territory, but were not a part of the agreement. The Army agreed to close all forts along the Bozeman Trail. The treaty created the Great Sioux Reservation, although the Lakota did not give up their hunting grounds. The Lakota were given the Black Hills. In exchange, the Indians agreed to "civilize themselves" and give up their nomadic lifestyle in exchange for government rations and land of their own, which was a large portion of what is now western South Dakota. Other leaders refused to sign the treaty because they did not want to give up their roaming lifestyle and freedom. Sitting Bull and Crazy Horse refused the proposed system and did not sign the treaty, so they were under no obligation to follow the treaty restrictions. That refusal made them heroes among young warriors who were oppressed on the reservations.

1868: George Armstrong Custer gained the reputation as a successful Indian fighter by leading his troops at the Washita Massacre, where Black Kettle was killed. This was Custer's first significant Indian War battle.

1870: The Massacre on the Marias. United States soldiers massacred 173 Blackfeet men, women, and children on the Marias River in Montana as retribution for the actions of a small group of Blackfeet men who killed Malcolm Clarke and wounded his son.

1870: The Sioux killed fifteen white men who were along the Missouri River below Fort Peck.

1871: Thirty-nine white men were slain along the same area of the Missouri River.

1872: White men started trespassing into the Black Hills in search of gold.

1873: George Custer and the Seventh Cavalry moved to the northern plains to protect surveyors for the Northern Pacific Railroad. Custer had a chance encounter with Crazy Horse, resulting in Custer's second and third battles, of four total, during the Indian Wars.

1873: A United States financial panic turned into a depression that lasted until 1877. Grasshopper plagues swept the plains where the grasshoppers piled two feet deep in places. A yellow fever epidemic also struck.

1873: The Sioux killed fourteen soldiers near Fort Rice.

1874: United States Army Lieutenant Colonel George Armstrong Custer led one thousand mounted soldiers on an exploration expedition into the Black Hills. This was a direct violation of the 1868 Fort Laramie Treaty because the land had been designated for the Lakota. General Alfred Terry drew up written orders for

Custer to explore the Black Hills for natural resources and for a logical location for a fort. On the expedition, gold was indeed discovered by geologists in the party and word spread quickly. Upon learning of the gold, The United States government unsuccessfully attempted to purchase the Black Hills. Settlers rushed into the Black Hills, an act that was strictly forbidden by the Fort Laramie Treaty.

1874-1875: Sioux killed 137 whites within the south border of the Niobrara River (Nebraska) and the north border of the Yellowstone River (Montana).

1874–1875: The winter was extremely cold on the plains, with heavy snow and temperatures reaching below negative forty-five degrees Fahrenheit. Touch the Clouds moved to the Red Cloud Agency and did not stay long because he found the life unfulfilling. He fled back to the Powder River area and rejoined Crazy Horse and the remaining hostile Indians.

1875: The Lakota flowed into the agencies and the number of hostiles shrunk from ten thousand to three thousand.

1875: By spring, hundreds of white prospectors were scattered throughout the Black Hills. A few miners were removed by the Army. Nonetheless, when no legal action was taken, word circulated and more prospectors flooded in, recognizing no punishment awaited them. Red Cloud and Spotted Tail complained to Washington officials.

1875: John Pearson discovered gold in Deadwood Creek.

1875: By summer, the 1868 treaty was violated again as white settlers and gold seekers flooded into the Black Hills. Lakota runners were sent to all the tribes, to request an assembly at the Red Cloud Agency on September 1, 1875. Red Cloud delegated Spotted Tail to visit the Black Hills and find out what the white man had discovered.

September 1875: The United States government was confident they would be able to purchase the Black Hills from the Lakota for five million dollars, but the amount was refused. The Treaty of 1868 stated that three-fourths of all Lakota men must sign any future agreements regarding the sale of land. During the meeting on the prairie, the Indians rode in war paint and threatened the white commissioners. The commission offered to pay the Indians four hundred thousand dollars a year for mining rights or six million dollars, in a lump sum, for the Black Hills. The twenty chiefs refused, and the conference ended on September 29, 1875. The Lakota were on shaky ground, but they did not cower. They moved with the migrating buffalo to Powder River.

November 3, 1875: As a result of the failed negotiations, President Grant held a top cabinet meeting, whose members agreed that all military restrictions on the gold rush were to be removed and the "hostiles" should be forced onto reservations because the Black Hills needed to be developed. General Sheridan attended.

December 1875: John Q. Smith, the commissioner of Indian affairs, ordered all Sioux to report to their respective reservations by January 31, 1876. He labeled those who did not comply as "hostile." The demand was impractical even for peaceful Lakota because they took cover from harsh winters in protected areas of the Black Hills. To report to a reservation on a treeless prairie in the middle of severe winter conditions made this forced travel a death sentence due to the lack of adequate food and shelter. Furthermore, most villages did not learn of the ultimatum until after the deadline.

January 31, 1876: Most Lakota did not report to their agency. The next day the Secretary of the Interior, Zachariah Chandler, handed the matter over to the War Department.

February 1876: The tide of compliant agency dwellers ceased and the majority of Indians moved back to the hostile camp. By May 1876, the agencies had lost fifty percent of their population as the Indians returned to roaming. While the government labeled them as noncompliant, they were not supplying food as promised, which caused the remaining agency dwellers to starve and in desperation, leave the agencies for the possibility of hunting near the Yellowstone River.

1876: General John Gibbon and 450 men moved out of Fort Ellis, near what is now Bozeman, Montana.

February 1876: Sitting Bull organized the final gathering of Indians on the northern plains. He sent out runners to the agencies to spread the word of the grand Sun Dance, real buffalo hunts, and a community of union. Sitting Bull prophesized, claiming his people would make a good fight against the soldiers and many would count coup. He invited the Cheyenne to join in the festivities and fighting. The Indians knew of the threat and banded together for safety.

March 1876: General Philip Sheridan ordered four columns of several thousand troops, both cavalry and infantry, to seek out hostile Lakota and force them back to the Great Sioux Reservation.

March 1876: Fifteen thousand white men lived in the Black Hills. Eleven thousand were in the town of Custer, in the southern Black Hills.

March 17, 1876: Originating at Fort Fetterman, Brigadier General George Crook, along with Colonel Joseph Reynolds, moved north and attacked a Northern Cheyenne village situated on the Powder River (Wyoming and Montana border). The village was the camp of He Dog and Two Moons. Crook claimed the village was led by Crazy Horse and destroyed the entire village. They attacked at dawn, with temperatures dipping under twenty degrees below zero. With the Army capturing supplies and horses, the survivors fled to Crazy Horse's camp. Not having enough supplies for the group, Crazy Horse led them to Sitting Bull, who provided only shelter, since their food rations were depleted.

April 9, 1876: Hank Harney and two brothers, Moses and Fred Manuel, discover an outcropping of gold ore where the Homestake Open Cut exists today. A new mining camp, called Lead City, appeared at the location.

May, 1876: Brigadier General George Crook left with one thousand men from Fort Fetterman, located in central Wyoming, with the directive to locate hostile Indians.

May 17, 1876: Brigadier General Alfred H. Terry and General George Custer departed from Fort Abraham Lincoln near

Bismarck, North Dakota, with 879 men. The lack of communication between the Terry, Custer and Crook was a known weakness that limited coordinated attacks on Indian villages. Furthermore, the Lakota frequently moved, which complicated strategies for uniting forces.

June 1876: In early June, the united Indians moved their camp to the Little Bighorn Valley. When the grass became thin, they moved to the Rosebud Valley. There, they held a Sun Dance, during which Sitting Bull had the vision of defeating the white man.

June 17, 1876: Battle of Rosebud (east of Billings, Montana). Crazy Horse, Gall and other warriors attacked General Crook. Twelve soldiers, and between twelve and twenty warriors, were killed before the Indians withdrew. Crook retreated south, up the Tongue River, to recover from the battle and wait for reinforcements. This action prevented his troops from assisting in the June 25th Battle of the Little Bighorn.

June 21, 1876: Terry held a council of war meeting with Gibbon and Custer on the steamboat *Far West*, located at the mouth of the Rosebud. Terry and Gibbon estimated they would have to fight one thousand warriors, while Custer estimated fifteen hundred. The meeting focused on not letting the villagers scatter when the soldiers approached. Custer left with fourteen days of rations and orders to complete the campaign as he determined, regardless of unforeseen circumstances.

June 25, 1876: The Battle of the Little Bighorn. General George Armstrong Custer led 210 men into a battle. All under his command were killed. Reno's command lost fifty-three men, for a total of 263 Army casualties. The Teton (Hunkpapa, Blackfoot, Oglala, Brulé, Two Kettle, Sans Arc, and Minniconjou) and the Northern Cheyenne were gathered together when Custer and his men attacked. The Indians suffered about sixty warrior casualties, and approximately eight women and children were killed. Gibbon's column was half a day behind schedule.

June 26, 1876: The battle continued in the morning of June 26 and then the Indians broke camp and departed. They stopped that night for a few hours but did not set up lodges. They continued to travel upstream through the Little Bighorn Valley.

June 27, 1876: Around 2 p.m., at their traditional summer hunting grounds, below the mouth of Lodge Grass Creek at the base of the Bighorn Mountains, the Indians stopped traveling. Finally, they celebrated.

June 27, 1876: The Seventh United States Infantry and Second Cavalry came upon the battlefield, only to find swelling soldier corpses rotting in the heat. Maggots already feasted where blowflies had laid eggs in the gaping wounds from cut-off body parts, gunshots, arrows, and blunt trauma. Blackened, scalped, and decapitated bodies were strung out in the field. Gibbon rescued Reno, Benteen, and the Seventh Cavalry survivors.

June 28, 1876: With only two shovels available, the surviving soldiers buried the dead in shallow graves, or covered with dirt or branches. General George Custer was said to have been buried the deepest, at only twelve inches. The soldiers found gravely wounded cavalry horses which were put out of their misery.

Comanche was the only horse who survived. Two skin funeral lodges held dead warriors and chiefs. The military men stole the dead warriors' and chiefs' robes, clothing, war bonnets, beaded shirts, moccasins, saddles, and Indian artifacts.

June-July 1876: Deadwood's first hotel, the Grand Central Hotel, was established and featured chef Lucretia "Aunt Lou" Marchbanks, an ex-slave. She offered flapjacks, bacon, and beans for $1.

July, 1876: Charlie Utter's wagon train arrived in Deadwood, bringing Wild Bill Hickok, Calamity Jane, a number of prostitutes and madams. Miners lined the street and cheered as they arrived.

July, 1876: The combined forces of Sioux and Northern Cheyenne which had prevailed at the Battle of the Little Bighorn, traditionally migrated north and east from the Big Horn Mountains toward Dakota Territory. They utilized their annual practice of setting the land on fire behind them.

July 26, 1876: Lawrence County Commission voted and approved the bounty of $25 for any Indian (dead or alive) brought to white authorities.

July 26, 1876: General Sheridan ordered the military to control the Sioux agencies (taking control from the established civilian-run agencies through the Department of the Interior). Sheridan ordered the troops to confiscate all Indian horses and guns. He instructed, "On no account will any Indians be allowed to return to the Agencies without unconditional surrender of their persons, ponies, guns, and ammunition."

320

August 1, 1876: Seth Bullock and Sol Star arrived in Deadwood to set up a hardware business.

August 2, 1876: Jack McCall shot and killed Wild Bill Hickok at Nuttall and Mann's No. 10 Saloon. The killing demanded a call for law in the town.

August 3, 1876: Jack McCall was tried by a jury of miners and was set free.

August 12, 1876: Smallpox Outbreak in Deadwood.

August 19, 1876: Seth Bullock was elected as Deadwood Commissioner and Fire Warden.

August 19, 2876: Pony Express rider, Charlie Nolan, was murdered by Indians near Sturgis.

August, 1876: The Cheyenne roamed with the Oglala Lakota and Crazy Horse and then separated, heading toward the foothills of the Bighorn Mountains.

August 20, 1876: Preacher Henry W. Smith was murdered on his way from Deadwood to Crook City. The community immediately blamed the murder on a band of Indians.

August, 1876: Seth Bullock raised the bounty for an Indian head to $50.

August, 1876: First Indian head was delivered to Deadwood for the bounty. The gathered crowd contributed $66 in personal funds. Bullock claimed the Board of Health gave $250 to the man. Originally, Brick Pomeroy had shot the Indian, claiming he stole Pomeroy's horses. Then, a man of Mexican decent cut the head off the body and took it to Deadwood. Once he received the bounty, he misspent the money. Pomeroy was angry and shot and killed the man in a Crook City bar.

August, 1876: A handful of Indian leaders signed off, releasing Sioux interest in the Black Hills in exchange for continued rations sent to the Reservation. This agreement was later amended and signed by 4,473 tribal members in 1889.

September 4, 1876: General Crook marched toward the Black Hills with two thousand soldiers in punishing conditions with rations running out. Soldiers killed their horses and mules to ward off starvation. Seventy played-out horses were shot in one day which destroyed morale among the exhausted troops even as they ate the remains. The march was referred to as the "mud and horsemeat" march.

September 9-10, 1876: The Battle of Slim Buttes. General Crook's men engaged on an American Horse's village of 37 tipis housing about 260 people, including thirty to forty warriors. Nearly two thousand soldiers were ultimately involved (150 soldiers initially). Weak from the previous month's campaign to locate non-compliant Indians, the soldiers did not mount an offensive on the Indians who fled their camp. In addition, General Crook had information that larger groups of Indians, including followers of Crazy Horse, were in the vicinity (twelve miles to the west) but they did not have the strength to pursue the other villages and continued to march toward the Black Hills.

September 11, 1876: E.B. Farnam, a real estate and mining entrepreneur, was elected the first mayor of Deadwood.

September, 1876: General George Crook's "mud and horsemeat" march from Montana to Deadwood concluded with crowds cheering as they entered Deadwood. Mayor E.B. Farnum showed the exhausted men to the bathhouse and clothing store. At the Grand Central Hotel, General Crook addressed the excited crowd for half an hour, describing his Indian War campaign and his Slim Butte victory. The locals hoped the troops would stay in the area for protection against Indians.

October, 1876: The Manypenny Commission demanded Red Cloud and Spotted Tail relocate to their respective reservations or threaten starvation. A group of chiefs signed over the Black Hills to the United States.

October 21, 1876: Colonel Nelson A. Miles met Sitting Bull near Cedar Creek, where Sitting Bull demanded all troops permanently leave the Yellowstone area. Colonel Miles refused and considered the Indians hostile, starting a battle. Two soldiers and five warriors were killed in this mainly strategic positioning skirmish.

October 25, 1876: Sioux leaders, including Hunkpapa Chief Gall, participated in peace negotiations with the United States government. Sitting Bull refused to attend.

November, 1876: The Northern Cheyenne raised two hundred lodges supplied with their winter stores, warm bedding and clothing at the Red Fork of Powder River.

November, 1876: Crazy Horse and his followers camped south of Yellowstone.

November 25, 1876: Five months to the day after the Battle of the Little Bighorn, Colonel Ranald S. Mackenzie attacked Dull Knife's Cheyenne village, camped at the edge of the Big Horn Mountains in a steep-walled canyon. Mackenzie's troops killed forty warriors and burned two hundred tipis in the Cheyenne village. The Army suffered five casualties. The Cheyenne survivors fled north to seek shelter with Crazy Horse, as the losses mounted and the temperatures dropped to negative thirty degrees. Approximately eighteen days later, the small group reached Crazy Horse's camp on the Tongue River. Mackenzie developed syphilitic degeneration of his brain, which caused insanity and death at age forty-eight.

December 18, 1876: Lieutenant Baldwin attacked Sitting Bull's village of 122 tipis near the Yellowstone-Missouri divide. No casualties resulted as the Army shot heavy artillery over the sleeping camp. Sitting Bull's village fled and lost all of their winter supplies, with temperatures of minus forty degrees.

January 8, 1877: General Miles attacked Crazy Horse's camp. (south of Billings, Montana, near the Wyoming border)

March, 1877: Seth Bullock was appointed Sheriff of Lawrence County.

March, 1877: Jack McCall was hanged in Yankton, Dakota Territory, for Wild Bill Hickok's murder.

April 21, 1877: Northern Cheyenne leader Dull Knife and 553 followers surrendered at Fort Robinson, Nebraska.

Spring, 1877: Wyatt and Morgan Earp, arrived in Deadwood, but Seth Bullock pushed them out, insisting he had the unruly town under his authority.

Spring, 1877: The Lame Deer Fight was the last battle of the Great Sioux War. Second Lieutenant Edward W. Casey attacked on Lame Deer's camp. They charged at dawn and drove the Indian horses through the camp. Facts are in dispute about the clash, but Lame Deer was killed even though he may have been surrendering.

June, 1877: Crazy Horse attended the last great Sun Dance at the foot of Beaver Mountain. The Sun Dance, a sacred religious ceremony, was a way to worship the Great Spirit when a problem was before them. They offered themselves by being pierced and dancing for days without food, water or sleep.

July, 1877: Lawrence County Board approved a higher bounty ($250) for each Indian captured, dead or alive.

September 4, 1877: (Northwest Nebraska) Crazy Horse took his wife to Spotted Tail.

September 5, 1877: Crazy Horse was killed at Fort Robinson.

NOTES

[1] Pemmican is sun-dried buffalo meat pounded into fine shreds and mixed with bone marrow, dried chokecherries, rosehips, and pin cherries. Once mixed into a paste, the high protein sustenance was squeezed into clean buffalo bladders and intestines for storage. Pemmican was prized during long, harsh winters. If prepared carefully, it lasted three years without molding, and was a nutrient-dense protein.

[2] Black Elk was an Oglala Lakota Holy Man, who was probably born near the Little Powder River during the Moon When Trees Crack from the Cold (December, 1858). Some family accounts place his birth year earlier. In 1872, at approximately nine to fourteen years of age, while questing on a high mountain peak in the southern Black Hills (originally named Harney Peak but has since been renamed Black Elk Peak), he received a vision to serve the Great Spirit, Wakantanka. Black Elk was an estimated twelve to seventeen years old when he participated in the Battle of the Little Bighorn in 1876.

Crazy Horse was Black Elk's second cousin (their fathers were first cousins). Black Elk surrendered with Crazy Horse's band at Fort Robinson on May 6, 1877. In approximately 1881, he exhibited the traits of a healer and medicine man and was quickly considered a Wichasha Wakon (holy man, priest). In 1890, he witnessed the Wounded Knee Massacre. In 1904, he was baptized in the Catholic Church and took the name Nicholas. He intertwined practicing his faiths of traditional Lakota Wakantanka (Great Spirit) and Catholicism. Black Elk's eyes failed and he was blind by 1931.

For the last season of his life, Black Elk lived in solitude at the end of a dirt road, in a one-room log cabin with weeds growing out of the dirt roof. It was a treeless, barren landscape approximately twenty miles east of the Pine Ridge Agency near the Manderson store and post office. He died in 1950. Brilliant Aurora Borealis danced above on the night of his wake. His friend, John Lone Goose, commented, "God sent lights to shine on that beautiful man."

[3] Northern Plains Native Americans used painting, quilling and beading to decorate their clothing and bags in elaborate designs. The designs were so specific they identified the maker, owner and from what tribe the items originated. Northern Plains tribes used sinew (animal tendons) to sew beads onto leather. Sinew was stronger than cotton thread brought into the area by white settlers.

[4] Mato Paha is a geological feature in western South Dakota, now known as Bear Butte.

[5] Henry Weston Smith was born on January 10, 1827. He lived in Connecticut and married at the age of 20. His wife and infant son died one year later. Smith became a Methodist preacher and married again in 1858. He had four children. He served in the Civil War with the Massachusetts 52nd Infantry and later moved his family to Kentucky. Smith felt called to minister in the Black Hills, so in May, 1876, he walked behind a wagon train from Cheyenne (Wyoming) to Deadwood (South Dakota). Smith was a

327

street preacher and a part-time prospector. He preached on Deadwood's main street in front of Bent and Deetken's drug store and he also walked to other camps in the hills to preach to gathered prospectors.

On Sunday, August 20, 1876, Smith walked toward Crook City to preach. The note on his cabin door said, "If God is willing, will be back at three o'clock." Smith was murdered on the side of the road, shot through the heart. Most residents blamed his death on Indians, while some believed he was killed by thieves or someone hired by the saloons and brothels to rid the town of a moral compass.

[6] The best gold pouches were made of bull scrotum because the slick texture held even the finest gold dust. An inferior alternative, still better than cloth, was the waxed buckskin pouch. Since nuggets over the size of a dime were quite rare, proper storage of hard-earned gold flakes and dust was critical in the success of a prospector.

[7] The injured horse was Comanche, owned by Captain Miles Keogh. When the soldiers assessed the battle scene, they heard a faint whinny from a ravine and discovered Comanche. They gave him water and urged him to his feet, as he had been shot and was unable to walk. The soldiers tended to his wounds and carried him to Grant Marsh's steamer, *Far West*, where he and wounded soldiers were transported back to Fort Abraham Lincoln at a record-breaking pace. Comanche was nursed back to health but was never ridden again. He lived out his life in the Seventh Cavalry. For ceremonies, he wore a saddle with military boots

turned backward in the stirrups and was draped in black. Comanche died at Fort Riley, Kansas, in 1891. His body was stuffed and exhibited at the 1893 Columbian Exposition in Chicago. He is now exhibited in the Natural Science Building at the campus of the University of Kansas.

[8] Mining claims were generally assigned on a first come - first serve basis. Lotteries were utilized when numerous miners demanded the same claim. An elected claims recorder documented all claims and the $1 or $2 fee. Three hundred claims lined the creek in Deadwood Gulch and were labeled in relation to "Discovery." For example, the tenth claim above Discovery would be called "Number 10 above Discovery." Each claim was 300 feet long and was required to be worked with pick and shovel at least two days each month.

[9] James "Scotty" Phillip was eighteen when he arrived in the Black Hills in July, 1876. He carried one hundred pounds of flour and intended to prospect until the flour ran out. Later, he married a Native American, Sarah Larribee, and settled the town of Phillip, located on the Great Sioux Indian Reservation. They were able to live on the reservation since Sarah was a member of the tribe. Scotty Phillip is credited with "saving the buffalo" because he purchased seventy-four head from the estate of Fred Dupree. He drove the herd to a pasture on the west side of the Missouri River north of Fort Pierre in 1901. In 1911, Phillip was buried near the buffalo pasture and some of the animals came near the funeral "showing their respect to the man who had saved them." (Black Hills Visitor Magazine)

[10] In 1876, the value of gold was approximately $22 per troy ounce. Approximately fourteen troy ounces equaled a pound. If Sara had sixty pounds of gold, it was worth approximately $18,000 in 1876. In 2021, the amount would be worth approximately $1,486,000.

[11] "Seen the Elephant" was a saying used by miners which meant someone had gained experience from another gold rush or mining town at a significant cost. Today, the phrase "seeing the elephant" refers to gaining worldly experience at a substantial cost.

[12] When in enemy territory, Lakota usually left their dead on the surface of the ground so their spirit would rise quickly. When in their own territory, scaffolding was typically erected to suspend the body for spiritual purposes and to keep scavengers away from the human remains.

Young Lakota men often aspired to membership in the Akicita Society, which was the group in the tribe who watched over their camp and preserved order. A young man was required to first prove himself through bravery, often by facing a battle before he was considered for the society. The Akicita was highly regarded as the men policed the movements of their group, keeping stress low and ethics high. They ensured adherence to buffalo hunt rules. They punished civil wrongdoers and left punishment for criminal wrongdoing in the hands of the family of the guilty.

[13] Grant Marsh was considered a great hero of the Indian Wars, due to his uncanny ability to safely and quickly move soldiers and freight. Marsh was born in 1834 and grew up in the riverside town of Rochester, Pennsylvania. At twelve, he was drawn to the river and became a cabin boy. In 1858, he worked under the direction of

Samuel Clemens who later became an author under the pen name of Mark Twain. Grant Marsh worked steamboats on the lower Mississippi River in the Union fleet during the Civil War. After the war, he was a captain for several steamboat companies and also worked independently. On the *Far West*, Grant Marsh steamed up 64 miles of the shallow and dangerous Big Horn River, rescuing fifty-one injured men from the Battle of the Little Bighorn at what is presently Hardin, Montana. General Terry had led litter bearers throughout the night by the light of fires. At 2a.m. on June 28, 1876, Grant Marsh transported the wounded soldiers and lone horse, Comanche, back to Fort Abraham Lincoln at a record-breaking pace. The 900-mile journey took only fifty-four hours to accomplish. Then, once the wounded soldiers and Comanche were escorted to care, Grant Marsh reloaded supplies for General Terry's expedition and returned for more wounded soldiers who were waiting along the Yellowstone River.

Marsh continued navigating the Missouri River but after 1883 steamboat traffic declined with railroad expansion. Marsh adapted and accepted jobs along the Mississippi River. On January 6, 1916, Marsh died in near poverty, with unpaid bills swallowing his estate. From Saint Mary's Cemetery, overlooking the Missouri River in Bismarck, North Dakota, Marsh's grave is marked with a rock tombstone engraved with a riverboat.

[14] Laudanum is a highly addictive opiate narcotic. Used in the late 1800s as a home remedy and as a prescription for the relief of various pains and diarrhea, the drug was a tincture of 10 percent opium mixed with alcohol, mercury, castor oil, musk, nutmeg, ether, chloroform, or whiskey. Laudanum was inexpensive in

comparison to a bottle of wine or gin because it was considered a medication and was not taxed. The drug was prevalent among all social classes and even prescribed for babies and children. Prominent people, for example, Mary Todd Lincoln, the wife of President Abraham Lincoln, were addicted to laudanum. Extremely potent, only two teaspoons of laudanum could cause overdose and death to a healthy adult, which made laudanum a common suicide tincture.

[15] James Butler Hickok was born in Illinois in 1837. He was best known for his Old West heroism as a gunman. However, his colorful life included running as a fugitive of justice, trapping, Union Army spying, Indian fighting, Army scouting, buffalo hunting, marshalling unruly frontier towns, freighting, gambling, and stage driving on routes that were harassed by hold-ups.

Hickok, knick-named the "Prince of Pistoleers," reportedly killed up to seventy-five men. He may have over-used his guns, since he was fast to the draw and an excellent shot. With $1,000 a month salary, he calmed the streets of Abilene and became a marked man. While well-respected by some, he was despised by outlaws who wanted him dead. In 1871, in a Texas shootout, Hickok accidentally killed a deputy and quit working as a marshal. He traveled with Buffalo Bill Cody's Wild West Show, but his eyesight failed, possibly from ophthalmic gonorrhea. In July, 1876, Hickok arrived in Deadwood, where he made a slim living playing poker, usually at the Nuttall & Mann's Saloon (later renamed No.10 Saloon).

On August 1, 1876, Hickok played poker with Jack McCall and tried to persuade him to quit playing because McCall could not cover his losses. McCall was insulted and on the next day, on August 2, 1876, Hickok went back to the Nuttall & Mann Saloon to play poker. Although he routinely refused to sit with his back toward the door, the other poker players would not move when he joined their game. Jack McCall, the young gunslinger from the previous day, walked into the saloon and shot Hickok in the back of the head with a .45 caliber gun, killing him instantly. Wild Bill was 39 years old when he took his last breath, never sensing his imminent murder. Wild Bill was reportedly holding a pair of black aces and black eights at the time of his murder. This card combination is still known as the Dead Man's Hand.

Shortly before his death, Hickok wrote a letter to his wife, Agnes Lake, who was a circus performer. The letter said, "Agnes Darling, if such should be we never meet again, while firing my last shot, I will gently breathe the name of my wife – Agnes – and with wishes even for my enemies I will make the plunge and try to swim to the other shore." Hickok is buried at Mount Moriah Cemetery in Deadwood.

[16] Bar towels were used as a community towel to wipe up alcohol spills, countertops and the beer foam faces of customers. The towels later became suspect for transferring epidemics, flus and viruses at a rapid rate.

[17] Al Swearengen was the owner of the Gem Theatre. He lured unsuspecting young women to Deadwood by advertising on the east coast. He offered to pay for their trip west and promised

high-paying respectable jobs as "stage performers" in the theatre as dancers, singers and actors. Instead, the women were forced into prostitution and saloon drink hustlers. Swearengen's life spanned between riches and poverty. He was known to gross $5,000 a night with his establishment proceeds from dancing, drinking, prostitution, and gambling. Yet, he fell into total destitution and died when he was crushed as he attempted to jump on a moving train.

[18] Charlie H. Utter, aka Colorado Charlie, was born in approximately 1838. He grew up in Illinois and moved west in search of a gold fortune in Colorado in the 1860's. Charlie Utter was of short stature (5'6") and was meticulous about his grooming and appearance, bathing every day. He enjoyed the finest of commodities, including high-quality bedding, and gold, silver and pearl handled pistols.

In July, 1876, Charlie Utter organized and led a 30-wagon train of prospectors, prostitutes and gamblers from Colorado to Deadwood. Close friend Wild Bill Hickok joined the train in Cheyenne, Wyoming. Later, Calamity Jane joined the train in Fort Laramie, Wyoming. When Wild Bill Hickok was murdered, Charlie Utter claimed his body and hosted the funeral at his camp. He marked Hickok's grave with a wooden identifier that said, "Wild Bill, J.B. Hickok killed by the assassin Jack McCall in Deadwood, Black Hills, August 2d, 1876. Pard, we will meet again in the happy hunting ground to part no more. Goodbye, Colorado Charlie, C.H. Utter."

Utter later left the area, chasing other gold rushes.

[19] John "Jack" McCall was born in Kentucky in the early 1850's. He reportedly moved west to become a buffalo hunter. By 1876, he was living in Deadwood under the alias of "Bill Sutherland" and the nickname "Broken Nose Jack." After shooting Hickok with a .45-caliber Sharps revolver, he fled from the saloon but was quickly apprehended. Since Deadwood had no legal system, the prospectors and businessmen formed an impromptu court and held a trial the next day at McDaniel's Theatre. McCall's explanation for murdering Hickok was that it was payback for when Hickok murdered McCall's brother in Kansas. The group acquitted McCall and he fled to Wyoming Territory where he bragged about killing Hickok. Less than one month later, he was arrested for the murder and brought to Yankton, the capital of Dakota Territory, for a retrial. He was found guilty and hung on March 1, 1877. Later, when his body was exhumed, the noose was still around his neck.

[20] Doctor William Worrall Mayo was born in 1819. In 1859, he set up his first medical practice and was known as the "little doctor" because he was only 5'4" tall. His son, William James Mayo, was born in 1861. Doctor Mayo applied to be a Civil War surgeon, but he was rejected. In 1862, after thirty-eight Indians were executed for a fight near New Ulm, Minnesota, Doctor Mayo stole Stands on Cloud's corpse, dissected the remains, and displayed them in Le Sueur, Minnesota. The family settled in Rochester, Minnesota, in 1863. William James and his brother Charles Horace followed in their father's footsteps by becoming doctors. William James Mayo joined his father's medical practice in 1883, when a tornado caused great injuries throughout Rochester. Charles Horace Mayo

335

joined his father and brother's practice in 1888. As their practice expanded, they added additional physicians and focused on a team approach to medical care, which was unique in those years. Eventually, the Mayo Clinic was created and is still well known today throughout the world as a premier medical treatment center.

[21]Martha Jane Canary, known as Calamity Jane, was born between 1852 and 1856. Martha's father was a gambler and her mother was a prostitute. The family traveled from mining camp to mining camp and she was orphaned at a young age. In her early years alone, she continued to survive at mining camps and on wagon trains with various jobs to get her by. She wandered from place to place, usually dressed in men's clothing. Although glamorized by the press as a unique Wild West character, Martha was a complex woman with a life full of bad choices and mistreatment. Women in the west had few opportunities to stay single and survive.

A great debate exists regarding the source of her nickname, Calamity Jane. One extreme suggests that losing her parents at such a young age was a "calamity." The other extreme suggests that men who "socialized" with her, contracted a "calamity" of diseases.

Martha was rumored to be a "scout" for General George Custer on his first expedition to the Black Hills. In actuality, she was not a scout, but what the men called a "hanger-on." She snuck onto the expedition and was disruptive to the party. She offered basic talents as a teamster, resold clothing and supplies, cooked and was "willing to pull down a pant leg" with any man wanting to go into the bushes.

She was often hungry, spending her money on drinking binges. She worked in brothels and slept on bar floors, which led to frequent mistreatment from men. She was represented by the press as bold, crude, feminine, and strong.

Martha was honest and if she gave her word to someone, she kept it. She was protective of other women and a generous philanthropist when she had spare money. She was fearless in protecting the unprotected. Once, she wrapped a black whip around a man beating his weary ox in order to stop the injustice. When a smallpox epidemic struck Deadwood, Martha cared for eight quarantined men. Five survived, brought out of the shadow of death. Martha personally wrapped up three dead men and rolled them to their burial.

In the 1890's, Martha tended to a girl named Jesse who most locals assumed was her daughter. Today, it is speculated that the girl was simply someone in need that crossed Martha's path. At one point, Martha wanted to put Jesse in school at the Convent School in Sturgis, SD. She started a fundraiser for the girl and sold tickets. When people donated, she bought drinks for the entire bar, and by the end of the evening, the money was gone and the girl's education was on hold. Martha worked for the Wild West Show for only a few weeks before being fired for intoxication. In the late 1890's, Martha was broke and living destitute in the Deadwood area. By 1903, her rough lifestyle had taken its toll. She only possessed a worn suitcase, a few trinkets, and two calico dresses.

She wore out her welcome, wherever she went. At this point in Deadwood history, the town no longer welcomed her brash outbursts as entertainment and she moved to Belle Fourche in 1903.

In Belle Fourche, she was hired as a cook and possibly worked in a brothel. She lasted six weeks before having a drunken bender with a cowboy on the back of his horse, waving and hollering in the street. Martha opened a laundry after asking for a loan from the first mayor of Belle Fourche. She diligently made payments on the loan as she washed prostitutes' laundry for a living.

She moved back to Terryville and in August, 1903. Martha collapsed and died at the approximate age of fifty. Her casket was covered with flowers. Contrary to popular belief, Martha did not request to be buried beside Wild Bill Hickok. She was laid to rest beside him because the town committee decided to make an everlasting joke, forcing Wild Bill to spend eternity beside her. The locals knew Wild Bill was never fond of Calamity Jane, and her obsession with him was not reciprocated. One committee member said, "Good thing he's dead because he would never tolerate it."

[22] Ohiyesa, also known as Charles Alexander Eastman, was a Santee Sioux, born in 1858. Ohiyesa was born in Redwood Falls, Minnesota. He was the first Native American to complete a formal medical education, with a bachelor's degree from Dartmouth College and a medical degree from Boston University. Ohiyesa believed that understanding and immersing in nature was critical for white immigrants to experience if there was to be any

understanding of the Native American culture. Ohiyesa founded the Boy Scouts of America and the Campfire Girls. He died in 1939 in Detroit, Michigan.

[23] Hannibal Morris, nicknamed Old Frenchy, was born in French Guiana in 1819. He was born a slave and was sold five times, bearing striking scars from the mistreatment. He lived in a one-room log cabin and was considered a moral gift to the Deadwood community from the moment he arrived in 1876. He was not a prospector but met the needs of the gulch as a laborer, never passing up an offered chore. The town cared for Old Frenchy in his final months of life and upon his death, the town mourned.

[24] Seth Bullock was born in Ontario, Canada on July 23, 1849, the son of a strict British Sergeant Major. Bullock left home in 1867, at age 18. He became a law officer in Montana and a state senator in 1871. On August 1, 1876, Bullock arrived in Deadwood with a party of thirty-five men consisting of many businessmen who left a lasting economic impression on Deadwood. He became Sheriff and was said to have the confidence to outstare an angry cobra. He also owned businesses and invested in cattle and horses. Bullock was not without conflict with other business owners. For example, in his hardware store he sold a supply of cigars, whiskey, milk, and tea, which were not typical hardware goods and certainly not appreciated competition by grocers and saloons.

Bullock became friends with Theodore Roosevelt in 1884. Roosevelt was a sheriff in Medora, North Dakota and Bullock was the sheriff of Deadwood, South Dakota. They met as they tracked a horse thief named Crazy Steve. Bullock benefitted by the relationship, being appointed captain of a cowboy regiment in 1898. He received training yet saw no live action in the Spanish-American War. In 1905, Roosevelt appointed Bullock United States Marshal. He led Roosevelt's sons on hunting expeditions throughout the plains and Roosevelt traveled internationally with Bullock as his guest. On July 4, 1919, Bullock dedicated a 31-foot stone tower to his friend on top of Mount Roosevelt, outside of Deadwood. A few months later, on September 23, 1919, Bullock died from colon cancer in Deadwood. He is buried in Mount Moriah Cemetery.

[25] General Crook was born in 1828. He was an 1852 West Point graduate, ranking thirty-eight in a class of forty-three. He rose to the rank of major general of volunteers during the Civil War, fighting for the Union. After the Civil War, he played a major role in the Indian campaigns. He was promoted to brigadier general in the regular Army in 1873.

In 1871, General Crook was described by Inyo Independent, a California newspaper, as follows: "The fact is, Crook is nothing but an Indian…He can take his gun and cross the desert, subsisting on the way where you or I would starve. Perfectly self-reliant for any venture, delighted with lonely travel and personal hazard, carrying nothing but his arms, he will walk after a trail all day and when night comes, no matter how cold, he wraps himself in an Indian blanket, humped up, Indian fashion, and pitches himself into a sage brush, there to be perfectly easy till morning. He will follow an antelope for three days. He requires nothing to drink or smoke, and very little to eat…utterly ignorant of fear, and yet stealthy as a cat, shy of women and strangers; and when he was a cadet, he had all the same traits."

On June 17, 1876, Crazy Horse, Gall, and other warriors attacked General Crook at the Battle of Rosebud. (Battle Where the Girl Saved Her Brother). With twice the men of Custer's force, Crook fought against half of the warriors which had collected at Greasy Grass. Reports of General Crook's casualty numbers were greatly varied, which were between twelve and twenty deaths and thirty wounded. About the same number of warriors were lost, but the Lakota remained on the battlefield as General Crook retreated. Crook stubbornly called the battle a "victory" while retreating south, up the Tongue River. This prevented his troops' assistance at the Battle of the Little Bighorn. Crook bivouacked at Goose Creek and waited until early August for what he considered sufficient reinforcements.

Custer was not aware of Crook's battle as he entered his last day on earth. It is unclear whether the knowledge of the battle would have altered Custer's aggressive action on June 25.

On August 5, 1876, feeling pressure to catch up with the Indians, Gibbons ordered movement with only fourteen days of rations. The reinforcements had been in the field for months and their horses were undernourished and "well-fitted for the bone yard." The men routinely covered twenty miles of difficult terrain in 105-degree temperatures each day.

When General Terry's troops arrived and joined forces, some speculated that the march was a "wandering the prairie exercise" with no interest in confrontation. Clearly, the soldiers were recovering from the Battle of the Little Bighorn and at the very least, were exhausted. They received fifteen days of rations on August 23 and Crook ordered his men to only carry a blanket, overcoat and a rubber blanket.

On August 26, General Terry separated from General Gibbons as he pursued a group of Indians possibly heading for Canada. General Crook departed from the Powder River, which culminated in a torturous experience for the men and animals involved. Mud, rain, hailstorms, diarrhea, neuralgia, rheumatism, malaria, and a rattlesnake bite burdened the campaign.

Instead of a four-day traverse to Fort Lincoln for resupply, General Crook ordered a march to the Black Hills to protect the mining communities and raise moral with a battle victory on the way. Facing muddy conditions and exhausted men and animals, General Crook forced the men to continue pursuing Indians. Short of supplies, Crook placed his men on half rations and they resorted to eating horses.

On September 8, 1876, a detachment of four officers and 150 enlisted men, led by Captain Anson Mills, discovered an Indian village of thirty-seven tipis. Before sunrise, on September 9, the detachment opened fire. The village warriors returned fire and American Horse was mortally wounded.

It is believed that fleeing Indians spread word of the attack. Crazy Horse and seven hundred warriors rode toward American Horse's village, creating a potentially grave situation for Captain Mills. Around noon on September 9, Crook and his relief column arrived, pressing Crazy Horse and his men back. The rest of

Crook's command, mostly on foot, arrived later that afternoon and evening. They seized 110 ponies from the village, as well as pemmican and other dried foods. They also recovered artifacts from the recent Battle of the Little Bighorn. Crook lost three in the fight and at least ten Sioux also perished.

General Crook died in 1890, while still on active duty after thirty-eight years of military service.

[26] Lucretia "Aunt Lou" Marchbanks was born on March 25, 1832. She was born a slave in Tennessee, and her father was the son of his slave-owner's brother who gained his freedom. The oldest of eleven children, Lucretia was trained in cooking and housekeeping on the Marchbanks' plantation. Prior to the Civil War, she traveled as a servant to the eldest Marchbanks daughter and they journeyed west. When she earned her freedom through the Emancipation Proclamation, Lucretia worked in the Colorado gold rush camps. She followed gold fever to Deadwood and arrived on June 1, 1876. She was employed as manager in the kitchen of the Grand Central Hotel. The restaurant was a favorite in Deadwood Gulch and Lucretia was nicknamed, "Aunt Lou." Single and determined, her creative menus labeled her in the community as the best chef in Deadwood and later of Dakota Territory. Her outgoing personality was noted, as well as the biscuits and plum pudding she created.

Aunt Lou was careful with her hard-earned money as she worked at different restaurants and mining companies in the hills. In 1878, she was lured away from the hotel kitchen by various mines, including the Father De Smet Mine and the Golden Gate Mine, earning $40 a month. By 1883, Lucretia managed the Rustic Hotel in Lead, Dakota Territory, which was a successful boarding house and restaurant. By 1883, she opened her own Rustic Hotel, which she sold two years later and purchased a ranch in Rocky Ford, Wyoming, where she ranched along the route between Sundance and Beulah, Wyoming. She hired a man, George Baggely, to help her raise horses and cattle. They worked together for the next twenty years. Marchbanks died in 1911. She is buried in the Beulah, Wyoming Cemetery. Her grave marker is the second to the left as one enters the cemetery gates.

[27] In late July of each year, the combined forces of Sioux and Northern Cheyenne traditionally migrated north and east from the Big Horn Mountains toward Dakota Territory. They utilized their annual practice of setting the land on fire behind them. Although many recollections describe this as a defensive tactical move against the United States Army, it was more likely a tradition where the burning of undergrowth on the grasslands produced healthy young grass for the next spring. The tender green grasses drew buffalo to the region which enhanced the food supply.

[28] Frederick Gustavus Schwatka was born in Illinois in 1849. He was a 1871 West Point graduate and United States Army second lieutenant in the Third Cavalry. He obtained his medical degree and law degree in 1875. A year later, he led the initial charge at the Battle of Slim Buttes at the age of 26. From 1878-1880, Schwatka led an expedition to the Canadian Antarctic and found remains of one member of Sir John Franklin's lost expedition. In 1883, he explored the Yukon River which included building rafts

and navigating 1300 miles, becoming the longest raft journey on record. He made other expeditions after his resignation from the Army in 1885. In 1892, Schwatka died in Portland, Oregon, at age 43. The cause of his death was reported as either an accidental overdose of morphine or as suicide by laudanum. His obituary noted his zeal, energy and intelligence.

[29] In 2001, an excavation in the former Chinatown area of Deadwood revealed a small oval-shaped pit, which was likely the result of a Chinese death ceremony. The site was named "Feature 17." According to Chinese culture, the symbolism of burning possessions was to convey the belongings into a spiritual smoke toward the afterlife. The deceased person's belongings were gathered together hours after the death. Items were broken and then wrapped in the deceased person's clothing. The bundle was placed in a hole and burned.

The 2001 excavation uncovered a beautifully embroidered floral pattern on the garment, suggesting a wealthy, prominent person wore the clothing. Chinese coins, glass seed beads, a hair comb, opium and smoking paraphernalia, fruit seeds, animal bones, and water pipes were recovered.

[30] Wing Tsue was a prosperous Chinese resident in Deadwood. He sold groceries and household goods, including intricately carved wooden utensils and knives. He sold opium throughout his time in Deadwood and played a significant complicated leadership role in the secretive Chinese community. His wife was a polite, beautiful entertainer which Wing Tsue routinely offered

to his friends. His wife and children returned to China in 1902 and he followed in 1919.

Opium is a powerful narcotic extracted from the seed capsules of the poppy plant. In the 1800's, the drug was imported from China to the United States and considered a lucrative crop, equivalent to tea and rice.

[31] A parfleche is a Native American rawhide container shaped like a large envelope, usually ornately beaded and quilled. It was used to hold items such as pemmican and maps.

[32] Hart Island is an island east of the Manhattan borough of New York City and at the western edge of Long Island Sound. The island was purchased in 1868 by New York City for a potter's field cemetery for the indigent or unclaimed dead. In 1865, the island was also used by the Union as a Civil War prison camp for Confederate soldiers. In 1870, a part of the island was used to confine people infected with yellow fever. Later, it became a lunatic asylum for women, and a tuberculosis sanatorium. During World War II, the Navy, Coast Guard, and Marines housed disciplinary barracks on the island and kept 2,800 servicemen in custody. During WWII, a German U-Boat surfaced near Long Island and its German soldiers were imprisoned on Hart Island. It continues to be used as a potter's field, where destitute and unidentified bodies are buried in mass graves. In the 1950's, the island housed a boys reformatory, and an overflow facility for New York City jails. From 1955 to 1961, a NIKE missile base occupied ten acres of the 100-acre island. Over the course of time, approximately one million bodies have been buried on the island.

[33] Deadwood Gulch was in desperate need of housecats and a bullwhacker named Phatty Thompson took upon an entrepreneurial spirit to fill the void. In Cheyenne, he offered boys twenty-five cents for each cat they caught and placed in his crate-filled wagon. With a load of alley cats, estimated at over 100 felines, Thompson returned to Deadwood Gulch after an incident where he overturned his wagon near Hill City and temporarily lost most of his cats. With the help of other travelers and prospectors, Thompson collected most of the cats and continued to Deadwood Gulch, where he sold them by the pound for a total profit of approximately $1,000.

[34] Harriet Tubman was born into slavery in Maryland in approximately 1822. She faced physical abuse and escaped in 1849. Later, she assisted seventy other slaves and led them to freedom using the Underground Railroad, a network of safe houses that allowed slaves to escape north. During the Civil War, Tubman assisted the Union Army as a spy, cook and armed scout. She later became an activist for women's suffrage. Tubman died in 1913.

[35] More than half of the 1877 population of Deadwood Gulch was foreign-born. While ethnicity was not overtly tied to inequality, each immigrant group tended to collect in specific sections of the community, self-segregating more for cultural comfort than ethnic bias. During the early years of the gold rush, approximately thirty Black people and thirty men of Jewish descent lived in the area. The vast majority of the prospectors and settlers came from Germany, Canada, Ireland and England. Immigrants from China were secluded and industrious, focusing on jobs from which

others turned away. For example, the Chinese reworked the tailings of abandoned mines, offered laundry services and ran restaurants which usually served American dishes rather than Chinese meals. The Chinese also believed in the community and formed a fire department in Deadwood. The Chinese volunteers were athletic and filled with stamina, endlessly hauling water up the gulch walls to contain fires.

[36] Crazy Horse was known by his people as a great warrior and battle leader. He used fasting and solitude to gain visions and power. He was nearly six feet tall and lean. His light brown hair, light complexion, high-bridged nose, and narrow face were not typical features of the Lakota. He was a quiet man until he was in battle. Crazy Horse had the childhood nickname of Curly. He carried a war club, a knife, and an eagle leg bone flute. He never wore a war bonnet and was adorned with a single red-tailed hawk feather or two bald eagle feathers in his loose hair.

Crazy Horse had two horses: a bay and a sorrel. The bay was his favorite ride in battle. In preparing for battle, he painted hailstones on his body, drew a lightning bolt across his face, and ate dried eagle heart and brain along with wild aster seeds. He passed a sacred stone over his horse's body, believing this would make him and the horse invisible to their enemy. The Oglala, Brulé, and Cheyenne were led by Crazy Horse.

After the Battle of the Little Bighorn, Crazy Horse led his Oglala people away with the intention of living and worshiping as his ancestors, living from the land and resisting government handouts. He was protective of his people and possessed the leadership and key survival skills which traditionally allowed his people to thrive. Crazy Horse found his former way of life impossible to reestablish since the buffalo were decimated and his primary food source was never to recover. He disappeared for days at a time and was said to roam the Black Hills on missions never identified.

Soldiers were ordered to pressure Indians to encourage Crazy Horse to settle on the government's reservations. While he camped at the mouth of Rosebud Creek, near Lame Deer, Montana, thirty volunteers went out and tried to persuade Crazy Horse to return. Then, Spotted Tail and several hundred warriors approached Crazy Horse, which he resisted. Finally, Red Cloud led another group who persuaded Crazy Horse and others to return in the late spring of 1877. As he left Rosebud Creek, he was heard saying, "All is lost anyway."

In June, 1877, Crazy Horse attended the last great Sun Dance at the foot of Beaver Mountain. Warriors volunteered to be pierced and danced for days without food, water or sleep.

[37] To date, no evidence of primitive life has been discovered within the Black Hills. Plains Indians and their ancestors likely avoided higher elevations since it was more difficult to navigate the terrain and endure the cold. Instead, they opted for the lower foothills that provided protection from winter winds and less severe conditions for hunting and daily life.

[38] Waglukhe is a Lakota term for the people who gave up their nomadic lifestyle and became "loafers at the forts." With the buffalo decimated, many of the Lakota accepted food and other

supplies from the Army forts, giving up their independent lifestyles instead of continuing their fight for independence.

Medicine bags were filled with a variety of different herbs picked from the plains and the Black Hills. Some of the most used herbs were purple coneflower (to treat inflammation, snakebites, and colds), blue flag (to treat earaches), mint (to treat colic), horsemint (to treat abdominal pain), sweet cicely (to treat wounds), and wild licorice (to treat intestinal distress and toothaches).

[39] "Hog Ranch" was a term used to describe the "end of the line" for prostitutes. Long sheds with separate doors for each "room" were placed along stage routes, including the Cheyenne-to-Deadwood stage route. The structures housed the spent women until desperate traveling customers passed by and did not object to the worn-out professionals.

[40] Swill Barrel Jimmy was rumored to be a Confederate officer who was traumatized by the Civil War and escaped to Deadwood to avoid the demons of war. He begged for food and scavenged the garbage of restaurants, saloons, and brothels. Saloon owners allowed him to sit inside their establishments on frigid days. In this book, when he claims Sara has "sand," he is referring to a contraction of the phrase used during the Civil War of "plenty of sand in his crop." This phrase has truncated into the popular term of "grit."

[41] Sir John Franklin was born in Lincolnshire, England on April 16, 1786. He became a British Royal Naval officer and a politician. Franklin was an explorer of the Arctic which culminated in his last expedition, at the age of 59, when he commanded an attempt to

navigate the Northwest Passage of the Arctic. With a three-year supply of canned goods, Franklin set sail on May 19, 1845 with 137 men as crew of two ships, the Erebus and the Terror. It is believed that Franklin's ships became icebound and the men tried to reach safety by traveling over land. Instead, the men died of various unidentified causes including starvation, hypothermia, botulism, scurvy, pneumonia, tuberculosis, and lead poisoning. Unknown to Franklin, lead had leeched into their food supply since the cans had been sealed with lead-based beads of solder.

On the expedition to determine the fate of Franklin and his crew, Frederick Schwatka verified Franklin likely died on June 7, 1847, although his body has never been recovered. Blade marks on some of the crew's remains indicate they resorted to cannibalism during their darkest moments.

[42] In the 1840's, over thirty million buffalo roamed the prairie, easily sustaining the Indians. With what seemed an unlimited resource, Native Americans hunted for their own needs and to trade hides and skulls for ammunition, rifles, clothing, and other white man goods. Two fur company records reflect over two hundred thousand hides a year were purchased from Native Americans. When ten thousand men initiated work on the first transcontinental railroad in 1863, tons of buffalo meat was harvested each day by contractors, including William F. Cody, nicknamed Buffalo Bill. Later, cattle ranchers shot buffalo, considering them a nuisance. Finally, tourists traveling west found it entertaining to shoot buffalo and some businesses actually harvested buffalo to sell processed carcasses back east.

In 1800, approximately one million Native Americans lived. By 1900, their population declined to 300,000.

[43] On November 25, 1876, five months to the day after the Battle of the Little Bighorn, Colonel Ranald S. Mackenzie, including seven hundred soldiers and four hundred Indian scouts, attacked the Northern Cheyenne's main winter camp at the edge of the Big Horn Mountains. Dull Knife's Cheyenne village was sleeping in the early morning hours when they were attacked by Mackenzie, who burned the village to the ground as soldiers shot into tipis. As the warriors attempted to defend their village during a brief futile effort, the surviving women, children, and elderly fled into the mountains. Eleven babies froze to death on the first night of the survivors' escape because a blizzard enveloped them. Starving and naked, numerous additional survivors froze to death during the 150-mile search, which took two weeks to cover before finally locating the camp of Black Elk and Crazy Horse on the Tongue River. Once at the camp, they were offered only clothing because Black Elk's camp was starving and had resorted to eating their emaciated ponies. On April 21, 1877, Dull Knife and 553 of his people surrendered at Fort Robinson, Nebraska. Dull Knife died in 1883 at the age of seventy-three.

[44] The single-shot Derringer was typically carried by gamblers in Deadwood. The .30 caliber was nicknamed "muff gun" because a woman could easily conceal the weapon for personal protection in her handmuff (a cylinder hand warmer made of fur). The gun was concealed in men's vest pockets.

[45] Charles S. Whiting was born on a farm in Olmsted County, Minnesota on May 25, 1863. His mother died in childbirth and as a result, he was raised by his paternal grandparents in Rochester, MN. He completed a public-school education and graduated in 1879. After high school, Whiting worked on his father's farm for three years. Then, he taught school and became a principal. In 1889, Whiting graduated from the first class of the University of Minnesota's newly established law school. Financially broke, he moved to DeSmet, South Dakota, where his first wife and daughter died of typhoid fever in 1897 and 1899. With a solid education and determination, Whiting ultimately became the sixth South Dakota Supreme Court Justice, serving from 1908 until the day of his death on March 25, 1922. His untimely demise was the result of a shoddy doctor who, while performing a tonsillectomy in his office, inadvertently injected Novocain into Justice Whiting's vein. Whiting's son watched from the waiting room as his father was instructed to run up and down the doctor's office hallway, desperately hoping the anesthetic would work through his system before stopping his heart. The effort was fruitless and the doctor left town in the middle of the night.

[46] Originally, Indian dogs were likely bred from the coyote, fox, and gray wolf. As generations progressed, specific traits of each tribe's beast of burden became evident. The Lakota used their dogs to pull 40-pound travois carrying water great distances. They also consumed dog meat, which was considered a prized protein source offered at special feasts. The flavor of dog meat has been described as resembling pork and bear. When Lakota learned the

white man considered their practice of eating dog to be offensive, they hid the practice.

[47] On September 5, 1877, Crazy Horse, age thirty-three, went to Fort Robinson. As he realized he was being arrested, he resisted and a soldier stabbed him in his right side through his kidney with a bayonet. He died later that night. Once he perished, American Horse took Crazy Horse's wrapped body to his parents. At Beaver Creek, they placed Crazy Horse on a scaffold and honored him. Then, in the darkness, his parents took him to an undisclosed location for burial. Given the elderly state of his parents, it is assumed he was possibly placed under the edge of a cliff and the rocks/dirt were collapsed above Crazy Horse, entombing his body. A peace pipe was found in 1957 on the Kadlecek ranch on Beaver Creek, located ten miles Northwest of Hay Springs, Nebraska. The ranch is on Beaver Creek Road, off Hwy 20.

[48] Patron Saint medals were frequently worn by the military. Some wore a particular medal because they were named after the saint. Others wore the medal with the feeling it would give them added protection. Still others wore the medal as a devotion to their faith. In the Catholic faith, followers believe saints intercede with God on their behalf. In this story, Sergeant Zito, Sara, and finally Rose clung to a Saint Michael medal. Saint Michael was considered a protector and leader of God's Army against evil. He is an archangel in Judaism, Christianity, and Islam. In the Bible's book of Daniel, Michael is referred to as a great prince who protects the children of Israel. In the book of Revelation, Michael leads God's Army and defeats Satan's forces.

[49] The golden eagle is considered the "chief of all birds" and is one of the fastest and largest raptors in North America. To the Lakota, the eagle is an emblem of strength and courage. He was admired for his great soaring heights, longevity, and extraordinary power of vision. The Lakota believe the eagle was given to them for decorative beauty and as a protection charm during battles. His lustrous gold feathers were fastened to hair, the manes of war ponies and to war bonnets. Typically, a warrior wore a golden eagle feather in his hair for each kill he had made in battle.

Golden eagles prefer open terrain near mountains and nest on cliffs or in trees. Their wingspan can reach seven feet. Females can weigh up to fifteen pounds and males weigh up to eight pounds. Their territory may be as great as seventy-seven square miles and their maximum airspeed is two hundred miles per hour.